Seven Days One Summer

KATE MORRIS

First published in 2011 by
Short Books
3A Exmouth House
Pine Street, EC1R 0JH

A CIP catalogue record for this book
is available from the British Library.

ISBN 978-1-907595-27-1

Printed in Great Britain by CPI Bookmarque, Croydon

Text design by Nicky Barneby @ Barneby Ltd
Jacket Design by Mark Ecob www.mecob.org

For Luke

February 13th

Alfie kicks me and I wake up. We are entwined like lovers in the large, warm bed. Alfie likes to sleep in our bed, squashed and hot and horizontal. He's six years old and should be sleeping on his own. I shiver and open the curtains. It's grey and dense; the pigeons perched on the television aerials are puffed up in the cold. I am not tired today because it is just me and Alfie in the bed, so there is space to stretch and sleep. Marcus is in Japan and I'm expecting him back some time this afternoon.

Marcus has become both richer in the last year or two and less available. Last week he said that the house looked tired and suggested that I take a sabbatical and concentrate on new carpets and paint. He knows how much I love my work, and how miserable I'd be if I spent all my time buying food and redecorating the house. "How is the house meant to look?" I joked, "Lively?" He didn't respond with a laugh, as he used to, but merely carried on staring out of the window, looking cross and preoccupied.

We live in a colourful, three-storey Victorian house near a park. The downstairs loo is painted pea green and the kitchen floor is yellow. The yellow rubber floor was a controversial choice. Marcus didn't like it, but I insisted. The floor looks constantly dirty and stained and I spend far too much time sweeping and cleaning it. Occasionally, I can feel depressed about my shabby home; particularly if I've just completed an assignment photographing a beautiful and stylish interior story where the bathroom tiles are duck-egg-coloured porcelain, the shower unit looks as though it could fly to the moon and the bespoke wallpaper, based on nineteenth-century Japanese prints, depicts tiny exotic birds perched on twigs.

Alfie and I make our way to the kitchen and I tell him it's my birthday. He processes this information for a second, with a sweet smile, and then he sits down and eats his cereal, while looking at the writing on the back of the packet. He wants me to tear off the voucher to take him to Legoland or Alton Towers or some other mecca for small children. He doesn't, of course, read the small print, which says he will get in free if two adults pay the full price.

We venture out into the bitter air. The cars have frost on their windows. I am gloveless and after five minutes my hands are freezing.

It's not as cold as last December when I was in Moscow taking photographs of an apartment designed by my friend Gaban. In Moscow it was cold enough to make the hairs in my nose freeze up, my eyes water and my hands turn numb inside my gloves. This London cold is different; damp and pervasive, creeping into our bedroom and blowing through the fireplace.

After dropping Alfie at school, my mother friend, Emma, and I, walk towards the bakery, where we usually stop to buy bread and croissants. Today I buy a small cake. Emma asks if I am shooting, but I'm not and that is why I have a little time to linger. Thankfully I don't shoot birds. I am a photographer and shoot houses mostly, and furniture catalogues and shops. Emma asks me if I'm lonely spending so much time on my own, with Marcus constantly abroad.

I think about this while I walk briskly back to the house. Marcus has been away so much this last year and the days are fine but the evenings are quiet and eerie. I make another cup of tea and help myself to a snack. At this point, ideally, it would be an apple, but instead I eat a cereal bar smothered with chocolate chips. I wander up to my study, where I sit and look blankly at my computer screen. I have to master some files on a story I shot for a designer. The photographs are interiors of offices she designed for a hedge fund

3

company and the furniture and fittings are brightly coloured, surprising and unusual. The photographs flash up on the screen and I clean and dust the scratches. When I've finished I adjust the cropping and hone it by changing the colour and contrast and then, perhaps most importantly, the sharpness. The time passes quickly because I enjoy this kind of work.

At about two, a withheld number rings on my mobile. I pick it up.

"Happy Birthday."

"Sam?" I recognise his voice. He always sounds as if he is on the verge of laughing.

"Yeah. Hi, beauty. It's me." It's strange and exciting to hear from him. We haven't spoken for a long time.

"Sam! How long has it been?" I am aware of my voice, of each word I am saying. I sound light and coquettish.

"Too long," he drawls.

"How did you remember?" My voice is a little too high.

"I remember, birthday girl. I always remember."

"Where are you?" I lean back in the rocking chair and point my toes.

"San Francisco."

"How are you doing?"

"Good," he pauses and takes a deep in-breath. "Great. But…"

4

"But?" I prompt him.

"I'll tell you another time," he laughs at last.

"What?"

"Don't worry. Listen, Dad owes me a favour, so he's offered me a week at his house in Italy. I was wondering if you guys would like to come? It's a week in August, I'll have to check which week." His accent, once British, now has a faint American tone.

"Wow! How amazing. Where is it?" I draw a heart on a yellow pad.

"Umbria."

"That sounds lovely. Let me get back to you after I've spoken to Marcus."

"Get back to me," he says, "and have a good day, kid."

"Thanks Sam."

I put the telephone down and tilt back my chair. How strange to hear from Sam. We haven't been in touch for a couple of years. I sometimes remember moments from our time together in Rome. We were always laughing, or talking, or zooming around on his Vespa. I was working as an assistant to a Swiss fashion photographer, and we travelled all the time, but when we weren't shooting we were based in Rome. Sam was there on a scholarship from an American college, where I was doing a part-time module in philosophy. He worked in the student bar on Tuesdays and Fridays, so after my Tuesday evening seminar, I always

5

stopped at the bar to see him.

When he wasn't working, we would meet in the Piazza Navona, near where he rented a room. We were just so thrilled to be in Rome, amongst the statues and beautiful buildings. If we weren't actually seeing each other we would talk on the telephone. He sometimes mentioned a girlfriend, who lived in England, but the details were vague and I told myself he didn't really care about her. One weekend he disappeared and I later found out she had been to visit. I was surprised at how jealous and betrayed I felt. I was irrationally possessive of him. Knowing there was a man I could chat to every day filled some need in me, though I wished that Sam would kiss me. I remember one evening, an ex-boyfriend who was visiting Rome took me out to dinner. It was the night I usually visited Sam at the bar and I told him I wouldn't be coming. When I got home there was a handwritten note, posted through my door, asking me to call. I didn't call that night, partly because I wanted him to think about how much he missed me.

Sometimes those celebrity questionnaires ask: What was the best kiss of your life? Mine was the kiss I eventually had with Sam just days before he left Rome for good. We were in the Piazza Navona, drinking coffee after a long dinner in our favourite restaurant. We really liked the restaurant, because the food was simple and delicious and cheap. It was tucked away, hidden from tourists, and the patron always gave us a glass of a dark medicinal-tasting liqueur on the house. I had finished my coffee, when he suddenly leant forward to wipe something off my face and then he kissed me.

At first we giggled at the strangeness of kissing each other, but soon we were kissing with depth and meaning, oblivious to the people who sat around us. The kiss made me giddy and light-headed. We went back to his top floor apartment, five floors up without a lift. We sat side by side on a white chair, and kissed again, until we fell onto the floor and rolled on a tatty rug. He kissed my neck and my arms and then finally, he led me to his bed. He took off his shirt and I took off mine and we lay side by side. We kissed again and then made love for a long time, on and on. When it was all over, I cried and so did he. "It's all right, baby," he whispered before falling asleep. I lay on his chest for a while, before turning away, curling up and trying to sleep. But I stayed awake thinking about what had happened and remembering how pleasurable it had been. I dared to hope that we would go further and be together.

In the morning, I wanted him to stroke me, or kiss me, or hold me some more, but he rushed around, joking with me, pulling on his jumper, gathering his books together and cleaning his teeth. We went for a coffee and a croissant at a stand-up bar, and then he kissed me goodbye, as he always used to, before we had slept together. After he left, a sickening, heavy wave of grief descended on me.

Later that day, as I was preparing to leave for Milan he telephoned and asked how I was, but he didn't mention what had happened the evening before. It was as though all the brightness had been taken out of my life. Everything, everybody, seemed dull to me. We no longer talked nearly every day as we used to; there was no call from him for a very long time. I missed him. I spent that Christmas in India with my mother and brother and was distracted by the smell, the colours, the filth and gnawing poverty, but returning to Rome in January was bleak. He was back in London as he'd graduated, and I had never been so alone. He sent me a few postcards, and we saw each other occasionally when we were both living in London, but our friendship was never the same. Now, all these years later, I sometimes wonder what he is doing, or remember something about our time together. Hearing his voice brings back fragments of those times: his smile, his laugh, and his bedroom. I remember the sound of a piano playing the evening we made love. Someone was playing scales in minor chords over and over again.

It's 3.50 and Alfie and I are blowing up balloons for

the birthday supper I have planned for us after Marcus returns this evening. Alfie has made two birthday banners and we have set the table. It's half an hour before we're meant to leave and pick up Marcus from the airport when his secretary, Jane, rings to say he won't be home until early evening tomorrow. I am disappointed and sad, but not surprised. She asks me whether I will pick him up or whether she should send a car for him and I advise her to send a car because I am shooting a lighting catalogue tomorrow. He's got to fit in one more meeting, Jane informs me in her brisk, unsentimental tone. Jane is not one to chitchat about the weather. She informs me that a birthday dinner has been booked for tomorrow anyway, which is lucky, as she won't need to cancel. Almost as an afterthought she actually wishes me a happy birthday. A few minutes later, I receive a long apologetic birthday text from Marcus and I'm sure that Jane has taken it upon herself to remind him.

After Alfie and I have had tea with a cake and three candles and long after he's gone to bed, I curl up on the sofa and listen to "Hurt" by Johnnie Cash. It's a powerful song about loss and people going away. This year Marcus and I have been estranged, not as together and tight as we used to be. I let my mind wander, and wonder what it would be like to be with Sam, now, all these years later.

I should be grateful that Marcus's business is doing well because it means he will no longer be anxious about money. Isn't that what I wanted? I remember thinking that if we had more money everything would be all right. When we wanted to save on our gas bill, we used to make real fires. I found it sexy that Marcus could make fires so easily. Now, though, he never has time to make a real fire, so we stick to central heating like everyone else.

About two weeks ago when Marcus and I were having a row about the house, he accused me of spending too much time thinking about work but not earning enough to justify it. He apologised pretty quickly and said he didn't mean it, but it hurt as the money I earn is not what it should be. My salary to myself has not increased for a few years. Editorial rates are low, and the competition for the more lucrative jobs is intense. I have at times been whittled down to the last two in an advertising campaign, but not secured the job. My overheads are very high. I have to spend so much on updating my camera equipment, leasing cameras and lenses and investing in a good-quality computer. There is no freedom to work and to travel as Marcus does, because I am the mother. One of us has to be at home. The truth is that I am known as an interiors photographer and I am trapped as one, even though I am tired of shiny kitchens and beautiful floors, vast windows and perfectly pruned gardens.

Now that we have a little financial freedom, I would like to take some time out to work towards an exhibition, but Marcus has other ideas. He'd probably like me to host a dinner party for his Japanese clients, and spend my days pampering and preparing, painting my toenails and making origami-style napkins for the table. This thought makes me depressed, so I put on "Hurt" again, because it suits my mood. It's frustrating to think of Marcus; he's like a trifle: somewhere down towards the jelly layer, I know he's still who he was. He's a wonderful, kind, funny, weird, original man.

The following morning, an extravagant bunch of lilies arrives and a note written by someone else, which simply says, 'Happy birthday to my wife.' Marcus and I are not married and the note seems impersonal and cold. The flowers are still in the sink, wrapped and waiting for me.

Marcus is home. He sits on the slickly designed kitchen chair; his long, slim legs stretched out in front of him. He's holding a bottle of lager in one hand and a cigarette in the other. His face is even more craggy than usual after the long flight from Tokyo. His dark blond hair is unruly and hangs at shoulder length, and the laughter lines in his face seem deeper and more ingrained than before. He has the demeanour of a man who is habitually stopped at customs and given a thorough body search, particularly when he's tired. I keep thinking that now he's richer, and has higher expectations, he will probably want to smarten up his look, but he hasn't yet and I am relieved because I like him the way he is.

"I'm hungry," he yawns.

"Would you like a sandwich? You look as though you're in need of some nourishment."

"Yes," he smiles, "bring it on. I never want to see another sushi, sashimi, miso soup again in my life."

I make him a sandwich with ham and mustard. He is quite particular about his sandwiches. He likes thick ham and English mustard. Marcus is a much better cook than I am, though recently he doesn't seem to have the time for anything but work. I'm very good at cooking for children. I make perfect spaghetti, eggs, baked beans, (not exactly cooking, more putting things on to boil), but Marcus is far more adventurous. He's a confident but somewhat haphazard cook and he enjoys entertaining large groups of people, using flamboyant and unusual ingredients; he grates chocolate in gazpacho soup and sprinkles cumin in his scrambled eggs. There was a time when he grated nutmeg in everything but that phase has passed. After the nutmeg it was red chilli.

"I'm knackered." He yawns again. "I couldn't get to sleep before four in the morning and they had scheduled me in for breakfast meetings every day. It was exhausting. My neck hurt, my temples throbbed, I probably got an ulcer, but I got through it. I was like Bill Murray in *Lost in Translation*. Remember the way he wandered around all night in that hotel in Tokyo unable to sleep?"

"Poor you." I massage his neck. He always exaggerates. "I suppose that's why I could never get through to you."

"Sorry darling. There was so much going on. They seemed to like my presentation. We've got the job." He smiles at me, briefly.

"Well done," I reply, kissing him. "It's a huge roof top garden isn't it?"

"Yes, on top of a bank," he says, surveying the washing-up. "We should refit the kitchen and buy you some clothes. Would you like that, darling?"

I look down at my perfectly good pair of boot-cut jeans and old tee shirt with the three buttons, and wonder what he would like me to wear now that he is an executive and travels business class. I imagine that he wants me to look more expensively-dressed. I would prefer to use the money to rent a cottage by the sea for all of us to enjoy.

Marcus has bought me a gift. 'Happy birthday,'

he says as he gives it to me. It's something from Asprey. I open the purple box and inside, amongst many layers of tissue paper is a silver photo frame. He also gives me an envelope with a voucher from Harvey Nichols, just to make the point about the clothes, I think, as I thank him. He's also bought something for Alfie. It's a fridge magnet of Mount Fuji and a series of Japanese graphic comic books; the content appears to be far too old for him – slick couples and people falling off roofs and cats with no heads.

When Marcus is away the house is quiet. When he's here, he sings in the bath, clanks around in the kitchen and shouts at the football on television. He also talks and laughs extremely loudly on the telephone. He is full of plans, which change from one week to the next. He is constantly planting and replanting the garden. At the moment, he has an all-consuming passion for bamboo, but I can't let myself become too attached to it; there will be a moment when he will decide to uproot the bamboo and experiment with something else.

He's eating his sandwich when I tell him about Sam telephoning and the villa in Italy. He's only met Sam a couple of times but they had enough in common to get on reasonably well.

"Yes," he says. "Sounds good. Let's go for it." Then he gets up and goes upstairs to have a shower. As far as he is concerned the discussion is over.

It turns out that Marcus booked my birthday treat four months ago. We are going to Pierre Blanc's restaurant – The Fattened Pig – and are meeting Dave and Tara there. Tara is one my closest friends; we go back about ten years or so. She got married last summer to Dave in a ceremony at her parents' house in Yorkshire. Dave is a journalist. He's dark and attractive. He's quite good in a crowd, energetic and over the top and complements Tara's more languorous nature. It rained the day of her wedding, and she took it as a bad omen, but she looked so beautiful. She's blonde and slim. She's prettier than I am and smarter and even though she's 40 she looks about the same age as me. She reminds me of Uma Thurman, or Grace Kelly, or a combination of the two. But she's been very out of touch since she married and at times her behaviour has astounded me.

When I leave a message, she often doesn't ring me back or if she does, it's days later. We email occasionally but she makes no effort to meet, or if we do make a date, she cancels. So when Marcus tells me they are coming, I am pleased though aware that I am still angry and upset by her seeming indifference to our friendship. I didn't hear from her for a couple of months, then four weeks ago, I left three messages and finally she emailed me. The email was in part an explanation about why she had been so elusive. She wrote about Dave and how disillusioned she was after her first year of marriage. She explained that he's incapable of doing chores around the house and can't even put a pizza in the oven without burning it around the edges. He locks himself away in his study and she isn't at all sure whether his writing is any good. She says that she was also unhappy about the wedding. There were too many people and too much rain and she said she would never get over the fact that the food ran out. She wrote that she had post-wedding depression or post-wedding stress, and I felt sorry for her.

We are driving to Windsor where the restaurant is situated on the river. Marcus is wearing a suit that he had made for himself recently by a tailor in Savile Row. I am wearing a vintage Pucci dress with the same white shoes I've had for years. I am not as slim as I used to be, so the bold patterns disguise the bumps. I used to be very slim, almost too thin. I am quite tall, and my legs are not too bad. I am kind of lanky with limp, long brown hair and big eyes, and quite untidy eyebrows and a nose with a bit of a bump. I am driving while Marcus makes business calls; when he's finished he leans his head against the window and naps for twenty minutes. We drive around searching for somewhere to park, but we can't find a single space and Marcus begins to swear.

We finally find a place in someone's private drive; it looks as though the house is deserted.

Dave and Tara are waiting for us at the bar. Tara gives me a big hug, then hands me some bath oil wrapped in lavish red paper with a black bow. She seems happy and completely normal, although perhaps she is making a huge effort. We sit down and toast each other with glasses of champagne. It's hard to get used to this extravagance, which at times seems almost vulgar. Marcus takes it all in his stride as though we have always lived like this. We used to be in a situation where we couldn't buy a new pair of curtains or mend the dent in the car. Now, of course, he is buying a new car. I wanted a Prius because of the low emissions, but Marcus wouldn't hear of it.

Marcus urges us all to have the tasting menu, which includes snail porridge, cauliflower risotto with chocolate jelly, and scrambled egg-and-bacon ice cream. The snail porridge sounds awful but is in fact rather delicious, savoury but sweet. During a dish called "sounds of the sea" we are given headphones, and instructions to listen to rolling waves crashing on the shore. Tara and I are consumed with giggles and we bend over the table, trying not to laugh, while the rather stiff waiter holds out the jug of chilled water, waiting to pour it into our glasses. Marcus and Dave completely ignore us as they discuss whether to enter the marathon in New York. About two years ago, they did the marathon in Paris together and we all went over to cheer.

Pierre comes to the table for one of the pudding courses, and heats up sugar, which is then zigzagged over a spoonful of pistachio-coloured tea-and-mint ice cream. The waiter offers us a selection of unusual mixed berries to accompany it. We are also given miniature puddings to taste – tiny and perfectly formed vanilla rice puddings in eggcups and hazelenut crème brûlées and frozen kiwi yoghurt presented in scooped-out kiwi's and finally some tiny coffee-flavoured éclairs. Everything is delicious, perfect, but I can't help wondering, what are we all doing here? Last year we celebrated in the local Tunisian, where you bring your own wine. This seems so ostentatious and I look at Marcus and wonder about him. Who is he trying to impress? Dave and Tara don't have much money and I suppose this is a treat – in fact, it's more like performance art.

"You'll never guess who has invited us on holiday." I knock over a glass as my hand stretches out to fiddle with my knife.

"Sam?"

"Yes. Has he invited you?"

"Yes." I'm surprised to register how disappointed I am.

"Really!" Tara seems excited. "Did you hear that

Dave? They've been invited to Italy."

"Good news," Dave says, smiling widely and flicking his hair with his hand before eating a tiny hazelnut crème brûlée in one mouthful.

I fiddle with my miniature mousse and wonder if Dave knows or cares that Sam was an ex-lover of Tara's. "Why do you think he's asked us out of the blue like that?"

"I think he has this wonderful house and he just wants to share it with us. Oh, and he told me something," Tara announces conspiratorially.

"What?" I ask.

"He's just got divorced."

"Divorced? I didn't know he was married."

"Yes." Tara is triumphant now. "He was married for seven months to this freak and then she one day she just left him."

The men are talking about the wine list and don't appear to be listening to our conversation, but I am left wondering why Sam didn't tell me he was about to get a divorce. It's becoming clearer why he telephoned his ex-girlfriends. People tend to do that, or at least think about doing that, after a relationship has broken down. I don't broadcast this thought, obviously, as I don't want Marcus and Dave to feel uncomfortable, and I'm not technically an ex-girlfriend, just a friend who had a one-night stand with him. I must remember that.

We talk about the holiday and then I drink fresh mint tea. Tara and I fiddle with chocolate truffles, sharing one and then two more, and by the time we have finished, it's nearly midnight. Tara and I moan in the ladies' about how full we are feeling and how we will have to starve ourselves for a few days. We don't touch on the subject of how distant she's been for the last few months, and now is the wrong time to bring it up. But I am doubtful there will ever be a good time. I find it hard to confront people and hard not to. Tara thanks me for the evening and hugs me tightly, and for that moment she is hugging me, she feels like the best, most treasured person in the world, but the hug won't sustain me; our friendship is so fragile.

I am driving as Marcus has drunk too much. He leans against the window again and within seconds he is asleep and snoring. I am thinking about Tara. We first met about ten years ago. We were hanging around with the same crowd, and so when I bumped into her at the opening of the Summer Exhibition at the Royal Academy, I introduced her to Sam, who had invited me along. Marcus and I had temporarily broken up and I was going out as much as possible to compensate. Sam was a partner in Small Films, a production company that made advertisements. He had earned so much money in the first two years that he had then gone on to invest in a feature-length film based on a literary novel. The film, which had been made for a relatively small budget, won an award at Sundance. He was happy and he glowed. I went to buy some post-cards and when I returned my whole body cramped and twisted as I saw that they were locked in a cluster, chatting. My reaction shocked me. Sam took Tara's telephone number that afternoon, and called a week later to invite her to dinner.

When he shared the news that he had started a rela-tionship with her, I was despondent, probably because Marcus and I were still separated. They went to Rome for a couple of days at the beginning of the Easter Hol-idays and Sam sent me a postcard of the Trevi Foun-tain: *I threw a coin into the fountain and thought of you. Remember all the good times we had?* I think I threw the postcard away, or at least let it rot in my bag. A few months into their affair, Sam invited me over to a dinner party with Marcus (we were back together by then), and I was happy for Sam, happy for both of us because we had found love, but it was hard to watch him being so attentive to Tara, the way he hovered near her and touched her all the time.

Then Tara telephoned me one afternoon and it was strange to hear from her because she had never called me before. She was frazzled and upset because Sam had gone to Paris for an ex-girlfriend's thirtieth birthday party, and he hadn't returned. He had said he was going for twenty-four hours, but two days later there was no sign of him and he hadn't called. She said it was heartbreaking, because up until that moment, they had done everything together and she had trusted him. It was hard to respond because I was in the middle of a shoot – in those days I was photographing products for supermarkets, and schedules were tight. I returned the call the next day and she sounded small and flat and empty. He was coming back that day she said, but she was unsure whether she would see him.

I heard from Sam a couple of weeks later. He said that Tara had ended the relationship and he asked if I would be his envoy and try to persuade her to have him back. I asked him why he hadn't taken her with him to Paris and he said something about how she hadn't been invited and that things hadn't ended that well with his ex, and he thought that bringing along Tara would have been provocative. He had stayed on in Paris to think things through, he said. He wanted a bit of distance from the intensity of the relationship and he'd been busy with meetings. But he said he loved Tara, and on reflection, he realised he hadn't handled the situation very well. He really wanted her back. He persuaded me to have dinner with her, although I really didn't want to.

Tara and I talked a couple of times on the telephone and she agreed to meet me in her local Indian. She arrived ten minutes late, with a wisp of an apology. She said she was tired, and she yawned and took off a Russian-style fur hat. She was beautiful as a wronged lover, pale and forlorn and vulnerable. We ordered modest starter dishes, and a bottle of wine. She confided that Sam was dynamic and interesting and that she had loved him but she said, in the end – and I remember her saying those words, "in the end", or "at the end of the day" – he had a real problem with commitment. I was strangely elated to hear her say it because it helped explain why he had rejected me, and I clung onto that explanation for many years.

Tara thought that he found it hard to be close to a woman because his mother had left when he was a few months old. I knew that his mother had abandoned him, because Sam had told me about a dreadful conversation he'd had with his father, when he was eight or nine. His father had taken him around the garden and explained that the woman he'd thought of as his mother was in fact his stepmother, and that his real mother, the woman who'd given birth to him, had left when he was a few months old, as she hadn't been able to cope. Sam was enraged by the news and had run to his room where he'd lain on his bed and sobbed. He said at that moment he hated everyone. He hated his father for not telling him before, he hated his stepmother for lying to him, and he hated his stepsisters for having a real mother. His stepmother had come to his bedroom and said she loved him like a son, but he'd shouted at her and told her to go away. He told me he felt like an outsider in the family and just so bewildered and sad. Gradually, though, he began to accept the situation because he loved his stepmother and the only one he hated was his own mother, for leaving. He didn't want to betray his step-mother by looking for his birth mother and so he never had. His real mother, Beth, had once sent a letter to an old address, which had been forwarded to him. He was fifteen years old at the time and didn't reply; in fact, he threw the letter away and later, when he went back to retrieve it, the rubbish had been taken away and he was both disappointed and relieved. He carried on with his life. We ordered mint teas and I told her that Sam wanted her back.

She made the point that she wasn't strong enough to return to a man who had hurt her so much. She said she had been doing some thinking. She confided that she didn't have enough verve and panache for Sam. Sam wanted her to be a little more vibrant and she couldn't be that person. "I don't have the ambition or the energy to be with a man like him," she told me.

"But maybe he doesn't want a girlfriend like that," I said. "He really loves you. He was persuaded to go to Paris against his will, really. He was weak: I don't know why he did it." As soon as I spoke, I wondered why I was trying to persuade her to go back to a man who had hurt me so much.

"Polly is a model," Tara said, "and that's the kind of thing he's into. Believe me. He likes glamour. I'm sure he slept with her in Paris and that's why he stayed on."

She was probably right and I didn't bother to deny it.

"I just don't trust him any more," she finished.

I reported back to Sam with the news that he had lost her and secretly I was relieved that it was all over. Sam spent another few months in London, before packing up and going to live in San Francisco. I got on with my life, and moved in with Marcus. Sam and I didn't see each other again until two years ago, when he was in London on business and he called me to invite me for lunch. It was late autumn and we met in the Café Anglais. He was as handsome as he had always been, perhaps a little thinner in the face, but still attractive and funny and sweet, and we lingered over coffee until the secretary from Alfie's school called to say that Alfie had hurt his ankle in football and asked if I could pick him up. I was heady and confused after leaving, and more than a little sad. But when I next spoke to Tara, she said she had seen him too, that evening for a drink. It was the first time they had met in years. I was disappointed that he had shared out his time with both of us and I tried once again to forget him.

Marcus is exhausted as Tokyo is nine hours ahead; he falls asleep within seconds of rolling onto his side. Every night before going to sleep, I thank God or the universe – I'm not completely sure who to thank – but feel that it is important to remember to thank someone. I remember my single days and most of my childhood with dread. Before I met Marcus, I spent all my time recovering from one passionate relationship or consumed by another, and most of my childhood wishing I was older so that I didn't have to feel so powerless all the time. I am grateful that I no longer have to live my life alone. I am not a person who is good at being single. I started the nightly ritual of thanking the universe about a year ago, and now I've started I can't seem to stop. It's as though if I stop thanking someone, my life will fall apart. Some days I forget to say thank you and then I worry that something dreadful will happen that will throw me off balance, or tip me over the edge.

Marcus is drinking coffee and yawning. He's standing up, poised to go. It seems he can't take the time now to sit down and eat breakfast. He's ruffled Alfie's hair, and kissed him and given him the present, but his mind is somewhere else. "Listen, guys, I've got good news and bad news. Which do you want first?"

"Good!" Alfie says.

"The good news is I'm home, the bad news is that I'm not going to be able to make the holiday at half-term."

"What? Why not? We've paid for it."

Alfie's face twists and falls. I think he may cry. We booked a couple of nights at Disneyland in Paris a few months ago and the date coincides with Alfie's seventh birthday.

"I'm sorry," he says, "I'm just too tied up with this new contract. Believe me, I'd rather be with you."

"It's a couple of days over a weekend," I persist, racking my brains at the same time about who I can invite in his place. I'd been so looking forward to the three of us spending some time together.

"I'm sorry," he repeats robotically. "There's nothing I can do. I'll make it up to you, mate," he says to Alfie. "Maybe we can go to a football match together. I'll get Jane to look into it."

He kisses me on the cheek. "I'll be home late," he says. "Business dinner."

There is nothing to say.

"Bye," I call out.

I am smiling but raging inside. Is this the price to pay for being together with a man who is enjoying success? I drop Alfie at school and then take the bus. I stare out of the window as great plops of rain begin to fall on the dirty grey pavement. I am so disappointed that when I get home, I go straight to the fridge and pick out some carrots and hummus and oatcakes. Then I help myself to a slice of my birthday cake. The rain slashes down on the windows, and in my bedroom I find my window open, and a small puddle on the floor.

Six Months later:

I just had the strangest telephone call from Sam. He won't be in Italy until two or three days after we all arrive, because his bathroom has flooded into his study and he needs to sort it out. He says we must all go ahead without him and are welcome to make ourselves at home. It's a strange situation but I'm not that surprised. I asked him a few details about who else was coming and he says he's going to send me an email about the other guests. I am slightly uncomfortable about sharing the holiday with Tara. We wouldn't have chosen to spend our summer holiday together, not this one at least. But perhaps, I think rationally, it will be a good way to reignite our friendship, as we have only seen each other a handful of times since my birthday dinner. Marcus and I have hardly seen each other at all these last few months. I want this holiday so that we can spend some time together and be close again. I hope for this, and at night, before I go to sleep, I wish for it.

I am packing, throwing bikinis and other summer clothes into the case. I remember as a child walking along Tarifa beach in Spain and seeing an old woman dressed in a bathing suit with pubic hair spreading in a grotesque but fascinating way down the insides of her thighs. I imagined the woman had great mounds of creeping, curling hair on her thighs because she was old, just as I imagined that women's breasts grew bigger as they aged. When I think about swimming costumes and bikinis, I always think about the woman I saw on Tarifa beach. She is probably dead now.

As I continue to pack, I think that it always seems so weird to be suddenly walking around in the equivalent of a bra and pants or skimpy leotard, just because it's hot. I've had a wax and a fake tan and have struggled for a couple of weeks with a 'no carbs/no alcohol' diet but have lost just two measly pounds and at most half an inch from my waist. My friends say I don't need to lose weight but I do, just a little more. My jeans are less tight now, but still not comfortable. I've recently done a shoot of a 1950s house and a portrait of the mother with her three beautiful teenage girls. The girls made me feel old and cumbersome. "Youth is so beautiful," I sighed to Tara on the telephone, while we were having a chat about the holiday.

"Not necessarily," Tara replied. "You should see some of the teenage boys on the bus to work. They have shadows of a moustache above the lip, red pimples, greasy hair, half-broken voices, dirty nails and they smell of BO. It's disgusting."

"Well, these girls were beautiful and with their whole lives ahead of them. It made me feel tired and wrung out."

"Well, you're not," Tara said. "Don't you remember being a teenage girl? Don't you remember how seedy it was to get so drunk that your head spun and then you threw up? Remember the pain of being chucked by some ridiculous boy?"

"I know. But I do wish, like everyone does, that I could go back ten years but live with the knowledge that I have now."

"Yes, but you wouldn't be you."

It's true that I would not take up an offer to be someone else, even someone I really admire. Everyone has their dark side, however perfect they seem to an onlooker. Shame, longing, envy, fury, wishing ill will on others – these are the qualities that most people hide from the world. We keep our more unappealing sides, our weird, crazed, hateful sides for husbands, boyfriends and partners, the people who love us. No one has everything – the perfect house, the perfect job and the perfect relationship. At least that's what I want to believe.

Hi Beauty,

I've invited an old school friend, Toby. Nice guy, doing well in a difficult property market. He's engaged to Miranda. She wants to upgrade him from an unfit, pale smoker and drinker into a new vibrant and healthy superman. She made him give up smoking by imposing a fine system. He says they have great sex. Sorry, maybe that's more than you need to know. Anyway, they only got engaged about a month ago. He's not entirely easy about it. He told me he's woken up a few times in the night and worried that things were out of his control and going too fast. Apparently she was on the phone to her parents seconds after he proposed and arranging the wedding. Now she spends any spare time designing the bridesmaids' dresses. More later… I'll tell you about Jack. He's got two kids: Maud 4 and Jed 7.

I read the email quickly; Sam should have been a scriptwriter, not a producer.

"Alfie!" I call over the banisters. "Are you OK?"

There is no reply. I find him playing with his Nintendo DS, hunched over the small white box, gripped in concentration.

"Are you excited?"

"Yes," he looks up. "Will there be any other children?"

"A little boy, same age as you. He's called Jed, he's seven, and Maud is four."

"Do you know them?"

"No, I don't."

"OK," Alfie nods. "OK, Mummy."

I climb back up the stairs knowing that I should make more of an effort. I can't leave Alfie there for much longer playing with his Nintendo even though he's perfectly happy. Marcus has gone to play tennis. There is just so much to do before leaving tomorrow. For the last two weeks I've been working most days on a kitchen catalogue and Alfie has been looked after by Viola, a woman from the Ukraine. I pick up the pile of ironed clothes on the landing and climb upstairs to my bedroom to finish the packing. I have a headache and my neck is stiff. I am longing to be by the pool, slumped in the sun, thinking about nothing.

When I check my computer again, another email has arrived from Sam.

OK. So, Jack Boore is a typical actor. He's loud and full of himself, but he's amusing and means well. He's separated from his wife and has two kids. I think he still drives his wife insane. He goes round to her house and says stuff like, "there's a fuck of a lot of dog shit in this garden". Then he walks around prodding shit with a stick and demanding plastic bags to put it in.

I know this because he told me! His estranged wife owns a café with a friend and it's going really well and she's renting a new house. Jack says that the style of her house is the exact opposite of the slick, minimalist white house they shared in Hampstead. He's very sore about the ex. Originally she had an affair with a neighbour and Jack found out and ended the relationship. She pleaded with him not to leave her, but he was too betrayed and outraged. He hated the fact that she'd lied. He still talks about it and can't seem to let it go. I think he feels expendable and that's why I've asked him along. Also he's got the kids for a week and hasn't made a plan to take them anywhere. I know it sounds as though he's probably a wreck, but he's good fun. See you soon, xxx Sam

PS Had a message from Dad, apparently the housekeeper had to leave suddenly, and he's trying to find a replacement. But he says it's very short notice, apologies etc.

After reading the email I decide to telephone Tara. Jack sounds like the house guest from hell, and I'd like to talk about it. "Hello!" she says. "I'm sitting in a towel." I imagine her studying herself in the mirror of her antique dresser. "I can't decide what to wear," she continues. I wonder when she is going to ask how I am as she used to. "I'm reading *Mrs Palfrey at the Claremont*, by Elizabeth Taylor. It's the story of a widow living in a hotel in 50s London, with other elderly inhabitants, 'waiting to die'. Have you heard about it?"

"No."

"Oh, you must read it. I'll bring it for you. Mrs Palfrey is having a mild flirtation with a young, impoverished man who is using her for her financial handouts and thoughtful gifts. It's dark but brilliant. I can imagine living alone and flirting pointlessly with a younger man when I'm old. It's such a good story I don't want to go to the party."

"You should go," I say, slipping into my role of advising and taking care of her, while she goes on about herself. "Once you're there and you've said hello to a couple of friends and had a drink, it will be fine. Anyway, I was just ringing to say hi and that I've had a long email from Sam about the other people coming."

"Oh really? Who?"

"I'll forward you the email." I am absurdly pleased that he has written to me exclusively. "He's invited an actor, Jack Boore."

"Oh yes, I know him. I mean I know who he is. He has a new show, you know, a soap about sailing. He's quite good-looking."

"I haven't seen it, but I've read an article about him. Also, I just wanted to say that I'm really looking forward to spending some time with you."

"Me too, it will be lovely to see you and I'm sorry that I haven't been a good friend this year. I'll try and explain some more when we see each other."

"OK."

I put the phone down, glad that she's acknowledged the state of our friendship. There is another issue that we have never discussed. About one month ago, when Marcus and I were having supper, he said something about Tara being unhappy in her marriage, and when I asked him how he knew, he said he'd bumped into her near his office. They went for coffee and she confided in him that Dave was frustrated by the constant rejections of his book by publishers and had become quite withdrawn. She had expected marriage to be comforting like hot toast and crumpets and she was finding it more difficult than she had imagined. I asked Marcus why he hadn't told me before, and he said he'd forgotten all about it. I wanted to know what she was doing near his office (which is on the canal in Little Venice) and he replied that he had no idea. She'd told him not to say anything to anyone because she didn't want to come across as being disloyal.

I wonder why she has never mentioned that she bumped into Marcus? Why do I feel uneasy about asking her?

SATURDAY

While we are waiting for a taxi to take us to Heathrow, Marcus decides to make a snack. Chocolate spread on toast. He breaks the chocolate into small pieces, which he then puts in a bowl on top of gently boiling water. He then adds some sugar and butter, creaming it all together to spread on bread. He carries on, seemingly oblivious to the chaos around him. I run from room to room, shutting windows, locking doors and picking up books that I want to read on holiday. Marcus calls out, "CHOCOLATE" at the same moment that Alfie is shouting out for loo paper. I rush towards the bathroom with the paper and trip over my camera bag and land on my knee. "Ow!" I moan, handing Alfie the paper before hobbling upstairs to fetch my diary and handbag.

"Marcus," I groan a few minutes later, when I discover the dirty saucepans, bowls and cutlery all smothered in chocolate. There is also chocolate spread all over Alfie's face. "Marcus," I sigh, as the taxi hoots outside the door, "what are you *doing*?"

"I bought this chocolate from Selfridges and it seems like a good way to get us revved up for travelling."

"We've got to go," I say, pulling Alfie's jean jacket on, while Marcus chomps on his piece of bread and begins to wash up, flinging the wet saucepans into the rack and sweeping the chocolate crumbs into his hand.

"Careful with crumbs," I screech. "Don't forget we have mice!"

"Bloody bastards," Marcus swears, "I'm going to leave some poison."

"You can't. We'll come back to a house stinking of dead mice."

"Well, it's better than having them shitting all over the food shelves."

"No, it isn't." We continue arguing right up to the moment when we actually get into the taxi. We then drive to the airport in silence.

We seem to make up without talking about it, while queuing up to check in. We have been doing that a lot these last few months, arguing and then forgetting to make up but moving on anyway. I am dealing with the tickets when Tara telephones. We haven't spoken this much in a very long time, but we have fallen back into the role of good friends easily. "We're on our way to Stansted," she sighs, "and the traffic is at a complete standstill. People have begun to climb out of their cars and are asking each other what's going on."

I hand my passport to Marcus.

"What's happened?" I ask her.

"Well, the rumour is that a lorry has collided with a car further up the motorway and there's a five-mile tailback. Just to let you know, I think we're going to miss our flight. Dave is on the phone at the moment, trying to book something else. The taxi driver thinks it's something to do with a leak."

I can hear Dave talking to her in the background.

"There is a BA flight to Pisa this evening," he says, "but it's going to cost us £800 pounds and it's from Gatwick."

"Eight hundred!" Tara gasps. "We can't spend that. What the hell are we going to do?"

I have to help Marcus with the suitcases and the checking-in and I can't hold on any longer listening to her talking to Dave. "Good luck darling. I'm going to have to go."

"OK, I'll keep you updated. Think of us," she laughs, "stuck on the motorway, spending our last savings on a new flight. Keep your fingers crossed."

"I will."

It is awful for them, really awful. I will keep my fingers crossed. I know they are hard up. It will be difficult for them to pay for a new ticket. Dave only works part-time as he wants to keep two days a week for his writing, and Tara is a teacher. I know Tara finds it hard that he works part-time when they are struggling.

Tara has recently left a large multicultural primary school, where 53 per cent of the children had English as a second language. Some of the children were refugees, mostly from Somalia, and she was finding that it was often difficult to communicate with the parents.

The teachers at this school were some of the best that Tara had ever come across, but after three years she had had enough of suffering with a permanent cold and runny nose brought on by her constant tiredness. Officially, she should have been at school from 8.45 to 3.45 but really, she was often at work by 7.30 and finishing by 6 or 6.30. She told me all this when we were chatting about the holiday last week. Next term she starts at a smaller school, where the parents are pushier, and so the school achieves better results.

I tell Marcus what has happened to Dave and Tara while we are waiting in the business class lounge and ask him if we should offer to pay for their new ticket.

"No, we can't," he replies bluntly. "They're not our teenage children and I think Dave would find it patronising." He's right. It would probably make them uncomfortable.

On the aeroplane, I pick up my copy of *House & Garden* magazine, and find the story of a barn conversion I shot in Oxfordshire. My agent Nadine has already told me that I have the cover – a still life of a white vase on a hall table. I have been given three full pages and they have chosen the photographs I would have chosen. The barn is well lit and the walled garden looks really gorgeous and enticing – the perfect secret garden filled with herbs, flowers and vegetables, with an ancient glass house in one corner. Marcus leans over Alfie who is reading *Beast Quest*, and takes my hand. I close my eyes and imagine that in Italy, Marcus and I will fall in love again.

When we arrive at Pisa, I can't find a euro to put in the luggage trolley and Marcus strides off to change some money. As we walk into the arrivals hall I am excited, the sun is shining, and the women are darkly tanned like gypsies. Some are extravagantly made up and wearing shiny jewellery and high-heeled sandals, and despite my fake tan I am aware of how pale I am. The building smells of coffee. There is a café in the arrivals hall and we buy two coffees and three freshly made Parma ham and cheese sandwiches. I never usually eat sandwiches but I can't resist this one. Marcus also has a beer and Alfie a Coca Cola.

Marcus's secretary, Jane, has booked the wrong kind of car, and Marcus is sweating and still hungry. I can't see why it is wrong, but Marcus says it's something to do with the size of the engine and he thinks that the air-conditioning isn't good enough. While he is looking at the map, Marcus takes large greedy bites of an apple that I've found in my bag and then he lights a cigarette. He's wearing new Prada dark glasses that he's bought at the duty free shop, a blue shirt with the first three buttons undone and a pair of battered jeans. I am looking quite boyish today, in a pair of slim white jeans and a large and loose shirt. Marcus shoves his apple core into the ashtray and starts the engine.

I am reading the directions that someone from Sam's office has emailed me. "Turn right at Via Engenio 111 which is signposted Pisa/Rome/Aurelia/Viareggio."

"Shit!" Marcus says.

"Mum, can I have something to eat?" Alfie asks from the back seat.

I rummage in my bag and find some stale Hula-Hoops.

"Mum, can I sleep near you and Dad?" Alfie asks. "Because of my nightmares."

"Yes, I'm sure you can. Don't worry." We all know that Alfie will be sleeping with us, even though we will all go along with the charade of giving him his own room.

"Do you promise?"

"Yes."

"Thank God for air-conditioning," Marcus says wiping his forehead. "I'm still feeling queasy from the aeroplane."

"Taken your tablets, Marcus?" I joke.

"Which ones?" he laughs back. "Stomach, heart or hearing?"

"All three?"

"This is a shit car," Marcus, says. "I wanted the Alfa Romeo but at least we do have air-conditioning."

"We are climate criminals, flying on aeroplanes,

using air-conditioning, driving a petrol car."

"Actually, it's diesel. What do you mean, flying on aeroplanes? How else are we going to get here?"

"Train?"

"Yeah, right, I've really got the time."

"We should use trains as much as possible."

"How do you think I'm going to get to Japan for work?"

"You could take a cargo ship." I laugh at the absurdity of this idea.

Marcus opens the window and shuts it again. "I won't even bother to reply to that," he remarks with a sidelong glance at me. "The price of fuel is stopping people buying aeroplane tickets. It shouldn't be cheap to fly. That's the way to cut down flying."

"Yes, there should be more government restrictions on how much people can fly, or penalties for flying over a certain number of miles."

"Mum, you already recycle," Alfie says. "You're always telling us to put glass and paper in the orange bags, and we do it at school."

"Yes, but that's not enough."

"You're a good eco-warrior. You'll be storming parliament next." Marcus is already clearly bored.

"Well, I'd like to do something rather than just sitting around talking about it. If we don't, our grandchildren won't be able to live a normal life. We already have burning forests, dissolving coral reefs and some day soon there won't be any more polar bears."

Marcus turns the radio on and leans back on his seat. "You know what," he sighs. "I have no space to think about anything else in my head except work right now."

"Why not?" I snap, because this issue is something I worry about. "We have about six years to act and to make a significant impact on CO_2 and other greenhouse gas emissions."

"OK," he says, "if you insist on talking about this matter, what's your view on wind farms? We passed one just now."

I am thinking about how to respond; in theory, I think they are a great idea. I don't object to what they look like and surely using wind to produce energy is a good idea, but I don't know enough to create a coherent, convincing argument.

"Well –" we both start at the same time.

"Well, I'll tell you what I think," he continues. "They don't work when there's no wind and they don't work when it's not windy enough."

"That's not true," I stutter. "That's not true at all. I've seen them working when there is very little wind."

"Where?" he challenges me.

"I can't remember. Where have you seen them not working?"

"I haven't. It's something I read. And they're ugly," he adds.

"I don't agree. I think they are rather beautiful, they're like random pieces of conceptual art."

"They are hideous and wreck the countryside. Also, large migrating birds are at risk when confronted by wind farms.

"Barbed wire and pylons are far uglier than wind farms. But you do have a point about the birds; I hadn't thought of that."

"Stop arguing," Alfie pleads.

"We're not," Marcus says. "We're having a discussion. Although I have to admit I don't know much about the whole thing."

I open the window and quickly shut it again. "I don't know every detail," I admit. 'But I know its unthinkable to do nothing. That's why we have to keep campaigning, we have to keep people aware of what could happen if we do nothing, and what better place to start than my own family?"

"Mum, you're being so boring," Alfie complains from the back.

"I'm doing this for your generation and for your children," I tell him.

"Give him a break," Marcus says. "He's eight!"

"OK. I won't say anything else," I promise.

Despite the lack of interest from Marcus and Alfie about the planet, I am happy to be in Italy. I still remember my first visit to Florence, aged about eighteen, and the moment I stood looking up at David by Michelangelo. I was struck by the size of David, the beauty of the smooth marble limbs, and surprised when my skin shivered. Now, of course, it leaves me cold, an image I have seen so many times reproduced on postcards and tablemats, it's like looking at the Eiffel Tower or the Mona Lisa or Trafalgar Square.

I've always liked to hear Italians speaking. The language sounds sensual like poetry and has the rhythm of a song. I know a little bit of Italian – enough to get by – but I haven't spoken it for a while. When I first arrived in Rome to work as an assistant photographer, I remember walking around just staring up at the buildings and the fountains and the piazzas and falling in love with the city and desperately wanting to speak to people. After a little time there, I could say that I was hot or cold or that I would like a fresh orange juice or a hot chocolate. I learnt to read the menus, but once made the mistake of going into a bar, thinking I was asking for a grapefruit juice: "*Posso avere un pompino?*" Everybody laughed at me because it translated as "Can I have a blowjob?"

And I love their food – the minestrone, the spinach

cooked with lemon and the risotto. I devour Parma ham, Parmesan; anything, really, that an Italian will put before me, I will eat.

We are driving on the motorway and cars are overtaking us randomly, on both sides, which is quite intimidating if you're not used to it. We drive by rolling hills dotted with castles and fortresses and past terraces of olive groves and sudden makeshift shrines. The landscape is like an elegant Renaissance painting. We eventually come off the motorway onto a smaller road and stop to buy a box of yellowy pink peaches and one of tomatoes, which are for sale at a little stall. The peaches are sweet and delicious.

We finally find our turn-off, a bumpy track which has no signpost, and drive up a hill and round some bends, as wasps buzz and bump at the windows. After a few moments, I can see a traditional stone farmhouse with painted green shutters and doors. It looks out onto the mountains across the valley. I step out of the car and stretch my arms to the sun and feel its warmth on my skin. It's very hot and the cicadas are strumming, and there is a faint breeze. I inhale the aroma coming from the vast pots of rosemary, lavender and thyme that are positioned at the foot of stone steps that lead up to the house.

I turn to Marcus, who is lifting luggage from the boot. "Isn't this heavenly?"

"It is," he agrees, as a small tabby cat crosses our path.

Alfie runs up the steps, followed by Marcus who needs a pee. A woman – it must be Miranda – is waving from the large shady terrace which runs in front of the building. She's wearing a halter-neck top and beige shorts that come to the knee, a large pair of sunglasses and a straw hat. Her legs are alpine white. Her boyfriend or fiancé, Toby, is standing behind her, sending a text or email.

"Hello," Miranda calls out.

Marcus returns with Alfie a moment later. "Have you said hello to Miranda?"

"Hello," Alfie says, staring down at his shoes.

"Hello," she bends down. "How are you?" she asks in a high, childish voice.

"Fine." He looks away and I'm conscious of how rude he seems. Toby finishes his telephone call and comes bounding down the steps.

"Hello." He shakes our hands. "I've already discovered the fig tree." He's quite camp, I think, looking at his clean fingernails and shiny signet ring. Miranda stands next to him and fiddles with his hair, until I imagine he would like to swat her away like a fly.

"There are lots of wasps," Miranda says smiling brightly, "but we've got an idea. Well, Tobs has an idea. What we're going to do is go out and buy a crate of beer and then leave a half-empty bottle on the table. Wasps are drawn to the smell of beer and so they'll flop in and die." She motions towards their glistening hire car that shines on the driveway, next to the ugly one that we have rented. "We'll go soon – won't we, Tobs?"

"We've only just arrived, darling."

"Maybe you should wait until it isn't quite so hot," I suggest, aware that I am siding with Toby. Miranda's voice has a slight nasal, tinny tone that grates on me.

"I love the heat," Miranda says, squinting up into the sun. "I thrive in the heat, maybe because I was brought up in the tropics."

Marcus sits down next to her, and Toby gives him a glass of water. He stretches out his long legs, while Alfie sits on the floor with his alien creatures. They begin chatting about Sam, our absent host, who I am longing to see.

Now I'm here, I want to explore the house. I walk along the terrace and through into the kitchen; the floor is covered in terracotta quarry tiles. It is modern and clean and cool, and the beams on the ceiling look as though they could be chestnut. I can't help but notice these details because of my job. There is an Aga and a large wooden refectory-style kitchen table and an old bread or pizza oven. I open the kitchen cupboard doors and find some tins of tomatoes, jars of dried herbs, pasta

49

and cereal packets. I am about to leave the kitchen with my suitcase when a woman in her sixties appears, almost from nowhere. She is rather plump, with greying blond hair, a long fringe and large, sad eyes; clearly not Italian. "Welcome," she smiles, "I'm Jill. I've come to welcome you all and show you around."

We say hello and I shake her hand.

"I offered to help Philip out, when the last housekeeper left suddenly. Are you a friend of Sam's?" she asks me.

"Yes," I say. "I've known him a while."

"Have you? Is he here yet?"

"No, he's been delayed so won't be here for a couple of days."

"Oh," she says. "Oh I see." She sounds disappointed. "His father, Philip, gave strict instructions to make sure I welcomed him."

We are standing, chatting, when Marcus and Alfie come into the kitchen and Jill introduces herself.

"I'm going to look after you all," she says. "Philip was most particular when he said I should look after his son and his house guests. I stepped in, you see, when the last housekeeper left."

"What happened to her?" Marcus asks.

"Far too pretty for her own good. Down at the bar, drinking all the time. It was just as well her mother got ill, really. It was something to do with a burst appendix. Anyway, it was time she left. Philip found her in the caravan with a married man." She's talking almost without drawing breath. Then she starts to cough and her eyes are watering, so I offer her a glass of water.

Marcus says he'd like to see the bedrooms. He sounds a bit abrupt, which makes me feel that I should compensate and ask her a question. "Why did you come to Italy?" I ask, and see Marcus raise his eyebrows at me.

"Ah," she says, smiling, pleased that I have asked. She says she was married to a man who has connections here. "Happy times. Such happy memories. Anyway," she says sadly, "he moved on."

I am worried that she may cry. She says she doesn't live here all year round, but has a flat back home in Marlow, which she rents out for short lets. Marcus is fiddling with his briefcase; he looks impatient.

"We'd like to take our suitcases to our rooms, now," Marcus says brusquely. Jill looks strangely crestfallen, as if Marcus has wounded her.

"Do you know where to go?" she asks. "I'd be happy to show you."

"Don't worry, I'll find it. Sam says we should take one of the doubles upstairs and we need to be near Alfie."

"Would you like a cup of tea?" Jill asks.

"Yes, that would be lovely," I reply, as Marcus and Alfie leave the kitchen. I am longing to go to my room, but I don't want to offend her.

"Have you had any lunch?"

"We had a few nuts on the aeroplane and some sandwiches at the airport."

"Well, I'll be around if you need some help."

"Thank you."

"That's my pleasure," she says. "Oh, and by the way, there are extra parasols in the swimming pool hut but you must remember to fold them up in the evening. The winds can be strong, and could blow them all down. They can cause an awful amount of damage. Oh, and I must tell you, medicines are ever so expensive here," she sighs, "but I've got a huge stock, so don't go wasting your money. And welcome to the *La Silerchie*."

"Well, thanks for everything."

Jill heaves herself up. "I'll show you around."

Jill shows me the sitting room first. It is white and light and very tasteful. It has the same chestnut beams and the same quarry tiles as the kitchen. There is a large open fireplace, two comfortable deep cream sofas, covered with delicately patterned silk cushions, and two pale brown-and-white cowhide rugs spread out on the floor. A round marble-topped coffee table holds a vase of liliesand there are brightly coloured throws on the chairs. It's a large room but manages to be cosy. There is a flat-screen television pinned to a wall and various modern paintings, juxtaposed with a couple of local landscapes, one of a winding path surrounded by pine trees and another of a small church.

"Are you OK?" I ask as Jill sighs again. She seems a bit confused. "Yes. I haven't been here for a while, you see. Well, I did put the flowers in the vase. Philip asked me to do that."

"Thank you. It's a beautiful room," I say. She nods in agreement. Then she grimaces. "Are you sure you're all right?" I ask her.

"It's just, well, that I get this twinge under my arm, quite often, not sure what it is. Anyway, you wanted to see the rooms. Well, there are two on the ground-floor, darker than the three upstairs." On the way out of the room, I notice that she glances at some family photographs that are displayed on a wall between the windows. The photographs are black and white, simply framed. There is a smiling grey-haired man, a blonde sensible-looking wife and two children.

The three downstairs bedrooms are small and simple. Two twin rooms share an interconnecting bathroom and one small queen-size double room looks out over the driveway. The queen-size bed is a four-poster, and in the back frame is a beautiful silk hanging decorated with red and white flowers. Jill walks slowly up the stairs and I follow behind. Upstairs, the bedrooms are far larger, with their own en-suite bathrooms. The master bedroom is enormous with a corridor containing a walk-in wardrobe and a view of the hills from the windows. Everything in this room is white, except for a chandelier, which is made of multi-coloured Venetian glass. There are white towelling dressing gowns hanging behind the doors, a white bedspread, white cushions on the bed, and a white chair. Even the mirror behind the bed is framed in white.

Marcus has put our case in one of the two larger bedrooms.

"Thanks, Jill, I think I'm just going to change into a swimming costume." I am hovering on the threshold of my bedroom.

"I'll scribble down my number in case you need me." She thrusts a note into my hand.

"Thank you so much, Jill," I say again. She doesn't leave, and I want to shut my door, and change into my swimsuit.

"All right," she says at last, "I'll head off now. So you're all here tonight, apart from Sam who's coming soon?"

"He'll be here Tuesday or Wednesday," I tell her, half-shutting the door.

"It'll be nice when he gets here," she says. "He's got an awful long way to go."

"Yes," I agree, moving towards my bed. "Yes, it's a long way."

"He's definitely coming? Is he?"

"Yes," I say. "Yes, definitely." She looks satisfied but her question has left me wondering whether he will come at all.

I lie down on the huge double bed and close my eyes. A gentle wind ruffles the plain white curtains in front of the shutters. I shut my eyes and hear Alfie shouting in the hallway. I catch a snatch of a conversation between Marcus and Toby and hear the slow plodding of Marcus's footsteps on the stairs.

"Jen!" he calls out. "Where are you?"

"I'm here! In our bedroom."

He comes in and puts his computer case on a chair. "It's a great room, isn't it?" he says. "Just went to fetch the last suitcase."

"It's fantastic."

"It's very odd that Sam would miss three days of a seven-day holiday. He didn't ask us to contribute to the rent did he?"

"No, he insisted that we didn't need to. I don't think he needs to either. It's his father's house."

"Well, we'll have to go and buy several cases of wine and all the food, and take him out to dinner."

"Yes, let's do that."

Sam has always been so generous. I look up at the

large colonial paddle fan as it whirls round and round, and then I lift myself up on my forearms and look out of the window at the view of the mountains.

Marcus kicks off his shoes and lies next to me.

"I think that woman Jill is a bit odd," I say.

"Why?"

"She looks sort of tragic."

"Give her a chance," he says. "But I do agree, she does rattle on a bit. Where are we going to put Alfie? Shall we just admit that he's actually going to sleep in our bed?" He sounds cross now and a bit stressed.

"I've put him in the room next to ours. It's a really grand room and it should probably be for Miranda and Toby or Jack."

"You can't put him in there," he says. "You can't take an adult room for a small child."

He's right, of course. I can't put him in a huge double bedroom, when we know he will sleep with us. It's awful having a large lumping boy with bruises on his knees and pointy elbows in our bed. Marcus is loath to kick him out because he has issues, bad memories of his own childhood. His parents had too many children to really focus on any one of them, and equally I don't want to oust Alfie, because I remember being really terrified in my dark room as a child. I was scared of what lurked in the darkness, witches in the cupboard and ghosts and ghouls behind the curtains. And I always think that Alfie suffered because there were complications at his birth and as soon as he was born he was snatched away from me. I have talked to a psychologist about this and she confirmed it. But we have to get him out of our bed. He is literally between us, a great barrier to any kind of intimacy, an excuse not to do anything about the state of our relationship. During my worst moments, I fear that the damage is done, and that Alfie sleeping between us symbolises the end of what we once had.

I am thinking about getting up and going for a swim and then lunch.

"I can't think of anything I'd like to do more," I say, "than swim in the pool. I'll move Alfie's things in here."

"I can think of something better." He rolls on top of me, cackling in a phoney evil way. He smells of aeroplanes and cigarettes.

"Help!" It's been so long since we lay down together on a bed in the daytime. It feels strange and a little awkward, and instead of kissing him, I giggle. I am giggling when Alfie comes into our room without knocking and demands that we take him down to the swimming pool. Marcus sighs heavily. He stands up and walks across to the window. He turns around and I see that he looks exhausted, pale; and older than he used to, even older than he looked six months ago.

We walk down towards the pool, which is surrounded by lavender bushes and has a small gazebo next to it. We overhear Miranda and Toby talking. "Why?" she asks in a baby voice. "Have I been really awful?"

"Never," he sounds sweet and happy.

"Do you think this bathing costume is too tight?"

"No."

"Are you sure?"

"Yes."

"Not just saying that?"

"No."

We appear at the pool and say hello. It's an infinity pool and it's long and wide and painted dark blue, with sumptuous cream-coloured deck chairs and sunbeds scattered around it. There are more pots of lavender by the pool house and big fluffy pool towels for us to use. Miranda is wearing a bright pink bathing costume. Toby sits up, picks up his digital camera and puts on his shades.

"Hello," she says to us. "I was just teasing Toby about his Hawaiian shirt." She's giggling and collapsing with laughter.

"Don't you like it? It was a present from my mum."

"I love it," Miranda replies, picking up her book. "You look like a gay bartender."

"I think it's great," Marcus says, pulling a sunbed

from the shade of an umbrella into the stunning brightness.

"Have you heard, that Jack Boore is coming?" Miranda asks. She's looking up at Marcus, almost fluttering her eyelashes. She is the kind of woman who must flirt with a man.

"Yes, we heard," I reply.

"Can't wait to meet him," she says, turning onto her stomach. "My mum loves him. Can you put some suncream on me?" she asks Toby. He gets up and squidges the cream between his fingers and massages her back in rather a sensual way, as though they are just about to make love. She squirms under his fingers. Then I ask Marcus to put some on me. He slaps the cream onto my shoulders and rubs it in briskly, losing interest by the time he gets to my back. His mind is on other things. I know this because as soon as he's finished with the cream, he wipes his hands and picks up his mobile to make a call.

Miranda insists on talking to me about her wedding and how excited she is, and how she's so glad not to be left on the shelf. I can't believe that she's actually saying things like this, but she really is. Every so often she takes a tiny bite of an apple and then a handful of what look like sunflower seeds. She asks about my wedding and when I explain that Marcus and I are not married, she seems visibly shocked and says "ah…" in a pitying manner, as though she feels really sorry for me.

"Do you mind?" she asks, and I am getting the impression that she just wants to know and wouldn't really care if I did mind. She's one of those women who chat for the sake of chatting, without any depth or meaning and who want to know everything about you, but only because they are looking for gossip ammunition. I know I am making my mind up pretty quickly about her, but that's how she seems to be. I could be wrong.

Alfie is jumping in and out and in and out of the pool. I stand and pull up my red bikini bottoms, and think again of the old lady in Tarifa beach. I hope my bottom isn't showing too much as I dive into the pool and swim as far as I can underwater. When I surface I see that Miranda is now reading a magazine. I climb out of the pool and walk slowly towards my chair and pick up my book before lying down on a lounger, hoping that she won't engage me in conversation again. Marcus is now talking to someone on his mobile. He's frowning and rubbing his hands through his hair. Toby appears to be asleep on his stomach. I look at him and worry that his shoulders will burn. This is the kind of thing I can't help but think since becoming a mother.

At about 2.30, I walk up to the house to prepare Alfie a snack – I know he'll be hungry soon. As I reach the house I can hear a car horn and the tinny sound of

Italian pop music, which sounds grotesquely loud in the still clear air. I move round to the drive to see who it is. A man is standing by a red convertible sports car. I say hello and the man, whom I vaguely recognise, introduces himself as Jack Boore, the soap actor. I am conscious of the fact that I am wearing a swimming suit and a flimsy wrap and pleased that I have had my eyebrows shaped. He looks like the kind of man who appreciates perfectly groomed females.

His hair is blond and greying at the temples and he has mischievous blue eyes, and a weirdly unlined forehead. He's smaller than I imagined him. I've noticed that many actors are smaller than you think they will be.

"Did you find it all right?"

"No, not really – we got lost," he replies with a crisply confident, smooth voice. "We had an Italian dominatrix trying to explain the directions on sat nav and I couldn't work out how to change it to English. This is Jed," he says, indicating the children that Sam had told me about in his email, "and this is Maud."

"Hello, Jed and Maud, it's really great to see you both. I'm Jen. Shall I show you your rooms?"

They are the sweetest children. Maud has a dimple and straight blonde hair with a long fringe, and she's taken my hand. Jed wears shorts and has thin white legs poking from underneath. He's smaller and much sweeter-looking than Alfie, who is tall for his age.

"Why are you called Jen?" Maud asks in a sing-song voice. "I have a book called *Jen the Hen*."

Jack laughs.

"I know, it's funny, isn't it? My real name is Jennifer."

"Funny about old Sammy," Jack says. "Leaving all his guests here like the Great Gatsby."

"He's had a flood."

"Flood!" Jack laughs. "He's probably scored himself a date. Can't imagine what he thinks he's doing flying halfway round the world for half a week."

"What's a date?" Maud asks.

"An oval, sweet fruit." Jack replies.

"Why is Jen short for Jennifer?" Maud asks, looking up at me.

"It's just the first three letters."

"Is this your house?" Jed asks. Jed is beautiful, almost like a girl, with long lashes and huge trusting brown eyes.

"You'll have to meet my son Alfie. He's seven, probably the same age as you."

"Actually, I'm eight, but don't worry," Jed says in a serious, grown-up voice. "I'm used to that. I'm quite small for my age."

He's adorable, and for one treacherous moment, I want to swap him for Alfie.

"Can I grab a glass of water?" Jack asks.

"What about the children? Would you like a glass of water?" I ask as we walk into the kitchen.

"We'd like juice," Maud says. "Mummy always asks us if we'd like juice or water or milk."

"Of course she does," I reply. "It's just we haven't done a big shop yet."

I walk towards the fridge and open it, and to my surprise, find it full of things – milk, juice, eggs, slices of Parma ham, a kind of fig tart, some home-made-looking pasta, yoghurts, butter and packets of meat, and on the oak kitchen table, an enormous loaf of bread, covered in paper. "Oh," I say, "it looks as though some lovely elves have come and filled up the fridge." The children laugh at this.

Jack sits down and drinks his water and mentions that he has an enthusiastic fan, Jean, who had heard he was going away with his children and sent him some home-made jams. "She's always writing these notes," he says, "with pressed flowers enclosed. She makes me knitted ties for my birthday. Anyway, I've brought some for you."

"What! Knitted ties?"

"No, you duck, the jams. Well, I brought them for our absent host Sam, but he's not here, so I'm giving them to you."

He hands me two jars of strawberry jam which

makes me feel slightly uncomfortable as I don't want to be the host in Sam's absence. Jack cuts a piece of bread and spreads it with butter and jam. The children ask if they can have some too and I cut them each a slice.

"I gave some of this to my friend, Stephen Fry," he says. "He really enjoyed it."

"Oh really?" I reply. "That's great, maybe I'll save some for my friend, Kenneth Branagh."

"Oh, Ken," Jack says. "Do you know him? Great guy. We had lunch together at the Groucho the other day."

"No, I don't know him," I smile.

He looks at me with surprise before laughing. "Don't mind me. I'm the world's worst namedropper. I can't help it."

We talk about the sleeping arrangements, as Sam has not left any instructions about who is to sleep where. When we reach the upstairs bedrooms, we find that Toby and Miranda have taken the large double room, which I had originally thought about giving to Alfie. Jack grunts and walks back downstairs and takes the twin with the interconnecting room, which is actually perfect for him, as it means he can be next to his children.

Jack and his children walk with me to the swimming pool and I introduce him to Miranda, Toby, Marcus and Alfie. I have brought down some homemade lemonade that was in the fridge, and four frosty plastic glasses. Jack sits down at the edge of a lounger and drinks two glasses of lemonade. Miranda immediately tells him how much she loves his show, and that she knows all the plot lines and all the actors. Jack visibly puffs up like the cold pigeons outside my bedroom window in winter. He turns towards her, so that I get a view of his back. Jed and Maud want to swim and take off their clothes. Jack moans about having to go back to the house to fetch the armbands and swimming suits and when Jed offers, he lets him go off on his own. I offer to help Jed. As we walk together to the house, he tells me that his parents split up last summer, and now he wishes that they would get back together. I take his hand, small and hot, in mine and he holds on tight.

When Marcus and I are changing out of our swimming things for lunch, I ask him what he thinks about Jack. Marcus umms and ahhs and doesn't answer the question, so I repeat it and he replies that he doesn't really know yet, that he hasn't had a chance to form an opinion.

"Well, you had an opinion about Jill."

Marcus doesn't say anything.

"Anyway," I go on. "Jack rolled up in a Mercedes

convertible blaring pop music and hooting the horn."

"Bastard," Marcus says. "He managed to get a decent car."

"His children are gorgeous. I bet his wife is lovely."

Alfie comes into our room in his towel. "I've had a shower."

I follow Alfie into the shower room. The floor is drenched. "Oh God. ALFIE!" I shout. I am relieved that Sam is not yet here to witness the mess.

"What?"

"Look at the mess you've made. I'll have to find a mop. Now what about your clothes?"

"I'll go and change into my shorts," he sniffs and then bursts into tears. He quite often cries if I try to reprimand him in any way. I hug him and kiss the top of his head. "Sorry, darling. So, what do you think of Maud and Jed?" I ask, rummaging through his suitcase and pulling out some shorts and a tee shirt.

"They're OK. I've only seen them for a minute."

"Jed is nice," I prompt but he doesn't reply.

"Are you hungry?" I realise I forgot to prepare Alfie's snack, with all the commotion of Jack's arrival.

"Very hungry, I haven't eaten for ages. I had breakfast and then only some nuts and a sandwich."

"Stay here, don't move. Don't do anything. I'm going to get the mop."

I run downstairs wondering where I'm going to find

a mop. "MUM!" I hear him scream. "Where are you going?"

"To get a mop! Sssh, don't make such a noise!" I call up the stairs.

The kitchen is less immaculate now, because I didn't wash up the lemonade jug and it looks as though someone else has helped themselves to some bread. The crumbs are spread around the board, so I quickly sweep them into my hand and dump them in the bin. I look around the kitchen and open cupboards and then search outside the kitchen, but can't find any cleaning products at all. Jill's number is pinned to the board, so I telephone her and ask where the mop lives. She doesn't seem to know, so I take a cloth from the cupboard under the sink and return to the bathroom to wipe up the water with a combination of cloth and paper. By the time I'm finished, I find Alfie sitting on Marcus in the bedroom. Marcus groans and lifts him off. "Come on, mate," he says. "Let's go downstairs." But we don't go just at that moment, we spend some time unpacking and tidying up and getting used to our room.

About twenty minutes later, I walk down the polished flagstone staircase to the kitchen, followed by Marcus and Alfie. I am surprised to find Jill has returned and is holding a mop and she's also bought a pasta sauce. "I couldn't leave you stranded. You just have to cook the pasta and heat up the sauce and I've thrown a salad together."

"Thank you, Jill, you really needn't have. But you are brilliant. I meant to make some pasta then got distracted. And thank you for putting all that food in the fridge. I presume it was you. You'll have to tell me how much we owe you."

"You don't owe me anything, don't you worry. It's a little welcome present." She twiddles with a strand of her hair, as if she were a young girl.

"No, I insist," I say more forcefully than I had intended. "Of course we must pay."

"Well we'll see," she says. "I'm off again now." She gathers together a wicker basket and shows me the mop. I notice it looks new – there's still a label on it. Jill leaves with a breezy goodbye and I switch the kettle on and then off again, as I don't want a cup of tea at all.

There is a text from Tara on my mobile. "Our plane arrives at 9.30 tonight. Should be with you by 11."

"Mum, when is lunch?"

Alfie has flung himself on the outside sofa and is lying flat, while Jed plays on the ground with some football cards. Miranda has come up from the pool and we have a quick talk about food. "Just going to heat a pasta sauce," I tell her. Miranda follows me back into the kitchen. She is wearing a little sundress and kitten-heeled sandals and she has lots of gold bangles that jiggle up and down her arm.

"Hope we don't have too much pasta," she says. "All those carbs."

"I wouldn't worry," Marcus, says lifting a saucepan of water onto the hob. "We're in Italy after all."

"So?" She looks at him quizzically.

"When in Rome…" He's leaving the room.

"What do you mean?" she calls out after him.

I wander out to join the children on the terrace. Jed is wearing beige shorts and a red Rolling Stones tee shirt, and Maud a very short summer dress. Jed has his arm around Maud. They really are so cute. Alfie charges up to them both with a toy aeroplane that he zooms around their heads. Jed smiles but doesn't join the game. Maud begins to laugh.

"Want to play it?" Alfie asks Jed.

"I'm looking after Maud."

"I want to play it," she says.

"OK," says Jed, "I'll play too."

They charge off down the terrace steps towards the walnut and acacia trees.

"Lunch in three minutes," Miranda calls after them.

Jack has changed into a pair of pressed maroon shorts and a white tee shirt. "Never really know whether I have the legs for shorts," he laugh. I laugh too, while Miranda looks on as though he is being serious.

"What's a man got to do to get a proper drink round

here?" he asks loudly, as I place a jug of chilled water on the table.

"Do you really think I have the legs for shorts?" he winks at me. I look down briefly at his legs. They are short and muscular.

"They're fine legs," Toby says, returning with some beer.

"What a lovely house," Jack says. "Do you have the telephone number here? I should really text my wife Ellie, and call my mother. She's 81 and likes to be in touch."

"How much?" Toby asks.

"Every day if she had her way. And every few hours would make her really happy."

"What about your ex-wife?" I laugh.

"She's not in touch at all, really, if I'm honest. And she's still my wife. I mean we're not divorced yet."

Marcus comes out onto the terrace with a boiling pot of pasta.

"My tummy is rumbling in pleasurable anticipation," Jack comments, helping himself to some wine.

We all busy ourselves looking for plates and cutlery, while Jack sits like a king waiting to be served.

"She's made the ragu with bay leaf instead of oregano or basil," Jack comments after sampling some pasta.

"Wow!" Marcus exclaims. "What a connoisseur."

"Not really." He pulls out a bay leaf and waves it, while we laugh like courtiers.

Jed and Maud eat their food without fussing, while Alfie complains about the tomato sauce, and I have to give him a separate bowl with just pasta and cheese.

I look down the garden towards the inky cypress trees and the distant hilltop village. I can hear the cicadas chirping loudly and the sun is still hot at 3.40. That's late to be having lunch and it makes me feel so happy not to be rushing somewhere. Marcus still looks tense, though. I take a sip of water and twist the oiled lengths of pasta around the prongs of my fork.

"Oh, I forgot something." Jack stands up, wiping his mouth with a huge napkin. "I've got something, a treat I picked up on the way back from the airport."

"What is it, Daddy? What is it, Daddy?" Jed asks.

"Wait and see," he says.

He comes back moments later, with a big grin on his face. "Wild boar salami. Yum. Now I just need a sharp knife. I'll go and have a look."

"Yuk." Maud screws up her face in a grimace. "Yuk. What is wild bore salami?"

"It's a delicacy, darling. You may not like it."

"And we bought some cold beers," Miranda adds, "Shall I leave the receipt in the kitchen? Then we can divvy everything up at the end of the week."

"If we must," Jack says, "though it's rather a bore to

scrabble around with money. I have to add here that my salami is a gift."

"Yes," Toby says. "And so is our beer." He misses the look that Miranda shoots at him from across the table, but I see it.

The wasps buzz around the glass of beer that Miranda has left out, some fall in, then struggle to get out, but don't make it and drown. Maud stands on her chair while eating her pasta. Jack occasionally tells her to sit down, but she completely ignores him. When she's had enough of her pasta, she sings a song to the table.

"In upsydowntown the sky is in the sea, the rabbits are in the nests where the birds should be, the rain is falling up instead of falling down, down in upsidowntown."

We all laugh and clap; it's such a lovely song and she has a sweet, little-girl voice.

"She's a show-off like me," Jack laughs. "Aren't you, darling?"

Maud shrugs her shoulders.

Jack helps himself to a third bowl of pasta and then tells a long story about the time he was up for a very small part in one of the Harry Potter movies. He was waiting at his agent Eden's office, where he met Halle Berry and boldly offered to cook her pasta. "Unbelievably, she agreed to come to my humble abode for pasta. She arrived looking so stunning I could hardly breathe. We ate the pasta, I remember it had pine nuts in it, which I have to say was delicious, and then we watched a movie. I thought she might expect me to make a pass at her or something, but I was embarrassed, so I made a kind of half-hearted pass, a vague pass, I grabbed her hand as she was leaving the room, but she just swung mine as if we were children at kindergarten. God, it was awful! So humiliating..."

We laugh hysterically, in an exaggerated fashion, mostly because it's so good to be here. He quickly tells another story about his grandfather who was hypnotised to give up smoking and was successful for thirty years, until the day he woke up and decided to have a cigarette. His grandfather couldn't think why he wanted a cigarette after such a long period of abstinence. It was such a strange compulsion. A few days later, he found out that the hypnotist had died the day he smoked that cigarette.

Alfie pulls at bits of pasta with his fingers, and finally gets up and demands ice cream, and I am very much aware of how badly behaved he is. Marcus asks him to wait for the other children and he responds by wailing and stomping around the table. Marcus can deal with it, I decide, as he's better at managing Alfie in public. He is less embarrassed and less worried about what other people think, but he doesn't appear to be doing anything about the situation so I have to get up and pull Alfie into the kitchen, and talk to him about his behaviour. He refuses to apologise but agrees to go back to the table and wait for his pudding.

Miranda is massaging Toby's shoulders, while Jack is talking on his mobile. Marcus is chatting to Toby. I sit back in my chair and drift out of the conversation. I am drinking my glass of wine and looking out at the garden. It is so wonderful to be here, sitting on my white canvas chair. I decide to text Sam and take a photograph of the garden to send him. I take a pile of plates to the sink and wander up to my room to fetch my camera and my mobile. The bed looks so inviting. I sit down, then lie back and close my eyes. Waves of tiredness grip me and within minutes I give in and turn to my side, like a baby, and pull the covers over me.

I wake from a deep sleep to hear Alfie asking me where his blow-up boat is. We bought the blow-up boat at the airport, without any idea how to blow it up and no time to buy a pump. I sit up and stretch and take a sip of water and for a moment I am dis-orientated and find that I have only slept for about ten minutes, but it feels like much longer. I walk to the car, with Alfie following me, and drag out the boat. I then change into a dry bikini, another wrap and brush my hair and put on my dark glasses. I walk down to the terrace to find that Jack is sitting with Miranda. Miranda is doing a crossword and Jack is talking on his mobile. He waves at me and winks, and oddly, I am pleased.

"Eden, darling. Is it really you? No. I'm in Tuscany. Just a week. Can I do a fashion shoot in sailing clothes? Now what do you think? Well, it depends who it's for? Men's *Vogue*? Well, yes, you might just persuade me. When is it? Can I do it? OK. Sign me up. Good, good." Jack puts his mobile down on the table and studies it for a minute or two. "That was my agent Eden. Wonderful woman, but she can be a right pain in the ass. *Vogue* want me."

"Fantastic," I say, as he is clearly expecting me to say something. He asks me where I've been and I say I've been having a siesta. Then his mobile rings again. Alfie gallops off to the pool with his unblown-up boat and I sit down and cut up a pear.

"Hi, Ma," Jack bellows into his mobile. "Yes, we've arrived. Yes, you're talking to me. You do realise how much this is costing me per minute? Fine, Ma, tomorrow!"

"What shall I make for dinner?" Jack asks when he's finished, "or shall we just eat what's in the fridge and find out about markets tomorrow?"

"Let's eat what we have," Miranda suggests, "then go to the supermarket tomorrow."

"Oh, I'd like to go to a proper market," Jack says.

"Me too," I agree.

"But we'll need essentials from the supermarket," Miranda insists. "Like washing-up liquid, loo paper, yoghurt, and berries for this diet I'm on. I've made a list."

"I'm sure darling Jill would make a trip to the supermarket for us."

Uncannily, just at that moment the house telephone rings and it's Jill, saying she's going to the supermarket and asking if we need anything. I thank Jill and pass Miranda the telephone so she can read out her list.

Jack is bored of talking about supplies and offers to make us tea and coffee. Miranda tells me she is a cranial osteopath and that she has a column in a magazine answering readers' questions. I find it hard to believe that anyone would want her advice. Jack returns with a pot of coffee and a mint tea for Miranda. He gives Miranda her tea, then he sips his coffee and lights a cigarette. He blows the smoke out and Miranda grimaces.

"Are you one of those tiresome people who doesn't like smoking?" Jack asks with a big grin. "You look so healthy, I almost feel I'm tainting you just by sitting in your presence, so tarnished am I by nicotine."

"I'm afraid so. I…"

"I'll tell you what then," Jack says, "I'll take my cigarette into the garden, and have a smoke out there."

"Sorry, Jack."

We watch as Jack goes down into the garden and inhales deeply on his cigarette. He paces around a bit and then comes back to the table and tells us it's too hot to be wandering around without a hat.

"I thought I'd go for a swim and check on the children. Are you coming?" I ask.

"Yes, I'm just going to find a book and a hat. I'd almost forgotten about the children," he jokes.

"Alfie is at the pool with Marcus and Toby and I suppose yours are too. Can Maud swim?"

"No, but she's got some armbands. Wait for a second while I find my book."

I stand on the terrace, clutching my towel and a bottle of sun cream. I stare down at my new pedicure. Green toes were quite a daring choice, I'm thinking, wondering why I have chosen it. It had looked very good on the beautician's toes, on a girl called Stacey, who is probably fifteen years younger than me.

Miranda takes off for the swimming pool; the heat is less intense now, the sun glows still but there is a breeze again. The bells chime from a distant church. A dragonfly hovers near by.

"What happened to Miranda?" Jack asks as he returns with his book. "She was here a minute ago, but I must have frightened her off with my smoking."

We giggle.

We walk together towards the pool. I am now

conscious of my legs, which are still quite pale despite the fake tan, and I am embarrassed about the dark purple vein behind my droopy knee. I am also aware of the lines that are beginning to appear between my nose and mouth. I worry that I look permanently tired. I am sure that Jack is a man who is interested in a woman's appearance, the younger the better probably. He notices everything, I decide – every vein, every stray unwanted hair. I imagine I am too boyish for him, that he likes his women more feminine.

"Well, you look fantastic, if I may say so," Jack comments. I smile at the ground. It's strange that he is reassuring me without being asked. "I am so pleased to be here with you all."

I smile at him, forgiving him for his loud, ostentatious arrival earlier. "I'm so happy to be here too. I need to relax."

"Yes. I do too," he laughs. "Maybe we could work on that."

I'm blushing, because it feels like he might be flirting with me.

Marcus is in the swimming pool with all three children. Alfie is sitting on his shoulders. Jed has been diving in from the side of the pool and his hair is darkened and clamped over his face.

"Hi, Daddy," he shrieks when Jack appears.

"Hello, my boy," Jack growls.

"Can I show you my dive?"

"Of course you can. Maud, have you learnt to dive too?"

Maud smiles up at him from the pool, where she circles in her armbands. "*No* Daddy!"

Jed flops into the water and emerges with a shiny, smiling face.

"Hello darling," Marcus calls to me.

"Hi," Jack waves. "You look happy."

Marcus waves back. "Yes, very happy to look after your children for the last hour," he murmurs, but Jack doesn't appear to hear. Jack is dive-bombing into the pool, splashing water over Miranda, who is sunbathing and reading a book.

"Oh fuck!" she squeals, flicking water off herself. "Nightmare!"

We spend a relaxed couple of hours by the pool, listening to the chirp of crickets, and the buzz of bees, and the children's shrieks. The sky is cloudless and the mountains gradually change colour as the light begins to fade. The hamlet on the hill looks golden, like a scene from a film. I sleep for a while, drifting in and out of daydreams, then swim and eat figs from the fig tree and I am happy.

I am lying on the bed reading to Alfie, when Marcus comes out of the shower and kisses me on the cheek.

He tells me that he is looking forward to a glass of wine and to preparing some simple pasta with anchovies and broccoli. We all go downstairs to the kitchen.

"So what do we feel about dinner?" Marcus asks Jack, who is already there, rooting around in the large fridge.

"Everything under control, my good man. When everybody was changing I drove off to Montenero and bought some *fiori di zucchini*! Absolutely delicious, don't you agree? We can have them as a starter. I just have to remember to barely coat the delicious flowers, or they will taste like fish and chips. I found some pancetta. I thought we could have it with pasta afterwards."

Marcus looks down at the courgette flowers that are waiting to be fried and nods in agreement. I know that he wishes it were him who'd had the initiative to drive off and buy something special for dinner.

"Did you know," Jack continues, "that these courgette flowers are the male rather than the female ones?"

"No, no, I didn't. Look, Jack, if you're in control I think I'll nip out and buy a bottle of chilled prosecco. I fancy a bit of prosecco, tonight."

"Bought a case," Jack says triumphantly. "Out there in the larder. Help yourself. Oh, and I got some olives too. Olives stuffed with red peppers, very piquant." He kisses his first finger and thumb.

"Right, well there's nothing I can offer tonight." Marcus slumps against the counter.

"What about your beautiful self." Jack sips a glass of wine. "And your wonderful, happy, together fucking family."

We laugh and help ourselves to drinks.

I follow Marcus out to the terrace, where he sits down on a white canvas and bamboo chair. I light a citronella candle that we found in the kitchen. He tells me that he had thought about offering his help, but decided he didn't want to be Jack's sous-chef, chopping and tidying and wiping down the table. We sit quietly together. Alfie is now is bed. I look at Marcus, and stretch out to take his hand, and he squeezes mine, kisses it and then absent-mindedly lets it drop. I wish things could go back to how they were when we first met, when his hand in mine was electrifying.

We met when a girlfriend invited me to an impromptu lunch party she was co-hosting with him at his studio in Hackney. He served me a portion of bean stew, dressed in a crumpled long-sleeved Aertex shirt, and I decided that I wanted him and would have him. He looked a little rough and he had a seductive smile and a deep laugh. He made me feel funny and special and I was drawn to him because he seemed so big, and at the time, aged 25, I was vulnerable and wanted a man to take care of me. I still felt embittered and frail after losing my heart to Sam. I thought Marcus would make me better. I didn't know then that you can only look to yourself to do that. I could tell that he had noticed me, and was possibly interested, the way you can; the little signs – a certain smile, a glance, the sensation when you accidentally-on-purpose touch each other. I lingered while the other guests were leaving and offered to help him clear up. We pulled plates from the table to the sink, and while he washed I dried. He took me onto a small terrace and we looked across the flat roofs and the television aerials, and then we kissed as though we weren't strangers at all.

We started seeing each other occasionally, twice a week at the most, but after two months, he confessed that he wasn't sure he was ready to be in a relationship. It's nothing to do with you, he assured me, with a pained and hopeless expression on his face. I feigned not caring too much and left the pub straight away. I cried a little in the car and wondered why I couldn't hook a man I loved. What was wrong with me?

A couple of weeks later, he telephoned late at night, to ask if I would meet him at a pub on Hampstead Heath for a drink, and when I sounded unsure, he tried to persuade me by telling me it was a great place for people-watching. I made an excuse and refused. One attempt at asking me on a reconciliatory date didn't seem good enough. Another tortuous month passed without a word from him. But in April he started bombarding me with letters. After a week or so, I gave in and telephoned because I could no longer think of a reason not to.

It's ten o'clock when Jack announces that dinner is ready. His children are still running around, playing hide-and-seek and he doesn't appear to be doing anything about sending them to bed. So as Jack tosses the salad, I gather up his children and take them to their room. Maud protests that she would like Jack to take her, but he keeps fussing over his salad and tells her he will be up later.

"Will you stay a little bit with me?" Maud asks as I switch off the main light.

"Sure," I say, wondering how much their mother is missing them. I kiss both children goodnight and then go upstairs to check on Alfie. He is asleep on our bed, stuck in the middle as always. Then I tiptoe back to Maud and Jeds's room and find that Maud is fast asleep, her little body curled around a white rabbit.

We are silent as we eat the courgette flowers. I am thinking how delicious they are when Marcus says, "Very good. You're a good cook, Jack."

"You're very good too," I say to Marcus. "Really good."

"Quite good, though completely self-taught." Marcus is obviously embarrassed that I have taken it upon myself to inform everyone about his culinary skills.

"Who taught you?" Toby asks Jack.

"No one really. My mother was an appalling cook. We'd have tins of tuna mixed with burnt rice, undercooked macaroni, tinned tomato crumble, leeks rolled in ham with a thin cheese sauce. She couldn't even make a sandwich taste good. When I was twelve I started cooking for myself and lived off tomato soup, savoury rice and bread. When I was sixteen, I began to read cookbooks and learnt to cook for myself. In fact, talking of my mother, here she is. Hello," he booms into his mobile, standing up and walking from the table.

"Your ears must be burning. What? No, we're talking about your terrible cooking. Terrible cooking. Can't talk now, Mother. EATING COURGETTE FLOWERS. NO, NOT FLOWERS, MOTHER. WHY WOULD I BE EATING FLOWERS? COURGETTE FLOWERS. Children are fine. Got to go now, I'm eating. Yes, we'll talk tomorrow. Or the next day. Bye."

He sits down and mops his brow with a large napkin. "She's a liability," he explains to the table. "Eighty-one years old, and dancing disco in her bedroom, dressed in nothing but a squaw outfit. Don't know where she finds the energy. She's got a trainer every morning at six."

We all relax and laugh, even Miranda, who is not eating the courgettes because they are fried. We laugh with Jack and exchange stories about our own mothers. Tara and Dave arrive in a taxi while we are eating peaches and I introduce them to Toby, Miranda and Jack. Tara gives me a big hug, and sits herself next to me, and tells me how good it is to see me. Dave and Marcus hug and slap each other on the back.

I hand them slices of cold ham and salad, and Marcus pours glasses of wine. Tara looks pale with fatigue, quiet as always. Dave is irrepressibly cheery, drinking, eating and asking questions.

"You won't believe what happened to us," Dave exclaims. "We missed the flight because there was a crazy situation on the M11 and so we were forced into buying a ticket with another crap airline that left much later, so we had hours to wander around the airport buying things we didn't need, trying to fill the time. We're queuing up to check in," Dave continues, "when this big Irish bloke begins to make a scene. He's got this suitcase that's the size of a house and the woman behind the desk is trying to get him to pay overweight, but rather than paying overweight, do you know what he does?"

"Offers to clean the planes for the rest of his life?" I

suggest. Toby and Marcus laugh.

"No! He opens the suitcase and dumps all his clothes on the floor. Then he disappears, leaving his girlfriend and two friends behind. His girlfriend is wearing tight black trousers and high heels and she's chewing gum. She shifts her weight from one leg to the other, like a prostitute peddling for business at the side of the road. His friend and the other woman look sheepish and embarrassed; the girl then takes to sitting on the suitcase, looking really *mortified*." Dave screams out the word mortified in a hysterical semi-American accent. "Then the big bloke returns about fifteen minutes later with two rubbish bags and proceeds to stuff all his clothes in the black bags and just leaves his comical-looking suitcase standing on its side."

"When he says clothes, what he *really* means is lurid g-strings, bits of cloth, nylon garments," Tara says. "Underwear basically."

"Lurid g-strings all over the airport floor? Thank God there were no children to witness such scenes." Marcus laughs.

"Thank God," Jack agrees.

"He then tries to check the rubbish bags in, before having a final row with the poor woman at the desk who I think, in the end, refused, and you can hardly blame her. They were filthy old rubbish bags filled with underwear, packets of condoms and other unsavoury items and probably about to burst."

"Dave then decided *he* wanted to *keep* the abandoned case!" Tara laughs, "because he'd paid for two cases to be checked in and in the end we'd only checked in one, but I refused to let him. It was huge and so ugly and I was sure that the Irish bloke would just demand to keep it once he saw it whirring around the carousel."

"Anyway, we're here," Dave says, "*thank God.*"

"Good for you," Jack smiles and raises his glass.

"Cheers," we all say clinking our glasses together. I begin to clear the plates and take them into the kitchen and Tara joins me and pours us some more wine. We scrape plates into the rubbish and put things in the dishwasher, then we sit down at the kitchen table and chat a bit more about our journeys and I ask her how she is. She is quiet for a moment and then she says that since marrying Dave last year, she has woken most days feeling slightly hollow and bleak and a little bit claustrophobic. Some days, she says, it was hard to get out of bed. At times, she adds, she was afraid.

I take her hand and ask her why she didn't return my calls and she looks at me and says she honestly couldn't, she was too depressed to make the effort. Now her life is interlinked with Dave's, she says she can no longer fantasise or plan her future. He is her future; it's all mapped out. She says she was profoundly moved by the marriage vows and loves Dave, but she can't control her negative thinking; it strikes in waves. Some days it's clear to her why she's married him. She says he's intense, loving, loyal and good company, but when he's at home, he's very different to how he is socially. At home, apparently, he's not very communicative. He likes to listen to music, watch films and write his book. She says it's strange how soon you begin to take each other for granted. She is concerned that she has stopped kissing him good morning and good night. When she says this I am struck that Marcus and I haven't kissed each other goodnight for months, and I say this out loud. Tara says perhaps we should both try to kiss our husbands, every day, with passion.

Part of the problem, she realises, is that she has never really lived with anyone else before, not since she was growing up with her parents. She has two elder brothers, but they are both much older than her and left home when she was still a child. She is used to finding things exactly as she leaves them. It upsets her to discover that the milk is empty, or find Dave's mess in the bathroom, cushions scattered, and windows open too wide.

There are aspects of their life together that she does appreciate. She enjoys sitting on the little terrace of their first-floor flat, overlooking the garden, drinking a bottle of wine and talking about the highs and lows of their respective days. She dreads reading his work, though. Dave often shows her an article he is working on or part of his novel and asks for feedback. She has to be careful not to offend him, and to balance the positive comments with the critical ones. She thinks his articles are much better than his fiction, but she doesn't want him to know. As far as she is concerned his acerbic, witty style suits journalism better.

"But I find him really sexy," she says, "and I like his energy. Neither of us are practical, though. We can't even change a plug."

We laugh at this.

"Do you have to hire someone to change a plug?"

"I don't even know what I mean when I say change a plug," she confesses, and we laugh again some more.

"But do you regret marrying him?"

"No," she replies. "No, I don't think so. We have fun together, we take care of each other, but there are big differences in our characters and what interests us. He loves fashion and I don't. You know me, I don't bother much with clothes. Dave says I am quicker at getting ready for a party than any other woman he has ever known."

Miranda and Toby come into the kitchen on their way to bed. After they've gone, Tara says, "I'm really sorry this has been all about me. How are you? Tell me about you. I've missed you."

"I'm not sure Marcus is still in love with me," I

confess after a pause. 'He's quite distant and so busy and preoccupied. He's richer and more successful, but we couldn't be further apart."

Now that we are talking about it, I can see that I could cry.

"I'm sure he's still in love with you," she says, looking worried. "Maybe you need to go away together or something like that."

"We are away together," I say and we both laugh. "But he can't commit to anything but work at the moment. It was a miracle to get him on this holiday."

"You should be pleased to have a little money. Look at us – a teacher and a part-time journalist." She sounds a little petulant. She probably thinks I am spoilt to complain about money.

"You're right, I should be grateful to be alive and to be on holiday and not dying of some disease or living in a refugee camp."

"That certainly puts our lives in perspective," she says. "You know, there is a mother at school who has three sons. The eldest is disabled, and the middle one has dyslexia and dyspraxia. She seems exhausted most of the time, and sad."

"Poor woman," I sympathise. We both begin to yawn and decide to go to bed. She hugs me and I hug her back, and despite everything, I am pleased that she's here, even though she's talked about herself for twenty minutes.

I fall asleep next to Alfie. Marcus and Dave carry on drinking outside; I can hear the voices drifting up from the terrace. Marcus wakes me as he comes to bed and I find it very difficult to fall back to sleep. I am suddenly alert and my heart is beating hard. I stay awake and listen to Marcus snore and after a long while, I turn on the light and start to read my book, and by the time I manage to feel drowsy and fall back to sleep, day is dawning.

SUNDAY

I have been asleep for a couple of hours when Alfie stirs next to me. It's eight o clock, but the house is quiet. I sigh and turn over and shut my eyes, but the sun's rays are poking through the shutters and I'm excited and know it will be impossible to go back to sleep. I look out into the garden and see the hard blue shadows on the lawn, and a light mist on the mountain, and I can smell lemon and mint in the air. The sprinklers are whirring on the grass, and the sound of the rotating click of the mechanism chimes with the cicadas. I move over onto my side away from Alfie, fall back to sleep for a minute or two and wake to find Alfie prodding me now, insisting that I get up.

I tiptoe down the stairs and hear muffled chatting.

I switch the kettle on and poke my head out of the kitchen door and catch a glimpse of Miranda and Toby. Miranda is wearing a pair of towelling shorts and running shoes. She's sitting on Toby's lap and he has his hand inside her top. She pushes it away. "No hanky-panky, the time to conceive is over. I'm due any day now."

"Oh." He sounds disappointed. "I thought if we wanted a child we had to fuck as much as possible."

"No, not for the whole cycle," she corrects him. I am embarrassed to be hearing this conversation. I slowly inch backwards, quietly, like a thief. "Does that mean that we can't fuck this whole week?" he asks.

"No, of course not, silly, it's just that… I'm sweaty. I've had a run. I'll have a quick shower and I'm ready to go."

"Where are you ready to go? Come here, I like you sweaty."

"To the supermarket."

"What time is it?"

"It's 8.30."

"Nine… it's still pretty early."

"No, but I want to get going."

"Can't you relax? Just for a moment. We're on holiday."

"Yes, but only for a week," she says. "Think of that – only seven days."

"That's quite a long time."

I'm wondering how I am going to reappear without surprising them in the middle of their chat about sex and conception, so I cough and sing a little song and put the kettle on, trying to make out that I've just arrived in the kitchen. The sound of my voice is out of tune and unbearable. I stop and hear her giggling and wiggling away from him and laughing.

I'm sitting at the table drinking very good coffee. Maud is eating a chocolate croissant, ravenously, stuffing it into her mouth. Chocolate is spreading over her cheeks and onto her shirt. The two boys are playing with plastic alien objects, zooming them over the table-top and onto the floor. Miranda and Toby are sitting side by side, dressed almost identically in white shorts and white tee shirts. Miranda is even wearing a white baseball cap. I really hope that they didn't both *plan* to dress in white. Miranda pours herself some cereal from a plastic container that she has clearly brought with her and adds a handful of blueberries, then sprinkles various seeds on top. Luckily for Toby, it seems he's managed to persuade her to postpone their trip to the supermarket for a little while.

"We're going to the supermarket," Miranda announces as Toby takes his last mouthful of croissant.

No such luck for him then.

"Shall we go, Tobs?"

Maud takes another croissant, which Marcus bought on an early-morning run to the local town. I think he's feeling competitive after Jack bought the zucchini flowers last night, and then I wonder where Jack is and how he has the nerve to leave his children unattended for all this time, when we only met yesterday.

"Hang on, hang on, I haven't finished my cup of coffee – do you want to go without me?"

"No, I want to go with you, of course."

She hovers over him while he sips his coffee.

I am about to go upstairs and cover Alfie with sun-cream when Jack appears.

"Daddy," his children cry, clamouring around him, "*Daddy!*"

"I'm *so* sorry," he says, "to leave you with the brood. The room was so dark behind those shutters."

"That's OK – you can look after mine tomorrow morning," I laugh.

For a moment Jack looks taken aback, then he regains his composure and laughs.

"Remember, Dad, when you didn't look out for me, and I disappeared for nearly a whole day and the police came and...."

"Yes, I do. Right, right," Jack sits down and pours himself a cup of tea. "And you won't be doing that again will you, Jed?"

"No. But are you going to play with us?"

"Why don't I organise races in the pool this morning to keep all you children amused?"

"Jack, that would be brilliant." I warm to him all over again; he's like a teddy bear. I imagine that he could be frightening when he's angry though. His mobile is ringing and he picks it up. "Yes, hello, Ma. Yes, the children have cream on. How are you? That sounds bad, Ma. Look, I've only just arrived. Can't someone else deliver the food for you?"

I pour a cup of coffee and take it upstairs to our room. I don't know how Jack can bear to have his mother telephoning at all hours of the day Maybe she calls him last thing at night too. Marcus is lying on his back with his mouth open and he's snoring. I envy him lying there so peacefully. Alfie never wakes Marcus, only me. It takes all my will power to remember that I shouldn't blame Marcus if I can't get back to sleep after he's woken me up. I am not a good sleeper. Unlike Marcus, who could sleep for 24 hours, possibly 36, if no one woke him. Marcus can sleep in planes, trains and automobiles, but I can't. I am a light sleeper, so whoever lies next to me, must lie still and silent, if I am to sleep through the night. I need to be in my own bed, in the dark, in silence, without anything to disturb me. I am insufferable in this respect. I often wonder why I am like this. What makes one person a good sleeper and the next a bad one? In the night, I toss and turn and am either too cold or too hot, or thirsty, or too tired to think. Anything can upset my quest for sleep: a new moon, hormones, caffeine after two pm, a change of location, an emotional upset, a bed that is too small, worrying, chocolate, noise, Marcus getting in or out of bed. Sometimes I wander around the house in the early hours eating bananas because I've heard they have sleep-inducing qualities. Then I try to read but I'm too tired to concentrate, so I close my eyes and meditate but am too tired to sit up properly as you are meant to. Then suddenly my heart is racing and, without any warning, I am totally alert and all thought of sleep has vanished.

I lie down next to Marcus. I love looking at him when he's asleep – I can see Alfie in him when his face is still. He stirs and then turns over. I want to wrap myself around him, lie with him and breathe him in. I imagine that every other couple in the world has a fabulous, regular sex life. I was comforted when a friend told me that it doesn't matter how often you make love, as long as when you do it is amazing and memorable, even if it's only once a year. I don't wear g-strings because they are so uncomfortable. I'd rather wear a vest than a corset. Sex toys are silly. Porn is vulgar. I am not sexy in this respect.

I read a letter in a problem page that worried me, but I am not sure how to broach the subject with Marcus.

The woman wanted to know if making love only twice a month was detrimental to her marriage. She explained that she had young children and she and her husband were both tired. Was twice a month reasonable, asked the wife from Nottingham? *Not at all*, wrote the problem page celebrity agony aunt, a young, loose kind of girl, who had made a name for herself writing columns and going to parties and having an ageing pop star father. Having sex 24 times a year is clearly not enough to nurture a marriage, she said, though I wonder how she knows anything about a mature relationship. I don't know if the agony aunt has young children; probably not. The problem is, I think, that I have lost the nerve to seduce my husband and so I wait for him to seduce me instead. I am concerned that he no longer finds me attractive. After all, I look different now from how I did when we met. Then, I was a size 8 and my feet were half a size smaller. My feet grew and widened after I had Alfie. God knows what happens to women who have four children. I am more sensible now – I don't drink as much, and perhaps I am boring. Perhaps I am so boring that I don't even know that I'm boring.

This is so silly. I reach out for him and he stirs, but then Alfie comes in without knocking. "I need my swimming shorts," he pleads.

"You're wearing them."

"Oh yes. Can I swim, Mum? Jack is taking us down to the pool."

"Yes, you can."

Marcus wakes up and gives me a kiss, then turns onto his stomach and pretends to snore. "Five more minutes," he begs. Alfie jumps on top of him, and pummels him until he is forced to defend himself and sit up. Marcus stands up and slips on a pair of swimming trunks and a tee shirt. He gives me a parcel from Prada that he retrieves from his suitcase. Inside there is a tiny black bikini which he urges me to try on. The bottom part is like a pair of very small shorts and has a gold buckle in the middle; the top just covers my breasts. He says I look great, but I think it would suit a seventeen-year-old far better. That is the flaw with these very expensive clothes: teenagers can't afford them and women like me don't look their best in them. I thank Marcus and give him a kiss. And he whispers into my ear that my hair needs washing. I laugh, as I have to laugh, because otherwise I would slap him.

A few minutes later, we make our way downstairs and he takes my hand, which I like, as it's the closest to intimacy that we get these days.

Marcus eats a couple of croissants. Alfie has gone off to swim with the other children.

"Can't wait to cook," Marcus says. "Maybe I should

start making lunch now, before Jack plants himself in the kitchen."

"Good idea. Perhaps we could have a picnic by the pool."

"I could toss together some salads. Do you want to come exploring with me to find something delicious to eat?" He wants my company and he looks great in the white tee shirt.

"Yeah, I'd really like to do that. Do you think we can leave Alfie with Jack?"

"He left me with his two children for most of yesterday."

"Go and ask him."

"No, you go."

"OK."

Marcus stands up. He is so tall, and gruff and sexy. I know women who don't find their husbands attractive across a crowded room, like I do. I have women friends who love their husbands, who know their husbands are good fathers but who don't find them sexy. One woman I know always rolls her eyes when she talks about her husband. It's sad, really. But women always gather around Marcus at parties. He is easy to talk to, flirtatious and funny. He is quick to laugh if someone is being amusing; he is observant and usually interested in what people have to say. He will tell a woman she looks less tired now than the previous time he saw her, he'll tell her if she's looking sexy, he'll notice her shoes, or her scent. He'll take the trouble to fill her glass, and he will always open a car door or let a woman through a door first, or help her on with her coat. He is tall and broad-shouldered and a little maverick. He doesn't make me feel jealous, though, as he gives me lots of attention in between the flirting. He'll always seek me out if he hasn't seen me for a while, and give me a kiss or bring me a drink, or ask me how I am.

Marcus gives the impression that he doesn't care about normal conventions - but paradoxically, he is responsible and works hard. He was brought up in Somerset on a remote farm with two brothers and a sister. His parents had quite a casual attitude to their children, never giving them a huge amount of attention and letting them run wild. They didn't bother with wiping their noses, or buying new socks, or making sure they got enough sleep on school days. His parents always made it very clear that they loved each other more deeply than they loved their children; the children were a by-product of their love, almost an afterthought.

I have a brother, but we don't see each other. My parents worry about him all the time. My mother smothers him with love. She does not smother me with love, although occasionally she will telephone to say she misses me. When we were young, she would sometimes rage, throwing things, shouting, banging doors. I had nowhere much to go with this madness and her undying love for my brother, so I put all my energy, both negative and positive, into my photography. I have been looking outside, seeking approval from others, all my life.

Marcus strolls across the lawn to find Jack, and while he is gone I read a magazine and sip my verbena tea. After about twenty minutes, Marcus returns with Alfie in tow. He tells me that Jack was shouting at his son to swim faster and faster, like a deranged Olympic coach, and asked Marcus if he'd come to relieve him of his babysitting duties. "So I said to him, 'not exactly, you've only had them half an hour.' I tried to sound reasonable and humorous and asked if he'd have Alfie for another hour while we went shopping. He sounded really unsure, so I had to remind him that two of the children were his own. He seemed to have forgotten that fact. He finally gave in and asked Alfie if he'd like to stay with him."

"But I asked if I could come with Dad. I don't know him well enough," Alfie informs me.

Marcus says later that it was easier to give in to Alfie than watch him collapse in tears, which is difficult and at times embarrassing.

Marcus goes into the house with Alfie traipsing behind him, asking questions.

"Whose house is this, Daddy? How long are we staying? What day is it today? What time are we having lunch?"

I know that Marcus loves Alfie and wants him to feel loved and special, because he didn't as a child, but sometimes we do discuss the fact that perhaps we have gone too far with all the loving and spoiling. Perhaps we have gone to the other extreme and have produced a monster who will not be quelled no matter how much loving we give him. We have a boy who needs to sleep between us every night but still doesn't feel secure.

Dave and Tara have arrived on the terrace to have breakfast.

Marcus returns with Alfie. I would treasure a moment alone with Marcus. I ask Alfie to go and change, with a hint of hardness in my tone, and for once he goes without complaining. I sit down on the comfortable sofa and curl my legs beneath me.

"Jack seems to forget that two of the children on this holiday belong to him," Marcus comments to Dave and Tara and they laugh.

"He seems quite fun," Dave says. "It's very amusing the way he talks to his mother on the telephone every few minutes. Poor bloke."

Alfie returns. He's changed into some nylon football shorts and a top. Even though I sometimes long for a break from him, for a little time alone, I am not looking forward to the day when his clothes begin to smell, particularly the nylon shorts, and his sheets are crusty, and he has no time for me. I am not excited about the day when he brings a teenage girl home and expects me to cook her breakfast.

Alfie stands in the doorway while I gather up the suncream and my bag. I put on my sunglasses, but then Alfie needs to pee and Marcus has lost his wallet, which involves a lot of running up and down stairs and shouting. Now Marcus is by the door, and we join him and walk out into the sun. It's so lovely to be hot. Sometimes in the winter, when I'm working on my computer, the house is warm, but my hands are cold and it's moments like those that I long for this Mediterranean summer heat.

We open the door to the car and I have to remove the bent cans, crisp packets and empty plastic water bottles and I stuff them all into a plastic bag. I drive down the bumpy dusty track lined on both sides by cypress trees. The wasps are buzzing and flicking themselves on the windows. Marcus turns up the airconditioning.

"Where are we going?" Alfie asks.

"We're exploring, looking for food and provisions," Marcus explains.

"Are we going to stay in a tent?" Alfie asks.

"No, sadly not," Marcus replies.

We drive out onto the dusty white road, through the village, past rolling hills and small hamlets.

"Shall we go to Montenero?" Marcus suggests.

"Yeah, let's."

"Mum, can I get some Match Attax?"

"Yes, if they have them."

"Matcha Attacka," Marcus says in a ridiculous Italian accent.

"And can I get an ice cream?"

"No, not now. Not before lunch."

"*Please*, Mum."

"No, we'll go with the other children, after lunch."

We take the road to Montenero, which is situated on the top of a hill. We drive through bland modern roads at the base of the medieval summit. "Built in order to control the connection between Rome and Umbria," Marcus reads out from a guide book. "During medieval times," he continues, "the town was fortified with a wall."

We park near the Piazza del Comune and find a small dark shop. Inside, a tiny hunched woman greets us with a nod. When she opens her mouth, I notice that she has two front teeth missing and Alfie points out in a loud stage whisper that she looks like a witch. I twist and turn with embarrassment, but she does not appear to have understood or to have heard him. There is a small deli section under some glass cabinets and a few loaves of focaccia bread. The shelves are packed with tins and packets of pasta. Marcus asks for some big balls of mozzarella cheese, in an Italian accent that sounds French. He indicates with impressive mime and a few words of Italian that he wants some *rucola*, and asks the old woman to cut some slices of ham. We watch her cutting the ham, very slowly – so slowly that Marcus begins to giggle, which sets me off. We laugh and laugh until my stomach is hurting from laughing, and I have to pull Alfie out of the shop into the hot sun, so that I can recover. He asks me what is so funny and I can't really explain – it doesn't make sense to say to a child that we are laughing because the lady is cutting the ham so slowly. And as I say it, I realise how rude we have been and go back in to see that Marcus has managed to engage the woman in a conversation of sorts and she is smiling. And all is all right, as it always is when Marcus is around. So we pay and my little bit of Italian comes back to me, as I thank the woman for our food. Marcus shakes the woman's hand and so do I, and I think the whole trip to Italy is worth it, just to laugh with Marcus like that.

Alfie is demanding money for the bubble gum machine in a pitch of a whine that makes me want to scream. We troop out of the dark little shop again into the bright light of the midday sun and I pull down the straw rim of my hat. Marcus strides ahead and I wish that he would hold my hand again.

We linger in the central piazza, which crowns the hill. In the spaces between the church, the old town hall and some other municipal and residential buildings, we glimpse a 360-degree view of the plain. I can see a woman taking down her laundry from the balcony of a top-floor terrace and a small cat scampering into the shadows.

In the cool church we discover peeling frescoes by a local artist painted in 1452. There are scenes from the life of St Francis in pale faded colours, a pink the colour of plaster, a burnt yellow and cornflower blue. There is a mural of St Francis surrounded by birds and another of him renouncing his wealth. When Alfie lies down on a pew, we decide to leave and head from the dark church back into the striking glare of the sun. We walk down a cobbled street and discover a smaller piazza, where we find a café and sit under an awning at a tin table, sipping espresso, while Alfie drinks a Fanta straight from the bottle.

I love being here. The café owner gives us such a warm welcome and his daughter delivers our drinks with a huge smile. Men on another table are smoking and playing chess, and an elderly woman has stopped to rest under the shade of a tree in the centre of the square. I am enjoying this moment. Alfie is reading a magazine and Marcus and I are chatting about the other guests, when Marcus's mobile rings out with "Hallelujah" by Leonard Cohen as its ring tone, which seems incongruous and very loud in the quiet piazza. Everyone looks round at us and Marcus smiles and waves, then picks up his mobile and walks away. He wanders off down the street. He walks quite a distance before returning to his chair.

"Do you want the good news or the bad news?" he asks.

"Oh God. What?"

"Well. The good news is that the Japanese want us to do some office gardens in Kyoto, but the bad news is that I have to go back to London this week to sign the contract."

I stare at him for a moment, without saying anything. I know I should congratulate him. "Well done," I say at last. "That's brilliant. That's really brilliant. Can't they fedex the contract across to you, though?" Underneath my cheery exterior I am devastated.

"No. They're in London for a conference and they want to meet up with me. We are talking an extra £20,000 or £30,000. We can always do with the money. Sorry, darling, I know it's a blow."

I understand that we will always need money no matter how well Marcus is doing. There is always the fear that the good times will come to an end. When I met Marcus I'd been working much more frequently than I am now. At the time I'd had a weekly slot in a magazine that was attached to an evening paper. Each week I would take photographs of an "interesting" person's house and an accompanying portrait, which paid really well. The slots featured interior designers, clothes designers, restaurant owners, actors and other minor celebrities. After three years, the editor changed, the slot abruptly finished and the income that I had relied on was gone. Since having Alfie, the work is even less frequent, and I am not so available as I was before. I can't travel to Switzerland at a moment's notice to take last-minute photographs of a chalet for a Christmas issue.

"I thought that you were doing really well at the moment," I say, staring into my empty coffee cup.

"Yes, but not so well that we can ignore that amount of money."

"No, of course not. So when will you go?"

"Daddy, can I come with you?" Alfie asks, as two American boys sit down on a table next to ours. They have American flags sewn onto the pockets of their rucksacks.

"No, darling, I'll only be gone for 24 hours."

"Where are we? It's Sunday today. They arrive Tuesday morning, and leave Friday. I think I need to get there on Wednesday morning and leave again Thursday to come back here. I've got to get back and go online to buy my ticket. Shall we go?"

My perfect moment has been spoiled.

"Can't Jane get you the ticket?"

"She's on holiday today. It's her brother's anniversary or something."

It's monstrously hot. Marcus pays and for a moment I hate him for deserting us all on holiday. His unruly hair just seems a mess, the bags under his eyes age him, and his cragginess makes him look like a drug runner. Then I calm myself, knowing that I'm lucky to have a husband who isn't idle, like my friend's husband Chris, who does nothing but make bread and describes himself as a "house-dad".

I rise from the table, and Alfie demands an ice cream again. "No. Not before lunch," I say, hating the sound of my nagging voice.

"I want an ice cream," he badgers.

"Yes, darling, but not now. I've already told you."

"You're not having an ice cream, you madman." Marcus says firmly. "You've had a fizzy drink. That's enough."

Alfie drags and scuffs his sandals as we walk towards the car. We drive in torpid heat, as the air-conditioning doesn't seem to work, back up the bumpy track lined with cypress trees. We park outside the house and are engulfed by the chorus of cicadas, sounding more urgent and ominous than yesterday.

Alfie finds the other children, who are playing with the hose. I go to the kitchen to fetch a glass of water, and while I am there I hear Miranda talking on her mobile in the sitting room. "I'll be back on the tenth. Jack Boore is staying, you know? The actor. He's pretty full of himself… the others are OK, I suppose." Then I hear her whisper something but can't quite make out what she says. I stand by the fridge and then tiptoe backwards out of the room. I laugh to myself as I realise this is the second time I have tiptoed out of a room backwards since I've been here.

I climb the wide stairs to my bedroom and lie down on the bed and drift into sleep. I wake moments later to hear everyone clattering around in the kitchen downstairs. The loo flushes in Tara's room. I cross the floor, open the door to Tara's room a fraction, and knock.

"Come in," she calls out. She is now lying on her bed.

"I just heard Miranda on the telephone. She was talking about us."

"What did she say?"

"Well, she started by saying that Jack was full of himself,"

"Really?"

"And the rest of us were OK, then she whispered something which I couldn't hear…"

"Really." Tara's eyes widen. "Oh, I wonder what she said?" Tara turns onto her side, but facing me. "I have to have a little rest," she sighs. "I know it's ridiculous, but I feel like a stone. In fact, I am strangely exhausted."

"Well, good idea. Rest up now," I say. "Why don't we have lunch here so you can take it easy, and go out tonight? The visitors' book says there's a restaurant down at the port that is very popular with the locals."

As I turn to leave the room, I notice that Tara curls up like a cat. "Yes, that sounds good," she says, but she is barely audible.

I go onto the terrace and find Dave looking at his mobile. I ask him if he's all right and in response he hands me the phone. He shows me an email that his agent has forwarded to him.

"Go on," he urges me. "Read it and you'll understand that it's not the best of days."

Dear Simon,
Thank you for sending us David White's manuscript. There is no doubt that he writes very well, I just didn't feel confident enough that I can do this book justice and therefore I have to say no. I do hope you find a good home for it.

"Not great," I admit.
He tells me that it's his tenth rejection. He says he

had been sure it was coming, but still, it was hard to read. He's chewing nicotine gum, but barely resisting the urge to smoke, he confides. I try and think of something to say and remind him that it's just one person's opinion; it's entirely subjective. He reminds me that it is now ten people's opinions, and they are all not interested in his book. He thinks it may be time to stop writing novels.

He's right, maybe he should stop, but I can't – I won't – say this.

"All the hard work…" he moans and he looks as though he wants to die. "All the months of hard work, what's it for?"

He says he would like to cry; then he changes his mind and instead says he'll do some yoga. I watch him leave with his towel and begin to understand what Tara means when she says that his social persona is very different from the man he really is. On holiday you start to see people up close, without their armour of make-up and evening drinks. This can be rewarding, or shocking, or both.

I watch him as he lies on his yoga mat. He pulls up his knees and rocks from side to side. He lifts his arms up above his head and gives each hand a pull. Then he sits up and crosses one knee over the other and turns his head and neck behind him. After he's done a few more poses, he lies on the grass and shuts his eyes.

Then he sits up and notices that I am watching him and asks if I would like to join him. I shake my head.

I am reading my book when he comes back to the terrace. He looks as though he wants to chat, so I put my book down. He sits next to me. His dark hair looks so black against the white of the sofa. He says that perhaps the book hasn't yet found the right publisher. Maybe the next submission will be successful.

"You deserve some good news," I say.

He stands up and says that he's not used to Tara being so quiet and that she seems to be inordinately tired, even more tired than her most tired days.

"I love her," he confides. "And I need her. She understands me. I'm not an easy person to live with. I know that."

I tell him that she's lovely but not easy either. Then I add that no one is as easy as they seem, and he smiles and stretches and says he's going for a swim.

"Can I tell you a secret?"

"Yes, do."

Tara and I are down by a stream that runs through the garden. I watch as the cold water tumbles over the stones, turning them shiny and bright. There are some church bells chiming and the air hums with heat and the insistent sound of the cicadas. I am sleepy and happy.

"I think I may be pregnant," she says. "I'm not sure.

But I feel so tired, I literally can't get up."

"That's fantastic!" I search her face but she looks miserable. "Do you feel sick?"

"No. I know this sounds awful, but I don't want to be pregnant. Not yet. This last year has been so strange. You know I've been quite depressed…" She trails off.

"But you love Dave and you married him. Don't you want his child?" I am surprised that she should be so casual about the timing of her child; she is, after all, 40.

She looks a bit uncomfortable, so I try another more sympathetic tone. "Is your period late?"

She leans back on her elbows and surveys me. "I'm about six days late. I'm on the pill, but there were a couple of days when I forgot, which was entirely stupid of me. It's not that I don't want his child – I just don't want to have a child with anyone. I'm terrified of childbirth."

"Well, what does Dave think? Have you discussed it with him?"

"No I haven't. I think he'd be really pleased, but he wouldn't be any practical help with a baby." Tara picks at a piece of grass.

"But Dave is great in so many other ways," I say, and then after a long pause, "Are you saying you'd have an abortion?"

"No, I don't think so. I'm just praying that I'm not pregnant."

"Well, I don't really know what to say, to be honest. But don't make any decisions until you know for sure. Why don't we go to town after lunch and pick up a test?"

Tara begs me not to say anything to Dave.

"Do you love Dave?" I ask her again. "He loves you; he needs you."

'How do you know?"

"He told me earlier."

"Really?" She seems surprised that he has confided in me.

"Yes. He was telling me about his novel being re-jected again."

"I do love him," she says. "But there are so many things that worry me about us. We are different in so many ways. Quite often he's out, or in his study not communicating. There are things he does that up-set me. He plays music too loudly and drenches the bathroom after a shower. And we are different. Dave likes to go to bed late and I prefer early nights. Dave is untidy and I am fastidious about keeping the flat clean."

"Well, that's OK, much better than if one of you was on drugs or something."

"Yes," she agrees, and she pulls the rim of her hat

further down over her face.

"I have a friend who said it took about five years to find the right balance after she got married. I suppose everyone expects you to be happy immediately after your wedding, but that's not always true. Not in your case anyway."

"Yes, but the more serious issue, one that we should have spoken about in more depth, is that Dave really wants children, and…" She pauses and sniffs and then she starts to cry. I hold her hand.

"I am such a fool," she says. "I can see that having a baby would make our lives more purposeful and I'm open to the idea of bringing someone into the world and cherishing them, but on a practical level I know I would find it hard to cope. I really enjoy teaching the children at school, but the possibility of having my own child terrifies me."

She lies on the grass and I find my hardness towards her melting and I lie next to her. "But why would you find it hard to cope? You're a teacher. You're surrounded by children all the time… What frightens you?"

She stands up now, and we walk together towards the gazebo, and sit there on a bench.

"When I think about being a mother, I can't really imagine it. I once read that families are more interesting than couples and I can see the logic behind that, being part of a couple seems easy in comparison with being a family, but I am afraid of giving birth and of not being in control. Whenever Dave broaches the subject, I try to stay calm, focused and positive, but inevitably, before long, I start panicking and find it hard to breathe and we end up rowing."

I am shocked because Tara seems so strange and fragile and also doesn't seem to be considering Dave at all in this decision, so I ask her how he is finding marriage. She responds by saying she's not sure. She changes the subject by saying she needs the bathroom and we stand up and she goes off to the house. "It will be all right," she says to me. "Don't worry about us."

I head towards the pool where everyone else is lying on loungers. The children are on their stomachs on the warm concrete, defacing the perfect pink surface with white chalk. Alfie and Jed are playing noughts and crosses and Maud is drawing figures with huge hands and stick legs. I dive into the pool knowing that Alfie is going to want to swim with me, and sure enough, within seconds of being in the water, he is climbing on my back, weighing me down as we swim together to the side. I stand up and he falls back, crashing into the water, laughing. I lift myself up out of the pool and he's calling to me, trying to get me to go back in but I don't want the weight of him. I dry myself off and then lie down on my towel on the warm concrete. Then I stand up and pull a chair up towards where Dave is lying in the hammock.

"How are you now?" I ask him.

He says he's OK. Just chilling. He tells me that he finds his work stressful – the constant deadlines and the need to produce stories and make money unnerve him at times. He says he's here to rest and do nothing, and I joke that he's having no problem doing that so far. He is not the Dave I know at parties and dinners and pub lunches; he is even different to the Dave who arrived last night. He looks different too, in the bright Italian sunshine: older. I can see the fine lines by his eyes and they are more hooded than ever. I imagine he can see my crow's feet and dry lips.

"How's marriage?"

"Good," he says. "How's your relationship?"

"Good. Very good."

"Great," he says.

I gather my sunglasses and hat and move back to a lounger; I can see there is nowhere else to go with the conversation.

I am feeling hungry and so announce to everyone that we have been shopping for lunch and I suggest that perhaps we could all go out tonight.

"Great idea." Jack takes off his hat and waves it at me. "And I'd love to make a risotto for lunch."

"We've actually bought some food for lunch already," Marcus announces rather sternly, tapping his foot and frowning.

"Great. I'll do my risotto as well." Jack is happy but Marcus is not.

"I'm going to go and book my ticket." Marcus pulls on a tee shirt and walks back to the house. I look at him and think how silly he's being.

"Would any of you like to watch me making risotto? I'm a very good teacher."

"I'd like to watch, Daddy," Maud volunteers, putting up her hand up, as though she were at school.

"Thank you darling. Anyone else?"

"Well, I wouldn't mind watching how to make a really good risotto. Are you really that good?" I'm giggling.

"My agent has put me forward for *Celebrity Master Chef*," Jack pronounces with a wave of his straw hat.

"Really?"

"Yes. Really."

Miranda is doing breaststroke and she stops by the side of the pool. "I saw a great place to eat for tonight. In that large town near the supermarket. It's right on the road, but they grow all their own vegetables and make their own pasta and I saw they have rabbit on the menu. It's recommended in the guide books but it's quite expensive."

"Quite a few visitors in the visitors' book recommend a little fish place down at the port too," I say, thinking of Dave and Tara who are broke.

"Right." Miranda pushes herself off from the side of the pool and manoeuvres into a slow backstroke.

"Oh, I have to say," Jack says a bit too loudly and a little too theatrically, "I would also prefer a little fish place."

"We like burger and chips," Jed chips in. Toby is reading the newspaper and doesn't look up.

"I could do with some fish," Dave adds, putting his book down.

"Yes, me too," I agree. "I'm craving a bit of fish."

I wonder if all these positive fish comments could count as ganging up on Miranda.

"I hate fish," Maud says. "It's yucky."

"You're a bit *sotto voce*," Jack says to Dave. "Are you all right?"

"Rejected again," Dave smiles. "By another publisher."

"Must be hard," Jack says. "I know what's that's like. Believe me."

"Well," Miranda says, pulling herself out of the pool, "perhaps Toby and I can go to the restaurant I found, and you can go to yours."

I am reminded of the school playground. There is something familiar about her tone.

We all continue to lie on the sun loungers, reading and occasionally getting up to swim. I'm reading Doris

Lessing's *The Grass is Singing*, which Tara has lent me. Inside the front cover there is an earnest, slightly depressing note scrawled in biro, probably written by Tara when she was studying the text at school: *Grass is Singing is about a historical and psychological stalemate, repression massed with oppression.*

It is almost a perfect day, apart from the news that Marcus will have to go back to London. I swim lengths of breaststroke, remembering my mother, who would never get her hair wet when she was swimming, and how old and boring that had made her seem. I dive under the cool water, and then flip on my back to backstroke to the end of the pool. When I surface for air, I glance over at Jack and see that he is watching me. He's singing "Perfect Day", the old Lou Reed song that used to make me cry, after a particularly harrowing break-up with an emotionally sadistic man.

> Just a perfect day,
> Drink sangria in the park,
> And then later, when it gets dark,
> We go home.

Jack knows all the words and soon we are all singing along, even Dave, who has cheered up and sings strumming an air guitar.

"I saw Lou Reed at a charity benefit the other night," Toby says. "He's still groovy. He has glasses and curly hair and looks a bit like a mechanic."

The children scream and jump in and out of the pool. Alfie looks tall and ungainly next to Jed. Jed and Maud start to play an imaginative game together. Alfie is allowed to join in and I listen to snatches of their games.

"Pretend that you can't see me. Pretend I'm invisible and I have this power and suddenly you can see me."

"Pretend that your mother is dead…"

"Yes, let's pretend that both our parents are dead…"

They continue the game for a while, before switching to a game about spying. They follow each other around, hiding behind loungers, and asking us not to notice them.

Marcus returns from the house and comes over to find me.

"I've got to go tomorrow," he says. "I couldn't find a ticket for Tuesday."

"So when are you coming back?"

"Thursday morning."

"Thursday morning? You'll be gone most of the holiday."

"I know and I'm sorry, but I have to sign the contract."

"Couldn't you come back on Wednesday night? Or

Tuesday? Can't you see them tomorrow and return the next day?"

"They aren't arriving until Tuesday," he reminds me. "I'm seeing them Wednesday and then returning Thursday, first thing on Thursday morning."

I take off my sunglasses and shield my eyes, even though he is standing between the sun and me.

"I'll make it up to you," he says.

"Look don't worry. That's how it is."

That's how it is, I think, as I turn onto my stomach, wishing he didn't have to go. This should be the holiday in which we reinvigorate our relationship, and now he's leaving. Marcus is sitting awkwardly at the end of my seat.

"How will you make it up to me?" I ask him, turning my head to face him and squinting up at the sun. He thinks for a minute and then Dave shouts out, "What shall we do about lunch? You could leave it to me, but I'm afraid I'm useless. I can make pasta with tomato sauce…"

"I'm going to prepare it now," Marcus replies, standing up. "Spanish omelette, with some salads, a nice bottle of rosé, some good bread, ham. Jack's risotto." Marcus seems almost jovial now after his earlier surly mood. He actually seems happy that he is going.

"I would offer to help," Dave laughs, "but I'm enjoying my time on this hammock. It swings beautifully."

Miranda heaves herself off the lounger. She has a classic Marilyn Monroe figure: full bust, tiny waist and big hips. "I'll help." She has pulled her umbrella into the shade but she is still wearing sunglasses and a wide-brimmed hat. She is tiny without her shoes and her hair is a strange colour, dark bronzed tints over what must be black hair. Her eyebrows are quite heavily plucked.

"Don't worry." Marcus says, "two of us in the kitchen should be fine."

"I'd like to get myself out of the heat anyway."

I watch them walking up the dusty track towards the house. Miranda is chatting to Marcus, while Tara drags behind. Dave is back in his hammock, reading and picking his toes. He is lazy. Jack has fallen asleep, and Toby is doing something on his laptop in the pool hut. "Children," I call out. "Time to get out of the sun. It's too hot now."

"One more jump – please, Mum." Alfie begs.

"One more."

Alfie jumps into the turquoise water and I glance at some poppies growing by the swimming pool hut. I hear the church bells ringing again and lean back on my chair and shut my eyes. The cicadas are strumming so loudly now; it's almost as if they are residing in my head.

By the time we are making our way to lunch, half an hour later, Alfie is whining that he is hungry and Maud is demanding an ice cream. Jack carries Maud on his shoulders; though halfway up the hill he flings her down, complaining that she is too heavy. She doesn't moan but races ahead of him, her back straight as a door and little legs moving fast. Alfie continues whining and demanding, while I attempt to soothe him with offers of ice cream after lunch. By the time we reach the table, he is shouting and hitting me.

"What a lot of noise," Miranda exclaims as she comes out with a bowl of salad. Alfie pulls out a chair, crosses his arms and sits down.

Lunch is laid out on the table.

"Do you mind if I start?" Jack asks sitting down. He starts piling the slices of prosciutto onto his plate, taking far more than his rightful share. The children are given pasta with tomato sauce and piles of cheese. Jack comments that a pasta pan should ideally be tall and thin-bottomed and not as wide as the one that Marcus has used. Marcus replies that it was all he could find. He sounds terse. The others sit down too and help themselves to a salad of rocket and Parmesan, another of Parma ham with figs and lastly, an impressive, huge platter, on which Marcus has arranged rolled prosciutto and slices of oranges with their skins on. It all looks beautiful. Marcus sits at the head of the table. He's telling everyone about a garden that he wants to visit twenty kilometres from the house. He'd like to go on Friday when he returns from his visit to London. He's promising that if anyone wants to come with him, they won't be disappointed. There will be hibiscus, acacia and rose trees blooming. Jack is sitting at the opposite end of the table and as soon as Marcus pauses for breath he is telling us about his co-star in the sailing soap, the actress Rowena Hamilton, known for the amount of plastic surgery she's had done on her face. "It's all true," Jack asserts. "She's even had her feet narrowed!"

Miranda has booked a tennis court for this evening and has made Toby promise to play with her. When she's finished her salad, she goes to the kitchen and returns with some sliced salami, which she offers to Toby. Jack asks if he can have a few slices, but Miranda explains that she has bought the salami, the only one left in the shop, for Toby, as it his favourite, and she has already used half of it so if he doesn't mind, she'd like to keep it for Toby. Toby doesn't say anything, but looks embarrassed. "Not that I approve of salami," she says. "But it's Toby's special treat."

"Miranda, I hope you aren't one of those people who mark the cereal packet, so that no one else can sneak a bowlful," Jack blurts out and we all laugh. Even Miranda smiles.

"We did a big shop and I've kept the receipt," she says, "so we can all divide everything at the end."

Dave pushes back his chair and stretches his feet out.

"Sounds all right," he says. "I'm going to get a beer." He seems agitated and we need more water for the table, so I follow him to the kitchen. He says he wouldn't normally worry about dividing everything up but they are really short of money, having overspent on their wedding and moving house, and he is wondering how he is going to make the August mortgage payment. He tells me he's desperate to relax, but like an insomniac who is worried about not falling asleep, the more he wishes it, the more he can't.

"I'm going to go and meditate," he says. "Perhaps that will calm me down."

I go back to the table and as soon as the children finish eating, they ask if they can get down.

"Go," Jack says, swatting at them distractedly as though they are flies. The children scrape their chairs over the flagstone floor and hurl themselves off down the steps into the garden, where they run shrieking through the sprinklers. It looks such fun, running through the water, and I think wistfully of my childhood, or rather, of being a child. I recall being constantly on the move, running and exploring and never worrying about being hot or cold. Adults had seemed so boring to me then, the way they sat around all day chatting, just as we are doing now, or lying still in the sun, burning away under the hot, fierce heat.

When lunch has finished, I take my tea to the gazebo by the pool, and shortly afterwards I am joined by Jack, who asks me if I'm coming to the pool.

The children are splashing and shouting and jumping in and out of the water. Maud seems fearless for someone so tiny and even though she wears armbands, she is jumping into the deep end and they are splashing each other and screaming hysterically. Jack says he'd love to let his wife Ellie know how much fun the children are having. He tells me that since they separated, she has kept in touch with short succinct texts. He thinks perhaps he should take a mobile phone photograph of the children and send it to her, but he isn't very good with gadgets and doesn't know how to, so I show him.

Jack pours himself a glass of rosé, leans back in his chair and then swings the bottle around, offering me a glass, which I decline. Then he lights a cigarette. Maud runs over to him dripping water, and asks him to blow up her armbands, as they have deflated. He follows her to the swimming pool and returns a few moments later. "Miranda is coughing, in an exaggerated way, to make a point about my cigarette."

"I can't work her out," I say. "I don't think she likes

us, well me, anyway. She was boasting about you being here! I heard her talking on the telephone."

"Oh really?" Jack seems interested. "How fascinating. But honestly, what was that all about? Why was she offering salami to her man and not to anyone else? Is that some kind of sexual phallic thing?"

We laugh at the absurdity of the salami question.

We are still laughing when Maud appears. She is crying and holding her stomach, and asking for her mother. "I've got a terrible tummy ache, Dada," she wails, collapsing onto the ground, holding her stomach and groaning. Jed follows her, with a wet shining face, and puts his arm around his sister.

"It's the wheat," Jed says very seriously. "She's eaten too much wheat."

"Mummy told me and I completely forgot."

"I want Mummy," Maud wails. "I want Mummy!" she shouts even louder now.

"We can call her," Jack says, putting his arm round her, but he sounds doubtful. He definitely doesn't want to be told off.

"Mummy!" she sobs.

"Do you want a big hug?" I ask, opening my arms and crouching down, waiting as she surveys me.

Maud looks at me, and then turns her mouth into a sulky, unhappy grimace. At last she walks over to me and I pull her into my arms, hugging her tight. I made a decision not to have another baby after three miscarriages and the life-threatening post-partum haemorrhage with Alfie. When I think about Tara not really wanting a baby, it's hard to be sympathetic.

Tara and I are walking to the village to buy the pregnancy test. The evening light makes the landscape more vivid, harder and clearer, but not harsh, and I stop a few times to take photographs.

"We're going to have to get a lift back," Tara gasps, "I am so unfit. I can hardly climb this hill. Miranda asked me if I wanted to play tennis! Can you imagine me on a tennis court?"

I laugh, because I can't even imagine Tara running for a bus. We walk past a field of giant sunflowers that look unreal, like an illustration in *Alice in Wonderland*; some have drooped like old arthritic people. We laugh about Jack and the constant calls from his mother. After a few minutes of silence, I ask Tara why she finds it so hard to be in touch with me when she's feeling low.

"You know how it is," she replies. "Sometimes when you're depressed, you just don't feel like seeing anyone. Or that's how I feel anyway."

But friendships need to be nurtured, strengthened with telephone calls and other gestures, I think but don't say. Friendship, like love, can fade away without care and consideration. I'd like to say this to her.

We reach the bottom of the hill and then walk through the outskirts of the village and past a playground and a football field, until we reach the older part where we walk down a narrow street. Elderly women sit on kitchen chairs outside their houses chatting; some are dressed entirely in black. Washing is strung across balconies. There is nothing open but a bar and a grocery shop.

"Oh well." Tara seems quite relieved.

"Let's have a drink," I suggest. We sit on green garden chairs outside a small bar that looks onto a side street. A dog lies on the ground with his head flopped over his front legs. A couple of men are having an animated conversation over a drink on the neighbouring table.

"Do you really not want to have a baby?" I ask as I sip a cold beer and fiddle with some nuts.

"I don't know. I've already had an abortion, before we got married. It was at a time when I really wasn't sure that I wanted to be with Dave."

"Did you? You didn't tell me."

"No, because you were going through the miscarriage. It would have seemed so tactless."

"Yes, you're right." I picture the Chinese ultrasound technician, who had slid the probe over my stomach and then announced, "Baby is dead."

"I know it's hard for you to understand, Jen, because you're a great mother, but I don't think I'd be very good at the job. Just because we are women, it doesn't necessarily mean we'll be good mothers. My mother wasn't a very good mother, and I'm afraid of being like her."

"If you are pregnant, perhaps that means your mission is to be a better mother than your mother was. We have to do everything we can in order that our children grow up stable and secure. And it's hard, that is true, and you're brave. I do think it's brave to consider whether you want a child or not. There are useless, damaging, uncaring mothers in the world; there is no doubt about that. I'm not a perfect parent; Alfie sleeps with us in the bed. Every night. Can you imagine that?"

"No," Tara replied, "I can't imagine it. What do you do about sex?"

"Very little," I laugh.

"That's one area where Dave and I don't have a problem. Well, he doesn't have a problem and my only problem is how tired I am."

She asks me if I want another beer, and I reply that I do, so she goes off to the bar to fetch it.

She returns with some beer and some nuts.

"What about Dave?" I ask as I sip my beer. "Do you think some men feel the overpowering need to have a child? Does he?"

Tara stares into the distance. I want to shake her. "Does Dave think you may be pregnant?"

"No," she says her smile dropping on her pale face. "Don't say anything. Not yet."

"No, of course I won't say anything. Come on, we should walk home. I don't want the rest of this beer."

We walk slowly up the hill. I walk faster than Tara and have to keep stopping so that she can catch up. I find that my inclination is to be horribly unsympathetic towards her. We walk in silence for a while, breathing heavily, as the hill is steep. By the time we reach the bumpy track, we are both out of breath. We stop and Tara is crying.

"I'm sorry," she sniffs. "I'm sorry, I know you think I'm selfish and I'm so sorry, there is something wrong with me. Perhaps I should be taking antidepressants or something. I know I've been a ridiculous friend. I can't help myself. It's hard to explain. The depression is so strange. It just comes on suddenly and then settles so heavily, like a stone."

"What's it like?" I ask, feeling naïve. "What's it like being so depressed that you can't be in touch with your friends? I know you said it was sometimes difficult to get out of bed, but what is the actual depression like?"

She thinks for a moment, bending over as she does

so, and letting her arms flop beneath her. "It's like you suddenly can't remember how you were brave enough to live your life as you knew it. It sounds so melodramatic, but it's a feeling of self-loathing and dread. It's just being totally afraid of life."

I give her a hug and she leans on to my shoulder.

"You'll have to see a doctor when you get home," I tell her, stroking her hair.

"Yes," she agrees. "You know what? I can't wait. You see there are days when things seem just great and days when everything is grey around the edges. And then days when I'm dark and scared."

"Do you think you'll change your mind about the baby?"

"No," she says. "I don't think so. That will probably stay the same."

I have sweat dripping down my face. We walk together towards the swimming pool and I am digesting the news about Tara. Dave is asleep in the hammock with a book folded open across his chest, but no one else is here, and when he hears us approaching, he wakes up. Dave says that Marcus and Jack are giving the children supper and they never got it together to go for a run. I climb into the pool, hoping that Dave is not scrutinising my thighs because although I am lanky and have slim legs, I have cellulite on my thighs and that vein behind my knee.

Tara lies on a lounger. I swim up and down a few times and then glide under the water, surface and dive down again. I swim up and down without thinking about anything, kicking my legs, stretching my arms, breathing in and out. Eventually I stop and hold on to the side. Dave climbs off the hammock and goes to sit on the edge of Tara's lounger. He takes her hand and kisses it.

We walk back together to the house. I have a towel pulled tightly around me. I'm a little cold and there are goosebumps on my arms. I'm regretting the whole idea of dinner in a restaurant, when I see Jill coming towards me and waving. I wave back at her. She is wearing a black kaftan top and wide trousers and her long fringe is covering her eyes. Dave and Tara walk past her on their way to change, but she is standing in front of me.

"I saw Jack," she says, "and I've offered to babysit."

"Have you? Thank you so much. I was just wondering what to do about the children." She is big around the middle, and still sad around the eyes.

"Don't you worry, we'll have a lovely time. I've brought over the *Jungle Book* DVD that my grandson enjoys so much."

"Lovely, and we'll pay you, of course."

"We'll sort it all out," she says as if it really doesn't matter at all.

"Thank you, Jill." I almost want to hug her. And then I do, and give her a kiss on the cheek, and she smiles. Toby and Miranda return from tennis. Miranda is red in the face and drinks two glasses of water, one after the other, and then reminds Toby that their table is booked in half an hour.

Alfie makes a huge fuss about Jill babysitting and refuses to say hello to her. Maud is also not that happy, and sits with a sulky down-turned smile in front of the oversized television. I am worried about leaving the children with someone they don't know, but Jill seems so lovely and I am ashamed that when we first met, I thought she was strange. By the time I have had a shower and changed, everybody is ready to leave and there is no time to worry.

The restaurant is hard to find, tucked away in a back street, and we would never have discovered it without the instructions from Sam's father written out in a big book of suggestions. There are about eight tables covered with paper tablecloths and candles stuck in bottles dripping with wax; the walls are decorated with photographs of wizened fisherman. A middle-aged waiter brings bread and oil, and a carafe of red wine. We toast each other and Jack stands up to make an impromptu speech. When he sits down I ask him whether he has Jill's number. But he doesn't. He thanks me for organising Jill.

"But I didn't," I say, pushing bread into the plate of oil. "She offered. She said she'd discussed it with you."

"Not to my knowledge," Jack says. "I wouldn't say we discussed it. In fact, I'd say she briefed me."

"But we didn't discuss it either. That's really strange."

"Maybe she was just confused, or maybe she just wanted to help."

"Oh, well, it's very nice of her to offer," I say but I am unnerved because I feel manipulated in some way.

Amongst the local diners, there is an elderly grey-haired British couple. The man is dressed in plain slacks and a beige jacket. The woman can't keep her eyes off Jack, and finally gathers courage, stands up and comes over to the table to ask him to sign her napkin. Jack writes his autograph on her wrist flirtatiously as well as on her napkin, and then slides out from the table to be photographed with her. He loves every moment and soon he is talking English with an Italian accent to the waiters and anyone who cares to listen. Marcus is chatting to Dave about schoolboy bands they were both in, while Tara and I watch Jack in amusement.

The food arrives and keeps arriving - bruschetta with tomato, a light fish soup, and *fagottini di pepperoni e coda di rospo* – bundles of monkfish and grilled peppers – tomato salad, mixed salad, *melanzane al limone*. We eat our way through the dinner and every morsel is delicious, each course delicately flavoured. After everything is finished, I order a curling length of lemon peel covered with hot water.

"I'm really pleased to slow down," Jack says. "I've been working all year on this new soap opera."

"What's it called?" Dave asks.

"It has the most ghastly title, an old Rod Stewart song, 'We are Sailing'. It's all centred around a yachting community."

"Who do you play?" I ask, laughing, and I'm relieved when Jack laughs too.

"I play the retired doctor, recently widowed, who sets all the local ladies' hearts a flutter, promising everything but not delivering anything. I've been living near Southampton, in a rented flat, working long hours."

"That must be tough," Marcus says, "living away from your children."

"Yes," he agrees, "but I do love being an actor. I'll admit it. I absolutely love it when people recognise me. I have a number one fan called Jean. She's been a fan for twenty years. She's as big as a boat with dazzling peroxide hair. She's a darling and put my wife Ellie to shame. Never forgets a birthday or Christmas.

Nothing sexual about it. She's in her fifties."

"Oh, she must fancy you a bit," Dave laughs.

"Maybe."

"Why does she put Ellie to shame?" I ask.

"Ellie completely forgot my birthday last year." He looks a little pensive for a moment. "I think that was a turning point for me, actually. It's a bit like my agent, Eden, who's been divorced for years. The final straw for her was when her husband forgot to order a taxi to take them to the airport. She decided at that very minute to end the marriage. You see, I knew something was wrong when she forgot my birthday. She had never forgotten it before."

I am thinking about my own birthday, last February, and the hasty misspelt text from Marcus.

The waiter brings the bill over to our table with a bottle of complimentary limoncello, "I insist," Jack says, taking the bill as it's being put down on the table. "It would be my pleasure to take everyone out."

We all protest, particularly Marcus, but Jack forces his card into the waiter's hands. "I'm earning a fortune," he laughs. "Believe me, I can afford it."

"We're all earning a fortune," Marcus laughs in reply.

"No, we're not," Dave smiles.

I take a sip of the bitter-sweet drink. Jack is quiet after paying the bill. He seems sad. There is something rather poignant about his perfectly pressed shirt. I wonder who ironed it for him. Did he do it himself? We all leave in good spirits and I drive with Marcus and Jack back to the house.

Jill greets us at the doorway, as Miranda and Toby are not yet back from their dinner. She has done a very good job of tidying up the ground floor and has washed up all the glasses we left on the terrace. She has also washed all the swimming suits and towels, and my earlier doubts about her dissipate a little, although I am still a bit uneasy.

"Oh, you needn't have done all that," I say. "Really, Jill. You are here to babysit and you should be sitting watching a film or something."

"It's not a problem. I do like to keep myself busy. You know how it is. There's not a lot on the television."

"How are you getting home?" Marcus asks.

"Oh, I've got the car."

She tells me how she read the children a story, and I give her a bit of a pat on the shoulder and ask her round for a cup of tea in the morning. Just before she goes, she asks if Sam is still expected and I tell her he is. After Jill goes, we sit around drinking a bit more. Toby and Miranda return and go straight to bed, and shortly afterwards I go to bed too.

I undress by the window. The moon is high and bright, and I'm too tired to put my clothes away.

Marcus is downstairs playing backgammon with Dave and I wish he'd come to bed. I wonder whether he is avoiding me. I hoist myself up and turn on the bed-side lamp, then pick up the leaflet that I found in the church, an English translation of St Francis's prayer. I read through it and think about loving Marcus, rather than expecting him to show his love to me, and then I begin to wonder what my life would be like without him.

When Marcus comes up to bed, I am still awake. "I'm just imagining what would happen if you met someone on the plane and fell in love with them, and I never saw you again."

"I'd have to see you because of Alfie and anyway –" he laughs, stretching out to take my hand, "it's not going to happen."

"Things like that do happen," I insist. "I know a woman who is happily married and has two beautiful sons, and her best friend and her husband took off together."

He turns away from me and takes off his watch. "It won't happen," he says. "I promise."

"Don't say never," I say. "Never say never."

I am aware, though, that I often fantasise about the worst possible outcomes. I wonder why I do that.

"I was thinking about my birthday. You know Jack said he knew it was the end when his wife forgot his birthday. You forgot mine, when you were away in Tokyo, didn't you? Didn't Jane have to remind you?"

"Possibly, if I was away." He looks vague. "But don't forget, I did book that restaurant. You must remember that? I had to book it two months before the actual date."

"Yes, of course." I am about to ask whether it was Jane's idea to book it, but I stop myself.

I am asleep very quickly, but wake suddenly in the night. It is still and very dark but I can hear voices on the terrace. Alfie is now lying next to me, having crept in while I was asleep. I turn around to find that Marcus isn't there. I go to the window and lean out and hear whispering. I am almost sure it is Marcus and Tara. I wonder what they could be discussing and strain to hear. "Don't tell him," I hear Marcus say. "Whatever you do. I don't think he'd be able to handle it."

His voice trails off into an inaudible whisper and I can't quite hear what Tara says in reply. I walk down the stairs, rehearsing what I will say. Maybe something like, "I heard some people talking and was just wondering who it was." I'm all too aware of the time that Tara met Marcus for coffee and she never told me about it, as though there was something to hide.

I turn on the light in the kitchen and pour myself a glass of water.

"Hello!" Marcus calls out. "Who's there?"

"Hi." I walk out onto the terrace and smile at them, sitting there together. They are sitting across from each other at the table and drinking tea. "I woke up and couldn't sleep," Marcus says smiling and pulls out a chair for me. He is somehow being too polite. "I came down and found Tara. Why don't you join us? We can start an insomniacs club. Inaugural meeting one am." He laughs and Tara smiles.

"I couldn't sleep," Tara yawns, "so I came downstairs, but I think I'll go back to bed. Night, Marcus, night, Jen." She kisses the top of my head.

Marcus watches her go in her short nightdress and tiny cardigan, and I say goodnight. We sit for a minute before Marcus suggests that we too go back to bed.

When we return to the bedroom, I question Marcus about what they were talking about and he says that he can't remember much about the conversation. He insists that it wasn't about anything substantial. I press to know more and Marcus says that Tara doesn't seem to be that happy. He goes to the bathroom and returns with a glass of water.

"Why were you talking so late?" I ask, and then I can't help myself. "And why did you have coffee together in London?"

"No reason at all," he says nonchalantly. "We bumped into each other and had a coffee. And tonight I couldn't sleep and found Tara downstairs. That's all there is to it. I promise." He puts his glass of water by the side of the bed, lies down and switches off his small glass-bottomed light. I climb into bed and open my book, but it suddenly seems too depressing to read. I lie awake, thinking about Marcus and Tara, and wonder what is going on. There must be something or I wouldn't be so churned up and uneasy.

MONDAY

When I wake, Marcus is already up and he's left the bedroom. I go to breakfast and he's not there either. I am about to go and look for him when Maud says to Jack, "Mummy has a friend."

"What do you mean, a friend?" Jack asks.

"He comes over a lot."

"What is she talking about, Jed?"

"There is a man who Mummy likes," Jed concurs. "And now he's moved in."

"What is he like, this man?" Jack is pouring himself a second cup of coffee.

"He's nice," Jed says.

"He has funny hair," Maud adds. "Kind of dark and spiky." She is eating yoghurt, with honey and peach, as Jack has now remembered the problem with wheat.

"What does he do? This man with the spiky hair?"

"He kisses mummy on the shoulder," Maud says.

"What's his job?" Jack asks, stabbing at the butter.

"We don't know," Jed replies.

"Well, it's good for Mummy to have a friend," Jack says but he sounds very unconvinced.

He leaves the table and returns with a pair of sunglasses on.

"Do you have a friend?" Maud asks.

"No, not at the moment."

"Well you have all of us," I say, because Jack seems very sad.

Jed asks if they can go and explore by the stream and Jack nods. I tell Alfie he can go if he's careful. We watch them running over the lawn, being sprinkled with water and he shouts after them not to go near the swimming pool on their own. Everyone gets up from the table until it's just Jack and me sitting together.

"I remember," he says, "talking to my agent, Eden, after I'd heard about Ellie's affair. She told me it didn't matter that Ellie had been unfaithful, because ultimately she had chosen me over the other guy, and she wanted me back. The jealousy, the rage I had been experiencing, would inject life into our marriage and our sex lives. The affair and its aftermath would stop us taking each other for granted. Eden considers herself something of a guru, as she was married to a Hungarian for 25 years. I think she was rather racy as a young woman and took lovers during her marriage. She instructed me to enjoy the agony of knowing that my wife had been wanted and desired by another man. But I was too full of rage and outrage to be turned on."

"Yes, I agree. I don't think the idea of Marcus having an affair would turn me on." I immediately think of Tara and Marcus and how horrible it would be if there was something between them. "Eden sounds a bit weird." I am sipping tea that is cold, and I want to make myself another cup, but don't feel that I can leave in the middle of this story.

"I wanted to teach Ellie a lesson and not forgive her under any circumstances. I really don't enjoy being a cuckold. She was distraught, but I was totally immune to her pleas; I felt she deserved it. She begged me not to destroy the marriage, but for me it was over. Recently, though, I've been thinking. Being here has given me time to think. Perhaps I was too unforgiving. I don't enjoy being half a family. It's lovely to watch you and the kids and Marcus."

"We don't have a perfect relationship; no one does." I don't want to elaborate on this so I change the subject. "But do you think it is too late to get Ellie back?"

"Well, after what Maud says, yes, I do."

"Maybe not. Write her a letter; tell her what you feel. Expose yourself. Men are so bad at exposing themselves."

"Oh, darling, I'm not a dirty old man in a mac."

146

"I meant, be vulnerable." But I'm smiling.

He stands up and asks me to wander through the garden with him. He picks at the heads of lavender, sniffing at them and then discarding them, and I want to tell him to stop it, as if he were a child. He is obviously very upset. He tells me that the new friend must be very special for her to want him.

"I know that I am jealous," he says, "but weirdly my feelings for Ellie have just rushed to the surface at the mention of this other man. I wasn't jealous about the neighbour – it was all so sudden and brief and she wanted me back right away, but this sounds more considered – and more final."

"Why do you think that?"

"I don't know," he admits. "I have no idea why I think that."

We sit in the gazebo and he says he would like to call her. He's twirling his mobile in his hand.

"What's this I hear about a man with spiky hair?" he says into the phone, and for a few seconds I actually believe that he's talking to his wife.

"Ha! Fooled you," he laughs at me. "I think I'll wait until the children want to speak to her and then I'll just ask them to pass me the phone."

We hear voices. Miranda and Toby push open the door of the gazebo.

"My gold bangle is missing," she moans, as though

she has lost her soul, not a bracelet.

"Are you sure? Have you looked everywhere?" I ask.

"It was by my bed and now it's missing."

"Are you a hundred per cent sure?" Toby asks.

"Well, now you're doubting me, I'm not so sure. Maybe I didn't bring it."

"You've got to stop being so suspicious of everyone and everything," Toby says.

"OK, OK."

"Better? Mood over?"

"Yes. Well, no. I'd still like you to keep to the 'no drinking' pact that we made."

"Can't a man have a drink?" Jack sounds outraged.

Toby smiles and says, "Jill showed up and said that you'd invited her for a cup of tea, Jen. I offered to come and find you, but she said it didn't matter and she's gone home. I think she left a note."

"Oh God. I thought she'd ring before she came. I didn't realise she would come so early. I hope she's not annoyed. I'll call her later." It's not as if she had far to come, I rationalise. Toby and Miranda walk away from us to continue their conversation in private.

"We must check on the children," I say to Jack, "and engage them in something."

"Don't children like to be left alone a little?" Jack suggests. "When I was a boy I was out all day on my own, bicycling to neighbouring villages, buying sweets and stuff. Don't you think we monitor our children a bit too much? Are we suffocating them? Making them afraid to do anything on their own?"

"Yes, perhaps, but ours are little children. Are you sure you were bicycling to neighbouring villages when you were seven?"

"Yes, I think so. Maybe I was nine or ten."

We find them under some trees playing an elaborate game on the floor with brightly coloured picnic plates and glasses. Maud is wearing bikini bottoms and huge flashing trainers. She looks cool, like a mini model at a music festival. Jack offers to sit near the pool while the children swim. We go together and flop back onto two loungers. It's 8.50 and already hot. Jack sits up and drags his lounger under the big white parasol. Maud is pulling on her armbands, and she pads towards him and asks him to blow. He blows a little and says he's exhausted. Then he puffs some more and falls to the floor with the effort. The children howl with laughter.

"Do it again, Daddy!" Maud yells. "Do it again!"

He plays dead, lying face down on the concrete and lets his daughter walk all over his back, weighing him down.

"Why have you got hairs on your shoulders?" Jed asks.

"Not sure," he mumbles. "I used to wax them off

when your mother and I were courting."

"What does courting mean?" Jed asks.

"Courting means when two people are extra spe-cially nice to each other, and think the best of each other, and really behave well, and want to be with each other all the time and the man takes the woman out to dinner and holds doors open for her and comments on her nice frock."

The children flop into the pool and splash the water and I think it's sweet that Jack calls a dress a frock.

"How are you feeling now?" I ask.

"Not having a great day."

"Well, it's only just begun. There's time for things to improve." I am wondering now where Marcus is; if he is somewhere with Tara, talking in that intimate way.

"I'm not sure. You see, I've found out that my wife has a new lover." He pulls a sad face.

"You don't know that for sure."

"Yes, the children told me."

"They said friend."

"They saw her kissing his shoulder."

"Right. Yes, but still…" I'm not sure what else to say as it does seem like a very intimate gesture. "Tara and Dave are going to spend the day in Rome. I imagine Toby and Miranda are going for a five-mile hike, so why don't we take the children for an ice cream after lunch?" I cover my knees, which seem very knobbly, with my towel.

Jack sits up. "I'd like that very much," he says, "very much indeed. Far more than a five-mile hike." I ask Jack to watch the children and go back to the house. Dave and Tara are having breakfast.

"Morning," Tara says.

"Morning. Where's Marcus?" I ask, looking at her.

"I don't know. But I think he's had breakfast."

"How did you sleep?" I ask Dave.

"I slept like a log, but Tara couldn't sleep."

"Must be a new moon or something. Marcus couldn't sleep either, he was on the terrace with Tara." I say this just so that Dave knows. "So," I continue brightly, "you two are off to Rome."

Tara pours me a cup of tea and passes it to me.

"We don't know where on earth we're going in Rome, or what we're going to do, and we've left it quite late to leave," says Dave.

"But we must see the Pantheon," Tara adds.

"Yes and the Trevi Fountain."

"And the Jewish quarter that apparently has a lovely dolphin fountain."

I'm thinking, how lovely, but how hot, and how glad I am that Tara won't be here today.

Marcus appears in his travelling clothes and I watch him and Tara carefully to see if they give each other a certain look, but there is nothing discernible. He's wearing navy-blue linen trousers and a starched white shirt and he already has the preoccupied, serious air of a man who is no longer on holiday. He's holding his computer case and he kisses me goodbye, then gives a quick kiss to Tara and shakes Dave's hand. "Say goodbye to Alfie for me," he shouts out to me. Then he's off, leaving me panicked and stranded, even more so as I realise that I won't have the car – so no means of escape if I need it.

A few minutes later, Dave and Tara leave too. Dave is wearing a short-sleeve shirt and a pair of very dark sunglasses and red trousers. He has a couple of cameras slung over his shoulder. Tara is wearing tortoiseshell glasses and a wide-brimmed straw hat with a ribbon around it, a white skirt and sandals. She looks very prim and neat and English. Dave kisses me goodbye, and asks me if I want a souvenir from Rome, but I can't think of anything.

I spend the rest of the morning swimming with the children and reading. All the talk of Rome has made me think about Sam and how much I was in love with him then. I remember writing his name over and over on a napkin; it seemed like the best name in the world.

At around one I go up to the house to do something about lunch. While I'm unloading the dishwasher, Miranda and Toby come home. Toby is quiet and disappears. I am cutting up ham and making a ragu sauce and Miranda is hanging around, taking things out of bags and putting them into the fridge. I am wary of her after hearing her on the telephone with her friends. She is silent but I get the distinct feeling that she would like to talk. I ask how her trip to town was. She sits down and says it was fine, then she sniffs and her face creases and she begins to cry. She sits up, waving her hands around her face and saying she's sorry. I tell her not to worry, and ask her what the matter is.

She describes how they were sitting at a café and she was listening to a couple of teenage English girls chatting on the table next to them. The girls were blonde, barefooted, wearing tee shirts with rips and jean shorts. They talked so fast it was almost impossible to understand a word they were saying, but she got the impression that they were talking about a party that they wanted to share for their birthdays and that it would be in a nightclub. She imagined they were about sixteen, but in fact she discovered a few minutes later it was going to be their fourteenth birthday party. The girls with their bare feet, sunny shaggy hair, tiny shorts and tanned limbs made her feel uncomfortable and uneasy and unsure.

"I know that's hard to understand."

"No, I understand," I say. "I understand completely."

They had gone out to visit the market before it was

too hot. They had started with a coffee in the small piazza. Toby sat opposite her, glancing at a paper, and she admits she was talking to him about his drinking.

"You must let him be," I tell her, "he's on holiday."

"I know", she says, "but he really wanted to have a break, you know like a kind of detox. I had devised a really good diet for him. We are meant to be doing it together. He got annoyed and then he disappeared. He told me he was going to buy a newspaper and I said I would pay the bill and meet him at the market. But then I realised I didn't have any cash to pay the bill, so I rung him to ask him to come back and pay. He didn't answer his phone though. So I explained in very bad Italian, mostly English, that I was going to find my fiancé because he had the money. I went to the market, but he wasn't there. I started going into all the shops to see if I could find him." She sounds really upset, but she has stopped crying. "Eventually I found him in a tobacconist shop, holding a packet of cigarettes, even though he is meant to have given up. I was shocked and confronted him. He said he had bought them for Dave so I reminded him that Dave's given up. Then he admitted that he'd bought them for himself. I just don't understand what's happened to him since we've been on holiday."

"Maybe he just wants a holiday from self-discipline. Maybe he just wants to do what he likes for a week."

She looks sad, as though she may cry again. "We're trying to conceive a baby. I share an office with a nutritionist and we talk all the time. It's hard to conceive if you're smoking cigarettes and drinking caffeine and alcohol; the three together is a disaster. She always tells her couples they must both give up. She asks her couples to stop drinking if they are having problems conceiving and are serious about wanting a child."

"Come on," I say. "How long have you been trying to have a baby?"

"Only a few days!" she laughs through her tears.

"So you're not having problems conceiving."

"No, not yet."

Now that she's upset, she's softened, like a sad little girl.

"Come on, let's go for a swim. He's just rebelling. If you leave him for a while, he'll probably change his mind."

She stands up and I check my sauce and turn it down and then we walk together towards the pool.

Jack is splashing and swimming with Maud on his back. She is clinging on like a little frog. He heaves himself out, pulls a towel off a chair and ties it around his waist.

"You all right?" he asks Toby, lowering Maud back into the pool.

Toby says he is, then he turns around and waves at

Miranda. She smiles as she approaches him and they have a quiet conversation. Then she spreads her towel on the floor and lies down next to him.

After lunch we decide to go on our ice cream expedition and Jack invites Miranda and Toby. Miranda decides that she will stay behind and read, but Toby says he'd like to come. We set off in two cars; the men drive together and I take the children. We go to the local town and walk together towards the piazza. There are lots of children playing and our children run off with their ice creams. We find a table and I sit in the middle of the two men. Toby is pale compared to the Italians, who sit at other tables drinking coffee, but Jack is tanned and everything about him is abundant. He has an enormous wad of euros in his wallet, and he gesticulates spreading his arms, talking loudly, laughing loudly like Marcus, but he's more present than Marcus and far more neat and orderly. He orders two beers for himself and then he reads us something about his show from an email his agent has sent him. I think he wants to impress me. Toby is leaning back in his char, smoking and drinking a beer. He is quiet, listening to Jack talk rather than telling us anything about himself, and seems very preoccupied. I ask him how he knows Sam and he tells us that Sam was his greatest friend at school. Neither of them particularly liked sport and both were into movies and comics and later girls. We take turns to say how we know Sam. I tell them about our time together in Rome and I try not to sound too sentimental. Jack says that hopefully he will be working with Sam on a feature-length film. "I'm perfect for the part," he says. "I play a slightly seedy arrogant detective."

"So what's so different about this seedy detective character?" Toby asks. "Haven't we seen a million detectives like that before?"

"He's commissioned a very young writer, who's written a great script. It's rare to read something this gripping." He rubs his hands together with glee. "But he has to confirm soon, as I am going to have to fit the shooting between the schedules for the soap."

Jack's mobile rings and he says he has to talk to his agent about the *Vogue* shoot. Toby doesn't make any effort to fill the silence Jack has left, so I ask him about the trip to the market. "We didn't actually get to the market," he admits. "I had a really powerful urge to smoke, so I left Miranda sitting at the café and went off to a tobacconist's."

I am drinking a Coke that is lukewarm. Toby is still so pale and English-looking, and his glasses are too big and too dark for him, and he doesn't seem to have much of a neck, but he has a sweet demeanour. He seems so malleable. I can see that someone like Miranda would boss him around, but he can't be as sweet as he looks; Sam said he'd done well in developing and selling property, so he must be pretty tough.

"I did give up smoking, but I am so bored of giving up things that I enjoy. I heard her calling after me but something inside me clicked and I ignored her," he says, brushing his fingers through his hair. "I went into a tobacconist's and bought the damn cigarettes and it gave me a real rush of pleasure. I had to go back and buy a lighter and she saw me coming out of the tobacconist's and confronted me. I said the cigarettes were for Dave and she replied that she knew I was lying as he'd given up." He laughs now. "I was on the spot. She was hysterical, really upset that I hadn't respected our agreement. I don't remember coming to an agreement, to be honest."

I signal a waiter and ask for some ice and lemon. Ice and lemon, I can remember the words in Italian: *limone* and *ghiaccio*. I remember once, when Sam and I were in Rome, a friend of his asked for Coke to go with his beautifully cooked liver, and the waiter threw up his arms in disgust.

"What do you think about smoking?" Toby asks me, as I finish my drink.

"I love smoking, but I hate the smell and it's definitely not healthy."

When I was a teenager we smoked because it was forbidden and it made us feel so grown-up and sophisticated and urbane. It was cool at school to share the cheapest brand of cigarettes with friends, all squeezed together in toilets that reeked of stale smoke. We shared cigarettes that we would then put out and relight in our next break. We thought we were the coolest girls in the school, but now that I look back, how cool could you be with a uniform that included wearing huge grey gym knickers over your underwear?

"So what did you do when you saw her?"

"I stood against the wall, inhaling slowly and blowing out smoke rings into the air. It was very arrogant of me."

"Yes, that was just a little bit provocative."

"She said it was her life too, not just mine, so I reminded her that we aren't yet married. We've still got to make it through to the wedding. So I told her: I'm on my holiday. I want to relax."

"Yes, I understand, but maybe she thinks you *want* to give up but can't. She told me she shares an office with a nutritionist who knows all about those kind of issues, so it's even more important for her."

"It was all her idea because she wants to get pregnant. But I don't see why we have to rush. There is so much pressure."

"She probably feels old. After the age of 35 a woman's fertility drops dramatically. How old is she?"

"Twenty-nine."

"Oh, really." I am surprised, but try not to show it, as I thought she was much older.

"She really wants to be married. I love her and want her to be happy, but it's all such a rush. We've only just got engaged."

"Children are part of getting married, though, aren't they?"

It is vaguely funny that I am trying to persuade a second person on the holiday to have a baby.

"Yes," he says. "Although I know couples that have decided not to have children and who are perfectly happy. Of course we will have children in time, but I just want to get married first."

"Maybe you could explain all that to her."

"We don't usually spend much time together," he says. "We are so busy that we seem to schedule each other into our lives." Jack is coming back towards us. "I know I should say sorry," he admits, "and I will."

Jack and Toby have a kind of mock fight about who is going to pay for the drinks and in the end I put the money on the table and the matter seems to be settled until Jack sweeps up my cash and surreptitiously puts it in my handbag. Just as the waiter is braced to take the card, Jack and Toby decide to order another quick beer, but I am worrying about the children, as once again Jill has offered to look after them and it is nearly six o'clock. Jack doesn't seem to be that concerned, but I don't want to be too indebted to Jill. Not in monetary terms, but in how much she wants back from us in some way that I can't really explain.

Jack is reading a cookbook for pleasure, which is called *The Real Flavour of Tuscany*, and it's full of fascinating facts.

"Did you know that San Lorenzo is the patron saint of pasta-makers?" he asks us.

We laugh.

"Tonight," Jack says, "I am going to make penne with prosciutto, cream and Parmesan." I think of the calories, but decide not to worry because I'm on holiday and a strange inertia has gripped me.

We return to the house to find that Jill has taken it upon herself to prepare supper for the children. Jack thanks her and says she's far superior to Mary Poppins. Jill looks so happy and pleased. She seems reluctant to leave so we offer her a drink, but she says she must get back to cook her dinner, and then she pauses and lingers slightly, looking for something in her bag.

"Well, just one," she says, changing her mind. "A nice glass of wine."

I open the fridge and pull out a bottle of white, and pour her a glass. Jack and Toby seem to have wandered off and no one else is around. Jill sits down at the table and starts to talk at me, about how she misses home, and as she talks, she punctuates her sentences with references to my name. "Jen," she says. "You probably understand what I'm saying, Jen. At the end of the day, if you're born British, you stay British wherever you happen to be."

She tells me about the pain in her chest, and how her heart was broken over 30 years ago and how she will never recover. "It was the death of love for me."

"You never met anyone else?"

"Yes but not to love... not to love."

She tells me she has never had children. "Well, there was one, but I lost him as a baby." I say how sorry I am, and then ask about the grandson she mentioned. "Oh, Rufus. I call him my grandson, but actually he's a godson."

She doesn't give me space or opportunity to contribute to the conversation, exactly like Tara. I stand up and say that I must really find the children and see if they are all right. She scrapes her chair, and sighs and says she's sorry if she talked too much. She stands up and walks to the door, and waves goodbye. "Cheerio," she calls out. "Catch you soon."

And for a moment, as she turns and waves, I'm not sure I would care if I never saw her again.

Alfie wants to talk to Marcus so we dial the number but his mobile is going straight to answerphone and

I'm wondering why he hasn't contacted me to say that he's arrived safely in London. I'm beginning to imagine that perhaps his plane has crashed and he's been rushed off to hospital. Whenever Marcus travels for work, I always have this absurd fear that his plane will crash, and it can be quite exhausting emotionally. I send him a text, asking him to call me when he arrives, and minutes later realise how melodramatic and needy that must seem, but the late-night meeting with Tara has thrown me off-balance.

Jack has started thinking about our dinner and it's quite a relief that Marcus isn't here to compete for the cooking crown. I am having a drink with Miranda and Toby, who seem to have made up, as she is sitting on his knee. We are stuffing ourselves with nuts, when Tara and Dave return from Rome. She says it was hot and very beautiful but a long way to go for the day. She yawns deeply as she says this and I think she should just go to bed. I can't get the intimacy of Tara and Marcus's whispering together out of my head.

Tara comes to sit down next to me and whispers that she has bought a pregnancy test and she'd like me to be there while she does it. I know that I must go upstairs with her, and be supportive, though I really don't want to. I follow her up to her bathroom and wait on her bed. I am strangely nervous and upset. She emerges and shows me the little white stick and we wait for it to change colour.

"Oh my God," she says, a few seconds later. "What does it mean?"

I see the line running through the little space. "You're pregnant."

In normal circumstances we would hug and I would congratulate her, but she's fallen back on the bed and she's just staring at the ceiling. I'm not sure what to say, so I say nothing.

"I know what you're thinking," she says, sitting up, "that I should have the baby – but I'm really not ready." She looks pale and ghostly. I suggest that perhaps if she is desperate she could have an abortion or have the baby and put him or her up for adoption. She stops crying and looks at me, widening her eyes. "You think that's OK?"

I nod coldly. "It's not up to me," I tell her. "You have to make the final decision."

"Yes," she agrees, biting her nail. The thought that the baby belongs to Marcus hits me in the gut and I feel faint.

"Why did you never tell me that you met Marcus and had a cup of coffee with him?"

"Oh, didn't I?" She seems vague, and if her vagueness isn't quite aggressive, it's certainly dismissive.

"No, you didn't."

"Sorry... I didn't think it was important. I just forgot."

"Have you ever met again – just the two of you?" I look down at my shoes. "I mean apart from late last night?"

"No," she says. "What is this? The coffee was just a random meeting. I confided in him. What made you suddenly think of it now?"

"I just wondered. It was strange to find you talking in the middle of the night last night." My heart is hammering against my chest.

"Yes, well, we were both up at the same time. And I told him I was maybe pregnant, and not wanting to be, and he advised me not to say anything to Dave until I had really thought it through. This is quite a weird conversation to be having now."

"Yes, it is and I'm sorry, but it's also quite weird of you to meet Marcus for coffee and not tell me. I've actually been really upset about it."

"Hey," she swings her legs off the bed and comes over to me. Kneeling in front of me, she looks up at me and takes my hand. "There isn't anything going on between us, I can assure you. Not a thing."

"I never suggested there was."

"No, but the implication..."

"I should apologise. I'm sorry. I'm not myself; I think it's the heat. And it's Marcus – he's been quite absent and uncaring recently, and when I found you two talking so late the other night, it seemed so intimate and I felt so excluded."

"I'm sorry if I've caused you to be so upset. Is there anything I can do?"

I shake my head. I want to change the subject now. It does seem really mad to persevere with this line of questioning, although nothing she has said convinces me that she is entirely innocent.

"So what are you going to do about Dave?"

"I'm not going to say anything right now, but I will talk to him at some point."

"Good." I breathe out deeply.

"He'll definitely want the baby." We are both now sitting on her bed. I can hear the shouts of the children from the garden and the little tabby cat is meowing outside the window. We sit in silence for a few minutes.

"How was Rome?" I ask to break the silence.

"We got very lost in the car and had a huge fight. Once we arrived, we ended up parking in a really expensive car park miles away from the city centre. We had a coffee in the Piazza del Popolo."

"Oh yes." I remember the one particular café in the Piazza del Popolo where Sam and I used to meet,

"And," she continues, "we looked at the *Crucifixion of St Peter*, by Caravaggio, which was lovely, and by then it was nearly lunchtime, but the restaurant that you recommended was fully booked, so we ate a plate of pasta in a stand-up bar. Then we walked around the streets, and ended up having ice cream outside a little café in the Piazza Navona."

"Sounds fun," I say.

"Yes, it was good to hang out with him for the day, although we didn't talk about anything much. But we held hands and were just slow together, instead of rushing. Do you know what I mean?"

The landline is ringing out and no one seems to be answering.

"It might be Marcus," I say, getting up quickly. I run downstairs, away from Tara, and pick up the receiver.

"Hello?"

"Hi, beauty." It's Sam.

"Sam! We were going to ring you."

"How is everything?"

"Everything is great, we're just missing you." Hearing his voice again, knowing that he is almost here, makes me both excited and nervous.

"Yes? I'll be there tomorrow, at about midday. I've just arrived in London and am taking the early plane tomorrow. How is everyone?"

"We're all having the best time and just wishing you were here."

"Marcus well?"

"He's gone back to London for a few days. He'll be back on Thursday."

"Why? Has he had enough?"

"Business as usual. He's gone home because there's a contract he has to sign."

I tell him about the figs and the watermelon we had for breakfast and how much we love the swimming pool and the gardens.

"I can't wait to see you."

"Can't wait," I say. "Bye, Sam."

"Is there anything you need?" he asks.

"Only you." I am surprised in which I say it, so boldly and flirtatiously. It is the manner that I say it; not really joking but matter-of-factly, as if it was the most natural thing in the world, and after I put down the receiver, I feel lighter and less concerned about Tara.

Toby and Miranda have now taken on the cooking tonight as Jack has disappeared somewhere on his phone. After putting Alfie to bed, I go to see if they need any help. Miranda has borrowed Jack's cookbook and is making a pasta dish but she has swapped the normal pasta for rice pasta, which is what I give Alfie sometimes so I don't overload him with wheat. Marcus thinks it's a travesty to call it pasta. I suggest that perhaps we make real pasta for the grown-ups and she says, "Go ahead if you really want to", in a sulky voice. The atmosphere seems to have gone back to being tense again between them. I put a big pan of boiling water on the gas ring and sprinkle in some salt and put a packet of pasta beside it. "OK," I instruct Toby, "I've put some water on to boil. You can put the pasta in when it boils."

"Sure thing," Toby says.

Tara is sitting on a white deckchair, drinking wine on the terrace with Jack, who has reappeared. We are chatting in an inconsequential way about Sam's arrival when Dave slinks onto the terrace carrying his hat. He's whistling and waving his hands around.

"Good news," he says to us, "really good news."

He pours himself a huge glass of wine and sits down at the table. "Random House wants to see the rest of my book. They've read three chapters. The bad news is I've now got to lock myself away and edit it for the millionth time. But hey!"

"Great news!" Jack raises his glass. "Will they take it?"

"Well, not definitely, but it's a good sign that they want to see more."

"It sounds great, but it's a shame we won't see you if you're hidden away working on it."

"Well, yes, but I've got to do it. By the way, I've lost a wodge of euros. It's disappeared – it must have slipped out of my jacket."

"Oh no! How much?" I ask.

"Not that much. About 150."

"That is a lot to lose," Jack says.

"Yes, but anyway, I'm celebrating." He takes a sip of wine. "The euros will turn up. I probably left them in a pair of soggy swimming trunks or something."

I wander down to the garden and look up at the stars. The air is cooler now, but the cicadas are still chirping loudly. I return to the terrace and light the citronella candles on the table and think about Sam. I can't wait to see him.

Tara joins me and in a hushed voice says that she's told Dave about the pregnancy.

"He wants the baby. I don't dare tell him that I've made a decision."

"Maybe you'll change your mind," I say a little harshly, lighting the last candle.

"No, I don't think so," she whispers. "I think he loves the *idea* of children but he hasn't thought about the reality. He hasn't realised that a baby will change our lives for ever."

I look over at Dave; he's talking animatedly on his mobile. I think Tara's convincing herself that he doesn't want children to assuage her guilt about not wanting to go through with the pregnancy.

"Why don't you believe him? I think you underestimate him."

"He hasn't thought it through."

"How do you know?"

"I just know."

"Maybe it's more to do with you not knowing," I say, walking away from her.

Later, we all sit down to eat. Tara picks at her food, like a teenager. Jack is quite quiet. When he lights a cigarette, Toby does too, but Miranda doesn't say anything. Dave eats quickly, like a dog, and he's drinking and filling up our glasses with wine. Everyone is drinking except Miranda, who is sticking rigidly to water. Jack sits next to me. He mostly talks about himself, as always, but he makes me laugh when he tells me how he pursued his wife Ellie. They met on a film set; he was acting, and she was first assistant director. He asked her out for lunch but she said she couldn't go, claiming she was on a melon diet and thinking that would put him off ever asking her out again. However, he turned up on the set the next day with a huge of box of melons, which she then had to eat.

After dinner, Dave suggests that we go for a swim, and everyone agrees except for Miranda.

"Come on," Toby says, attemping to pull her towards him but she resists a little too violently and he falls backwards.

"No, you go; I'll stay with the children. Has anyone

thought about the children?"

"Yes, Miranda, of course. We're only going for a quick swim."

"I'd forgotten about them actually," Jack jokes.

"Right, well, I'll stay here anyway," Miranda says.

"Look, if you want to go swimming, I'll stay with the children," I offer, as she's ruining the spontaneity of the adventure.

"Actually, I don't want to go,' she says. "It's pitch black and it's the middle of the night."

"Yes, exactly," Jack says. 'That's why it will be such fun."

"I'm not going to come," Tara says, "if you want to go, Miranda."

"No, I don't want to go."

Toby pours himself another glass of wine and Jack, Toby and I head off giggling like teenagers to change into our swimsuits. When I arrive at the pool, Jack grabs my hand and pulls me into the water with him and as I'm flailing around underwater, he grabs my legs and pulls me towards him and we float and glide around together in the dark water. We tread water side by side and then he quietly kisses me on the top of my head. He strokes my hair and then, because I have drunk too much and it's a starry night and Jack is giving me so much attention, and Marcus has possibly been unfaithful with Tara, I kiss him on the lips, and for a brief moment, we kiss fully and properly and his tongue finds mine.

The kiss lingers and he becomes forceful and more amorous, but his tongue is too harsh and too knowing and he's pushing his leg between mine, which I don't like. I gently push him away. I am suddenly horribly conscious and sober and worried that the others have seen us.

"You're a great girl," Jack whispers later as we are walking back to the house. "You're a good mother too. Are you missing your husband?"

"Not right now." I smile a little too flirtatiously. "Are you missing your ex-wife?"

"Never."

Dave joins us and says, "Well, hello, you two," in a silly voice that implies he saw us kissing.

"Hi," I reply, and then to distance myself from the whole situation, I fall behind and walk back with Toby, who is whistling.

Much later, alone in the bedroom, I wonder why Marcus hasn't called me and think about the scene in the pool with Jack. It wasn't a passionate kiss with Jack; it was more of a friendly, appreciative kiss and nothing to feel guilty about. I telephone Marcus again, just before going to sleep, and his answering machine clicks on. I say my usual thank-you to the universe. Thank you for this amazing house and the beautiful landscape. As I try to sleep, images of Jack and I in the dark pool flash before me. I don't know how to get through the rest of the holiday with Tara. I dislike her for confiding in my husband and for making me anxious and uneasy about her relationship with him, and for getting pregnant when she doesn't want a baby. The idea of aborting a baby can make me cry. I lost three unborn babies. Of course this is the issue. Of course it is.

TUESDAY

Sam wakes me with a kiss on my forehead. "Sam," I say, pushing myself up on my bed. He's wearing a navy-blue suit and light blue shirt. His eyes are the same sky-blue as his shirt and his face is tanned but there are more lines on his forehead than I remember. He moves towards me and kisses me on the mouth and he smells like pine. He stands back and surveys me and I remember with a rush of desire why I find him attractive.

I look to my left side to see if Alfie is there, but he's already got up. "Hi, beauty," Sam says, sitting on the edge of my bed and taking my hand. He has big hands that cover mine, but his fingers are long and slender. He lies down next to me, and I am consumed, almost impregnated, with a physical longing that spreads through my body. I want him on me. I want to feel the weight of him, and have him inside me, but I'm too shy to make my feelings known. I want him to know that without me having to tell him. This sensation is so intense that I am sure he must feel it too. He closes his eyes and whispers, "Come here, beauty", and soon we are kissing and I have never wanted anyone so much in my life. "I love you," I say to him. "I have always loved you." I am shocked that I have said this out loud. I wonder for a minute if I really have said this or if I have just thought it. I have always kept the knowledge that I loved him hidden somewhere deep inside, so deep that perhaps I have never admitted it even to myself.

He is kissing my neck, pulling up my nightshirt, and I want him. I have always wanted him. This is all very clear to me now. I have made a mistake in being with Marcus. Marcus is not my soul mate. I should have been with Sam.

"Mum! MUM!" I hear Alfie screaming at me. "Mum?"

I wake, without wanting to, very slowly, to find Alfie shaking me, pushing me. "Go away," I moan, desperate to get back to my dream. "Mum... it's Dad on the phone."

He forces the telephone into my hand and I sit up, pushing hair out of my eyes.

"Hi, darling,' Marcus says. He sounds smooth and

detached, as though he is calling from another planet and because he has to rather than because he wants to. I almost ask him if Jane asked him to call me.

"Hi…" I feel guilty and strange and adulterous from my dream. "Where have you been?"

"Busy," he sighs. "I'm going into a breakfast meeting now with the Japanese. They've organised a lunch and I'm having dinner later with my parents."

"Your parents?"

"Yes, they're up to see a show. They're celebrating their 50th wedding anniversary."

"Oh really?" Poor Marcus, I think, he's missing this holiday to see a show with his parents. Then suddenly I wonder if he made up the thing about the Japanese, and in fact he is in London on the pretext of a business meeting when really it's because he had forgotten that it was his parents' wedding anniversary. Or perhaps he's there to get away from the situation with Tara, which he is finding too intense.

"Oh, send our love." I lie down with the phone, and am aware that I don't really care what he's doing or why. I want to return to my dream.

"I will. And there's a big lunch in September that we are invited to. Look, I just called to say hi." He sounds impatient, and anxious to get off the phone. "Hope you're all OK."

"Yes, we are. See you on Thursday."

"Yes, see you then. Give a kiss to Alfie."

"I will."

I get up feeling disorientated, excited and nervous about seeing Sam. It is strange and oddly disappointing that he wasn't in my bedroom. There is still a connection there; he must sense it too. I can't shake off my desire for him, as I sit at breakfast with Alfie, Maud and Jed. I am looking at the view, and not really concentrating on what Alfie is saying to me. Miranda and Toby come and join us at the table. She pours out cereal mixed with berries and seeds into bowls for both of them. I notice that she uses longlife soya milk on top. Toby is smiling, though. Maybe they've made up after his midnight swim. Maybe they had a glorious night of hot and sweaty sex.

"How is everyone?" Miranda asks. "Did you sleep well?" She seems happier today.

"I had strange dreams," I reply. I feel loose and sexy as though I am embarking on an affair.

"Me too," she muses. "I dreamt that I was relaxing, doing nothing. So I've decided that is what I need to do. *Relax*." She sounds tense for a holistic kind of person.

"Yes, darling," Toby says. "After you've made all those calls you need to make."

"Yes, after that."

They eat their healthy breakfast. If I had any

discipline, I would be eating the same. I join in with the children and eat chocolate croissants. Just to remind myself why I shouldn't be eating chocolate croissants I look down at the roll of stomach that falls over my Marks and Spencer bikini which I have found refuge in now that Marcus has gone and I no longer have to wear the itzy-bitzy bikini that he bought me. The roll seems slightly less offensive than it did a few days ago. Perhaps the swimming has helped. Dave joins us and drinks coffee, then pours some more to take to the study where he says he's going to work. I am impressed that he can resist the gorgeous day.

Tara comes to the table and says she's tired already and she's only been up for about an hour. She says she feels as though she has reached a brick wall. For God's sake, I want to say, why don't you go back to bed then? She wants to stay on the terrace and read and she says that she's really excited about Sam coming.

I take the children down to the pool, because all they really want to do is swim. They are not interested in sightseeing or shopping, or walking or sunbathing or chatting like we are, and why should they be? I'm musing on photographs I would like to take one day, a series of chefs in their kitchen environments, and then I fall asleep. I'm woken by the sound of voices approaching the swimming pool. I sit up to find Sam walking towards me, followed by Dave and Tara.

"Hallelujah!" he shouts out. "Here I am!"

I stand up and he holds me tight and kisses me while Tara lingers behind him. Jack gives him a hug and he hugs him back and then, much to the amusement of the children, Sam strips off down to his speedo-style shorts and dives into the pool, causing an almighty splash. He swims a strong front crawl back and forth and then whooshes out of the pool, pulling himself out of the water.

He sits down. "Wow! That's better, can't stand airports." He pulls out several bags of sweets from his briefcase, which he gives to the children, who clamber around him and already think he is God. Dave slinks back to work, muttering about how he's going to have to lock himself away. Then we all sit around Sam, chatting about his journey, and the beautiful weather, until Jack goes off to the house for a shower, leaving Tara and me with Sam.

"My two favourite girls," he says. "Shall we slink off for a drink before lunch? Toby and Miranda are going to visit a church. We can ask Jack if he'd like to come with us."

"Well," I say, looking towards the children, "we can't leave them."

"No, of course not," Sam says. "They can come too."

Tara doesn't say anything but she is purring like a

cat all over Sam. She doesn't seem to mind that Dave is working instead of being on holiday.

"Why don't you two go off," I suggest, "and I'll stay with the children?"

Tara doesn't object, but Sam suggests again that we take the children with us.

"No, another time."

"We'll miss you," Sam says, but Tara still doesn't say anything. I have the distinct impression that she is pleased that I'm not coming. Sam squeezes my shoulders before he goes, and they trail off together and the exciting possibility of my dream is shattered. I realise after they've gone that perhaps Jack could have looked after the children, but between us we didn't think of that.

I am stuck by the pool with the children, feeling sad and irritated with Tara. I wonder if we met now whether we would become friends. I somehow doubt it. I wonder why we were ever friends. It was really all about Sam: knowing that he liked us both drew us together.

I have started another book but can't seem to concentrate on it. I read the same page over and over again without taking it in. I am pleased when Jack joins me and he seems happy to see me. "Great kiss," he says, somehow diminishing it, as though we had a great dinner last night, or great drinks, and I nod in agreement. I am relieved though that he is not attaching much importance to it. He says he's not in a good mood; he is despondent and depressed that he has lost his wife to a man who kisses her shoulder. He says he can't get hold of Ellie, and that she never answers the telephone, and he doesn't know what to do. "There is nothing you can do, from here," I say. "Maybe we should both learn to meditate with Dave; he does it all the time."

Jack says he'd rather jog than meditate and that meditating is for wimps. He swims with the children for a while and when he gets out, I see that he is looking another shade darker. I look down at myself and realise that I, too, am darker, and so I turn onto my tummy. I am slicker, possibly thinner, browner, sexier even.

"Sam's gone off for a drink," Jack says.

"I couldn't go as I had to watch the children." I am saying this rather pointedly, reminding him that he has two children of his own.

"I was actually in the shower at the time. Sorry to have left you so long. Why don't you have a drink this evening and I'll watch the kids?" He says "watch the kids' with an American accent, and I laugh.

"Thanks. Maybe I'll do that."

"Lovely to hang out with you last night." He squeezes my shoulders and I roll my head from side to side. I could do with a massage.

I would like to be able to tell Jack that Tara has secret

coffees with my husband and trysts with Sam but I won't. It would imply that I am jealous and that I have feelings for Sam and I don't want to give anything more of myself away. He's calling his mother. I hear him say that he went to buy a paper earlier and he decided to go to the museum to see the painting of the Annunciation, by a local sixteenth-century artist, and he was recognised by a group of tourists. I try to read again, but I can't. The words don't make sense. I read a bit more and then close my eyes. When I wake up, Jack is on the lounger next to me, reading. We exchange a few words about the beautiful day and I wonder what Sam and Tara are doing.

I make my way to the house and am agitated to discover that Sam and Tara have still not returned. But Jill is in the kitchen and she's preparing lunch. "I thought I'd give you all a break." She smiles at me, and tells me to sit down and to relax. "After all, you are on holiday," she says. Her eyes are wide and bright and she is talking quite fast.

"Thank you, Jill." She gives me a herbal tea, and asks me if everything is all right. I haven't really noticed before that she has a squint, which is rather alarming as it makes it hard to read her. She *seems* very sympathetic and understanding, but she may not be. She starts talking to me about some steroids she is taking and how much weight she has put on because of them, but before long I start confiding, partly because it's an effort to listen to her and partly because I need to talk to someone who is not involved with me in any way. I'm telling her how much I'd wanted some time alone with Marcus on this holiday and suddenly, without warning, I am crying and not enjoying my outburst of emotion in front of this woman I hardly know. I regret kissing Jack and dreaming wantonly about Sam, but of course I don't share this with her. Jill hands me a tissue, but there is something cold about the way she passes it to me, as though she is acting out of duty rather than from sympathy.

She washes her hands and tells me that Marcus must have a good reason to be in London. She's quite matter-of-fact, which surprises me. She's not gushing and sympathetic and tactile as I had imagined. He's signing a contract, I explain. She gives me a slice of cold, sweet ham and for some inexplicable reason, I want her on my side and I want her to like me.

"So he has to be in London? There isn't a choice?" she asks bluntly.

"Yes, he says he has to be in London." I am pouring myself a glass of water.

"So he's not escaping from you. He has to be there." She fixes me with her odd stare and it's hard to look away; there is something hypnotic about her eyes.

"Yes, I suppose so. Well, I think he could have had

the contract Fedexed here and then he could have signed it and sent it home."

She sighs and takes off a white apron. "He probably has to meet up with these people. They would like to see him in person." Although I know this, it is comforting to hear it. She gives me some tomatoes and a knife and asks me to slice.

"Sam has arrived," I tell her, cutting the tomato too thin. "He's gone off with Tara for a drink."

"Yes, he introduced himself to me. He's ever so good-looking. A real man."

She says this pointedly, I think, as though the other men on this holiday are not.

"Yes, he is good-looking," I agree. "So are the other men, though."

"But Sam has something," she insists, tearing some basil leaves. "Well, it's not surprising, so does his father Philip."

I am washing a few more tomatoes, when Jill suddenly says, "What do you mean he's gone off with Tara?"

"Well, she seems to want his exclusive attention, and keeps taking him off for secret chats." I pause. "Tara and I are not as close as we used to be. Actually, now I'm thinking about it, we were never that close." I bring the tomatoes back to the table and she sits down opposite me. "I suppose I thought she was a better friend than she has turned out to be."

"Well, it sounds like you and Tara have a few problems, but you don't want to fall out, do you? It would be pointless and sad never to talk again, such a shame."

"Yes, but what's the point of carrying on with a friendship if it's making you unhappy?"

"Have you tried talking to her? I do so believe in the power of a chat."

"A little, and she's apologised and I think she's quite depressed. She seems so removed, so capable of anything, of being disloyal, of sleeping with my husband…"

"Aren't you a one!" Jill laughs. "Well, I never. You're letting your imagination run away with you. Now give me back those tomatoes. She's probably having an off day. We all have them, you know."

I want to say "Do we?" But instead I hand Jill the tomatoes. "Yes, but her off days have gone on for months."

"Yes, well… take a step back from her. She's married to Dave so there's nothing much that's going to happen with Marcus, is there?"

"I don't know. I think she's a bit out of control. I get the feeling something happened between my husband and her."

"Well, there you go," she says. "You're jumping to conclusions."

I need her to understand me, but I am also a little

repelled by her. I find her unattractive and annoying. I explain how Tara had a coffee with Marcus and didn't tell me, and how I found them talking late at night. She says I mustn't assume anything, and for a moment I think how silly I'm being.

"Your husband's coming back, isn't he? You'll have a few days to be together and you'll relax and it will all be lovely by then. If you carry on as you are, thinking the worst of everyone, he won't want to stay with you, and Tara won't want much to do with you either."

Her tone has softened, but what she says has stunned me into silence. I instantly regret telling her so much. "I have learnt one thing," she says, waving the knife in her hand. "Life doesn't always turn out how you had planned."

She is standing up ready to leave, and I want to sit her down and ask, "What do you mean?" but I don't. I can't. She has left me uncomfortable and unnerved and not knowing what to do with myself. I have become far too introspective with far too much time on my hands. I don't usually have this much time to think.

I sit for a while on the terrace, brooding, and then I go to the garden and decide that there is something not quite right about Jill, but it's hard to define what it is that seems wrong.

Sam and Tara return from their drink just in time for lunch and they hover near each other, laughing at some private joke. Jill is still here, laying out the figs and ham and tomato salad, and I notice that after we've all sat down, she picks up plates and offers them to Sam who I am sitting next to. Jill lingers for a while, but soon there is no reason for her to stay and she leaves the terrace.

Sam sits next to me at lunch and tells me a little bit about his recent divorce. He says he first met his wife in Arizona at a health ranch. He found her sexy and kooky. "She's a natural sculptor," he tells me.

"What the hell is that?" I ask.

"She makes sculptures out of wood, driftwood, anything she finds. But she's volatile and too young for me. She wasn't used to hanging out with someone who was unavailable. I mean, she wasn't used to a grown-up man who has to work hard. She was used to surfer boys, and actors doing bar work. She made these almighty jealous scenes, and I couldn't take them."

Jack makes a toast to Sam and we all thank him for inviting us. He smiles and says how great it is to see us all. As lunch draws to a close, Dave appears from his bedroom, sits next to Tara and puts his arm around her. She falls onto his shoulder and says she is really tired and has to go to bed. I'd like to go and lie down with Sam and just chat and laugh about old times, while he stroked my hair.

After lunch everyone goes off for a siesta, including

the children. I lie on the terrace, sipping lemonade and when I look down at my hand, I realise with a sickening lurch of horror that the eternity ring Marcus gave me when I had Alfie is missing. A surge of terror and fear rushes through me. Where did I last see it? I'm almost sure it was on the side of the bath. I rush upstairs to the bathroom and search the room. I look in the plug-hole and behind the tooth mug, and in the bin. I search in my bed where Alfie is reading, and now I'm cry-ing, and Alfie is shouting after me, "Mum! Mum!" as I hurl myself down the stairs and across the hot grass towards the swimming pool. The water is shimmering in the heat and wasps are flying around the dregs of somebody's drink. I search frantically through a heap of wet towels and then look down at the lounger. I find some goggles and slip into the pool. I swim round and round, in a frenzied whirl, thinking that if I don't find this ring my relationship will not survive. I am quite sure I left it on the sink. I swim to the side of the pool and as I'm resting there, I remember Dave mentioning he'd lost a huge wodge of euros and Miranda lost a bangle. Did someone take my ring? Who? I lift myself out of the water and sit on the edge of the pool and sob and as I'm crying I know it is to do with more than the ring. I am the kind of person who loses things all the time: my car keys, my wallet, important bits of paper that I am sure I have stuck to the fridge with magnets.

Losing the ring is worse than all of those things put together and more; it is like losing the trust between Marcus and me.

I am staring at the sky, looking at a cloud the shape of a bay leaf, when I hear the shrieks of the children approaching. Sam arrives with them, looking very handsome in a pair of red shorts. "Hi there!" he calls out to me. The children shriek and rush towards me, and Sam must see the panic in my expression because he asks me if everything is all right. "You've been crying," he says, sitting next to me and putting his arms around me. I lean into him. "What is it?" He's stroking my hair, just like I wanted him to. I remember crying in front of Sam once before, after my grandmother died. He held my hand across a table and we drank coffee, and later wine, in a bar on the Via Condotti. But it was never the right time to tell him how much I loved him, even though, on reflection, that moment in the Via Condotti would have probably been it.

I am crying as I put Maud's armbands on for her.

"Why are you crying?" Maud asks me.

"I've lost something," I tell her.

"What?"

"A ring. My diamond ring. Marcus gave it to me after Alfie was born." I don't know how I am going to dare tell Marcus.

"Are you sure it's lost?" Sam asks.

"Well, I can't find it anywhere."

"Have you looked everywhere?"

Maud runs away from us, towards the pool.

"Yes, well I think so."

"Let's look again," he suggests, pulling at my hand.

"We can't leave the children," I remind him

"Well, if you give me permission, I'll go and look."

"Yes, do. Please do. I last saw it by the basin in my bedroom."

I lie back. He won't find my ring. He won't be able to. Time passes and Sam doesn't return. Tara and Dave arrive at the pool. They are arm in arm; I have noticed that since Tara announced that she is pregnant, Dave is being protective and Tara more affectionate than usual. All my old suspicions return. I wonder if she is covering something up. Does she really love Dave? Or is there someone else that she is involved with? They ask if I'm all right and I tell them about the lost ring. Dave thinks we should search the pool again, so we find a mask and he splashes around the pool popping up for air because there is no snorkel. He can't find my ring either. He gets out and dries himself and he and Tara go back to the house, saying they will look around for it.

Sam returns with a defeated expression. I knew he wouldn't find it. He sits down next to me and opens his hand with a flourish, and there, sitting on his palm, is my ring. A great rush of relief makes everything bearable again.

"Oh my God, where was it?" I am laughing and crying with happiness and relief.

"It was under your bed," he says.

"Under my bed?"

"Yes."

"How did you find it? Thank you, Sam." I stretch forward to kiss him on the cheek, and to my surprise, find that he smells of pine, as he did in the dream. Maybe he has always smelt of pine.

"Jill found it. I told everyone how upset you were. Jill was ironing and said she'd have a look. Anyway, she found it under the bed and brought it to me with a triumphant smile. And then she went home."

I put my ring back on my finger where it belongs. The ring will never leave my finger again. It will stay with me. I don't remember leaving it near the bed, though, but perhaps I did. Once again, having been annoyed with Jill, I am now grateful to her for finding my ring.

"I'll have to give her a reward," I say.

"Yeah, that would be nice," Sam agrees.

"I don't know what we'd do without her," I say. "I mean, sometimes she seems so annoying and then she has an uncanny way of knowing exactly when we need help."

"She seems perfectly nice, and a little familiar.

She reminds me of a teacher or somebody I used to know."

I want to touch Sam, I want him to hold me again, but it seems inappropriate now. There is no reason to comfort me any more.

"I have a lock on my briefcase," Sam says. "Do you want to leave your ring in there?"

"No, I don't want to take it off ever again. Thanks, Sam. I'm just going to go and get my book."

"No," he says pulling me back. "Stay and chat – it's been so long. You can go later."

We sit side by side and talk about the last few years and we are back to where we used to be, chatting in an easy manner. I almost confide in him my fear that Marcus is no longer in love with me, but I hold back. Instead, I tell him about how Alfie always sleeps in our bed. I explain that Marcus and I are both weak and that we can't get him out. He has the same reaction as most people. He can't believe we still let him sleep with us. He thinks it will ruin our marriage and our sex life.

"But why don't you redecorate his room?" Sam suggests. "Get a really cool bed on stilts or something, a few posters, some glow stars, a 'Keep Out' sign and anything else he could possibly want so that he won't want to leave his bedroom. Even better, ask him what he'd like in his ideal bedroom and go along with that. A spaceship bunk, toys hanging from the ceiling, secret drawers…"

"That's a brilliant idea, Sam. You're a genius. I never thought of that."

When Alfie was born, I wanted to ask Sam to be god-father but Marcus rejected him in favour of a couple of his friends, men who live abroad and who he talks to about once a year. I should have been more persist-ent. I tell Sam about my work, and how compromised I sometimes feel by clients, when they stand over my shoulder and expect a photograph to be a certain way. When I started photography I shot everything on film, but these days everyone expects digital and the process is so fast; I take far more photographs than I used to and the editing process is much more time-consuming. I don't think I concentrate as much as I should do at the moment the photograph is being taken. Sam talks about his film projects, and how long they all take to get off the ground. He says the world is a harder place to crack; agents make tougher and tougher financial demands. It's a miracle that any films are made at all.

As we are talking, Tara appears at the pool with a backgammon board and asks Sam if he would like to play. She is wearing a black bathing suit and her hair is up on her head. She looks beautiful and winsome, but she has dark circles under her eyes. Sam says he'll play, but then he hesitates and asks if I would like a game.

He is being polite; he wants to play with Tara and we both know this, so I refuse. Tara sits down next to me, and while Sam goes to fetch a beer, she says she's told Dave that she's not sure she wants the baby.

"He shouted at me," Tara whispers. "He says I'm selfish and silly. He really wants a child."

I am about to ask her if Dave's strong desire to have a child will make her change her mind, when Sam re-appears. She smiles up at him, a sly intimate gesture, which makes me feel like an intruder. I swim up and down while they concentrate on the game and then I sit at the other end of the pool reading my book and hear them laughing and joking and having eyes only for each other. When the game is finished, they walk together towards the gazebo. I want to follow them, but am reluctant to leave the children. They stay there, locked away together, and every so often I look up from my book to see if they have reappeared. I bite my nails, I can't concentrate on my book and am becoming more and more agitated.

Ten minutes later, I gather my things up and decide to walk quickly to the gazebo. When I open the door, I find Sam leaning against the bar and Tara sitting on a lilo. Tara is examining her foot. She looks up at me. "I think I have a splinter," she says. "Would you mind going to fetch my make-up bag? I think there are some tweezers in there. I could pick it out."

I look at her sitting there like a fallen queen, a precious princess, and I glance at Sam lapping her up. I fetch myself a glass of water and say, "I'm really sorry, but I have to watch the children."

"OK," Tara says. Sam smiles at me and offers to go himself, so we leave the gazebo and I go back to lying by the pool. Does Sam even realise she's pregnant?

A while later, I watch Sam walk up to the house, with Tara hopping beside him, leaning on him. It brings back those weeks when they first started seeing each other and Sam wrote me the postcard from Rome. It was during the time that I had split from Marcus and everything had seemed so bleak. I realise that for the first time in years I am not myself. There is nothing I want to do. I go back to my book and read, trying to lose myself in the story. While I am reading, Marcus's secretary calls to tell me she's managed to get Marcus back on a plane tomorrow night, very late. I register this news and somewhere deep inside I am pleased he's coming back, even though on the surface I feel quite indifferent – losing the ring feels like some kind of portent, and finding it like a second chance for us.

I am alone when Jack comes to find me. He looks well rested and cuddly. He's holding a pile of newspapers and magazines and a beer. He urges me to leave the pool and have a rest, so I walk back to the house and find a magazine in the kitchen and walk slowly up the stairs to our bedroom, where I flop on the bed and attempt to focus on an article about how to lose weight. I am halfway through the article when there is a gentle knock on the door. It's Sam. I wonder for a moment if I am dreaming.

He sits on the edge of the bed as he did in the dream. "Hey, babe!" he says, "Are you OK?" He looks concerned. "Just came to see how you are. I couldn't get away from Tara. You know she's pregnant?" He looks surprised, almost happy.

"What did she say?" I ask. Sam leans back so he is lying right next to me. He is easy with me as though we have been married for years.

"She's very distressed. She feels inadequate. Well, I'm sure she's told you, but she'll come round to the idea in the end."

"What did you advise?"

"I let her do the talking." He crosses his arms behind his head.

I sit up against the headboard.

"I think she should have the baby," he says.

We both say nothing for what seems like the longest time, then he asks, "Do you want to go for a walk?" I'd love to go for a walk with Sam, but I can't leave the children for much longer. "I should go back to the pool," I say. "The children will be like prunes by now."

"Shame," he sighs. "Let me walk you there." I stand up and he looks at me and I look downwards, away from his gaze, because it's too intense.

We walk downstairs and out into the brilliant day.

"Sam?" My heart is really thudding now.

"Yes."

"Do you ever think about me? I mean, when we're not together." I am worried that I sound petulant.

"Hey, beauty," he puts his arm around me. "I've never forgotten that night we had."

"Fifteen years ago," I remind him. "I've never forgotten it either." I am sure that I am blushing.

"It wasn't the right time," he suggests and I nod my head as if I agree, but I'm not quite sure what he means by that. Is he suggesting there could have been a right time? Is the right time now? He is whistling, looking at his watch, and I sense that this is not the right time to talk about this any more. There is much that has been left unsaid, but I am comforted to know that I am still important to him.

We have never talked about our night together before, not even two years ago when we met briefly in London, and I am surprised at how the subject has slipped into our conversation so naturally, so many years later.

"Why did you invite us all here?" We have returned to the kitchen, as Sam wants a glass of water.

"I wanted to see you," he replies with an inviting smile. "Come on," he says pulling me off the chair. "Let's play a game of boule."

I stand up and wonder at his energy and am disappointed that he's pulling me up rather than lingering with me in the kitchen. He has this quality about him that always leaves me wanting more.

"Why did you want to see us after all this time?"

"I always want to see you guys," he says, "but everyone has moved on. We all live in different countries. I thought it was about time we had a reunion."

I am following him out of the kitchen and we are walking towards the terrace.

"You have so much energy for a man who has been flying all night."

"I was in London yesterday. I had dinner with one of the financing partners and took the first plane out this morning."

"Oh yes, of course, I forgot. You said you were going to be in London."

I wonder if he has a mistress in London. I always wondered whether he had a mistress in Rome, but he never mentioned other women, not until he met Tara.

Dave joins us. I have never seen him look so dark and foreboding.

"Hi," he mutters.

"How's the writing going?"

"Not bad," he mumbles. "I think I'm getting somewhere but everything else is a mess."

Miranda and Toby are on the terrace playing backgammon. They both look up at Dave.

"How about a game of boule?" Sam asks.

"Yes," Toby replies. "Great idea."

"I won't," Dave, says. "I've still got work to do."

"I'm going to make some quinoa," Miranda says. "I'm a bit peckish."

"I'd love something really unhealthy," Toby jokes. "Something like sugar-coated chocolate cereal, just for a change."

Miranda shoots him a dark look.

Tara, Toby, Sam and I decide to play boule. There is a special course set up in the woods behind the house, where the heat is not so fierce. The boule pitch is a long stretch of sandy earth surrounded by a net. There is an ancient set of balls, all very similar in colour and hard to tell apart. Tara suggests that she and Sam play in a team against Toby and me. She is more like a single girl than a pregnant woman. She would never normally play a game. What is it about Sam that makes us behave like this? Part of it is that he is single, unattached and available, but never fully available either. The children and Jack join us, and they make up a third team. Toby turns out to be quite good at throwing the ball, and after an hour or so of fooling around, shouting at each other and laughing a lot, we beat them. Sam is full of praise for me, as I lean down to throw my last ball, which knocks his out of the way.

I'd like to take up Jack's offer of babysitting for me, and while Sam and I are walking back together, I ask if he'd like to go for a drink. I don't add "just the two of us", but that is what I am hoping. He says he has a business call to make, but suggests that we go out after dinner. I can't wait to have time alone with Sam, just like Tara did earlier.

The children are all in a tent in the garden. Jack is preparing dinner, sardines in a sweet and sour sauce. The recipe has been taken from a cookbook that he found in the house. He says it is an ancient recipe that was prepared for the sailors to take on their voyages. The amount of onion in the sauce was meant to protect the men from scurvy. We have a discussion about what else protected men from scurvy and we all remember citrus fruits. "Yes," Jack agrees, "it was a lack of vitamin C that caused scurvy." While we wait, we are all picking at bits of bread dipped in oil, and olives and slices of salami.

We are laughing when Miranda arrives to see Toby drinking and smoking and all of us eating her salami. "What the fuck?" she explodes before storming off. Toby follows her and a few moments later she returns and apologises, explaining that she's just had some bad news. She sits down and Toby puts his arm around her, which she shrugs off. Sam arrives and has luckily missed the explosion. I don't want his first night here ruined by more scenes and dramas. Miranda gets up and takes a glass of water and wanders off into the garden.

Sam asks what's going on, so Toby explains that things are a bit tense between him and Miranda. He thinks it may be pre-wedding stress.

"You have to be careful about getting married," Sam warns. "I mean, look what happened to me. Don't rush into anything, old man."

"What did happen?" Toby asks in a very genial manner. "I mean, I know a little. It was rushed, wasn't it?"

"Yes, it was rushed, she really wanted to do it. She'd had a weird childhood and needed the security, but nothing, not even getting married, was going to fill her up and help her. I made a mistake, what can I say? I was nearly old enough to be her father, which was pretty weird too. My stepsister had just got married and she's seven years younger than me. I think I thought it was time I got on with it."

I look at Sam as he's talking. He is unusually candid for a man. I remember all too well why I used to love spending time with him in Rome. The sardines arrive. Jack presents the dish to us in an earthenware pot; the fish are covered in sweet sultanas. Once we have the food on our plates, Jack goes back to the kitchen to fetch something and we hear him wail, "OH NO!"

He returns to the table and asks us all to stop eating, but it's too late.

"I was meant to cover the dish with clingfilm and leave for at least 24 hours," he moans. "It just won't be any good."

"Its all right, Jack," Sam comforts him. "It's very good."

"It could have been really tremendous."

"But it is," I say, and because he looks so dejected, I go and sit on his lap and kiss the top of his head. And he puts his arms around me, and we stay like that for a while. He's warm and cosy, and lovely. He's like a big bear. I see Sam wink at me and I wink back. And I am still sitting on Jack's lap when Alfie returns from his tent to say that he's had enough and would like to go to bed.

I take Alfie upstairs and watch him clean his teeth. He walks around chewing his brush rather than brushing and I tell him to clean them properly. When he's finished, he climbs into our bed and I hand him his teddy and he asks me to read him some of his book. I pick up *The Faraway Tree* by Enid Blyton and begin to read without taking anything in. I could be reading anything – a manual about aeroplane engines, soft porn, an academic book. I am an expert at this and manage to make my voice sound interested and upbeat. I read and read, until my voice is hoarse, and when I kiss him goodnight he asks me why I was sitting on Jack's lap. "Just for fun," I say. "Don't worry about it."

"But why?"

"No reason," I insist. "Just for fun."

"Do you like him like you like Daddy?"

"No, no." He keeps me for a little while longer, by saying he's thirsty and then that he needs a pee. I really want to get away, desperate to leave the dark shuttered bedroom. I tell him I must go and he shouts after me to leave the door open. When I am finally free, I run back down the stairs and join the others at the table.

We are chatting, sharing a bowl of cold peaches and cream. I am waiting for Tara to go to bed. I know that she has to and she will. She is tired and she's pregnant, and finally, after two teas, she does excuse herself from the table and goes upstairs, blowing kisses and is clearly quite drunk. After she's gone, Dave worries aloud about Tara drinking while she's pregnant. None of us say anything much, not wanting to come between them. We have all had too much wine and while everyone is clearing plates, I ask Sam if he wants to go for a drink now. He says he'd love to, and I'm wondering if he's going to invite anyone else. The saner part of me is worrying now about driving when we've had so much to drink, but the roads are not exactly busy.

We prepare to leave. I rush upstairs, check on Alfie, brush my hair and put on some lipstick. I like the way my face glows from the sun. We go off in his car, which is so much smoother than ours. We don't feel the bumps as we manoeuvre up the dirt track. We drive through Montenero and find one bar that is open and we stop. We park very badly, so that the end of his car is jutting onto the narrow road, but in the moment, we don't seem to notice or care and he grabs my hand and pulls me into the bar. A group sitting at a table look us up and down. I wonder for a sobering moment what we are doing here, but Sam has taken charge and is ordering us drinks. A man stands up. He is tall and quite old. He wears a cowboy hat and looks as though he has just walked out of a Robert Altman film. Sam and I squash together at the bar while the barman fixes our drinks slowly.

Sam and I take our drinks outside and find a table. We talk about stories he'd like to option, and how the top actors are difficult and demand far too much money and as soon as you pin them down for a film and book them in, a few weeks later, other options come up for them and they want to change the shooting dates. This is really bad news for the director as he's already fallen in love with the cameraman, etc, and the cameraman can't do the new dates. We don't talk about Tara and neither do we talk any further about the night we spent together. The time never seems to be quite right. He finally signals for the bill and I am drunk now and think it is now or never. I am imagining so many inappropriate things. The dream-kiss has fooled me into thinking that I can flirt with him even though I am in a lifelong relationship. We are talking, and I casually brush my hand over his thigh and he takes my hand and kisses it. Then my mobile rings out, and I answer because it would be strange not to.

It's Tara. She sounds sleepy, and she tells me that Alfie has woken up; he's had a nightmare and he's demanding that I see him. "Can't you read to him or something?" I glance at Sam, but he's already moved on, he's at the bar, talking to the barman. "Actually, listen, it's midnight, and I'm asleep." Tara sounds sleepy and slightly hoarse.

"Yes, of course you are. We'll be right back."

She wants me away from Sam. Sam is paying the bill and the moment has gone now. By the time we are back in the car, I wonder if there ever was a moment. I know now that during the fifteen years I have known Marcus I have never found another man as attractive, except for Sam. Sam is so easy to talk to, and he's bright and funny and sensitive and interested in what I have to say and who I am. I've always thought that he wasn't able to communicate that he wanted a relationship with me back in Rome. I have been thinking about asking him if I could be the stills photographer on his next movie, but I know that a project like that would take me away from Alfie and Marcus, and for a moment, just now, as I am being dragged back to the villa towards my son, that is just how I would like it to be. I would like to be away from my day-to-day life, away just for a month or two.

By the time I have comforted Alfie and lain down next to him, my head is spinning. I wonder if I have made a fool of myself. Does Sam no longer find me the least bit attractive? Did he ever? "Oh God," I moan into my pillow.

"What is it?" Alfie asks, waking up.

"Nothing." I stroke his head. "Nothing important."

"Are you sure, Mummy?"

"Yes, I'm sure." I am sure now that I have been ridiculous. I lie awake worrying about how foolish I am for a couple of hours until my hangover really sets in. Then I take some pills and finally fall asleep, forgetting to thank the universe for anything at all.

WEDNESDAY

I wake up with a dull headache that shoots pockets of sharp pain to different parts of my head. I drink a glass of water. The water tastes chemical and warm and does not quench my thirst. It's been a while since

I've had a hangover. The headache is acute and persistent. When I sit up the pain moves from the back of my head to the front and my nose is blocked and my ears need to pop. My mouth is dry too.

Alfie insists on joining me in the shower. The shower rains down like a tropical storm and it feels good – hard and warm and refreshing. When Alfie has finished and has left the shower cubicle, I lean against the wall and let the water pound over me, until my skin begins to wrinkle. I turn off the tap and rub my hair with a towel and dress in a pink Moroccan nightshirt. Alfie insists on wearing his pyjamas today and I don't have the energy to persuade him to change.

Someone has cut up some fruit and made fruit salad, but because of my blocked nose and lack of smell, I can't taste anything. The fruit is slippery and wet and the lack of taste makes the experience mechanical and not at all enjoyable. I wonder if this would be a good dieting gimmick: a pill that left a person without taste? When Sam joins me at the breakfast table, he nods and smiles in a rather distant way, as though we were acquaintances passing each other on the daily route to work. He asks me how I slept and I am about to reply when Tara sits down and he diverts his attention to her. He stands up and brings her a plate and pours her a cup of tea. She has a shawl pulled around her, as if it's very cold. She smiles at me, though, and is polite and friendly. She is nibbling on a biscuit and asks Sam for some ginger tea. "Ginger tea?" he enquires looking at me. "Do we have ginger tea?"

"I don't think so," I reply, "but I'm not sure." He's addressing me as though I was his housekeeper or restaurant manager. "Could you look?" Tara asks, glancing at me, and for some reason I am enraged and remain seated and don't answer.

"I'll look," Sam says after a few seconds, standing up again. I am under the impression that he wants me to search for the ginger tea, that somehow it is my duty to do so.

"Just look for fresh ginger," Tara calls after him. "God, I feel so sick."

Tara and I are left together and it's now awkward and charged between us. Sam is so taken with her. He always has been, he probably always will be, and that is how it is. It is a familiar feeling; a familiar pain I know well. It comes to me so clearly now, on this Italian terrace, drinking tea. It is the same sensation as longing for my mother to love me as much as she did my older brother, but there was nothing I could do or achieve that would make her notice me, or care about me, or even love me as much as him. And I achieved a lot. I won prizes, races, and was appointed prefect, head girl, monitor, but still my mother would not love me as much as my brother Tom, even though he did badly at school and was always being sent home. He refused to work or to conform and later to earn any substantial amount of money. But still, my brother could simply do no wrong. My mother's unflinching love for her son made me want to distance myself from my brother because it was too painful to be up close to him. Sadly all that is left is our family connection. As we grow older, my mother continues to be his ally, even though he is hopeless and can't get a job.

He trained at LAMDA and wanted to be an actor, and my parents subsidised him, and paid for his accommodation. They have never helped me. They still pay his rent, but now he has a girlfriend dressed in black and a baby dressed in hand-me-downs. My parents still talk about Tom as if he were a little boy, delighting in his small triumphs and hoping that his potential jobs will work out and that one day he'll get something big. "Oh, he's up for an airline ad," my mother will say, "or a small part in Holby City", but of course nothing ever comes of it, and nothing ever will – although he did once star in an ad about mortgages.

This is a little of what it feels like to be part of the triangle with Sam and Tara. Up until this holiday, I had never seen them together for any proper length of time. I have thought about them and wondered about their relationship, but I have not witnessed it up close.

We are left together on the terrace while Sam hunts down some ginger, and Tara says, "This pregnancy is making me feel so sick. How do women go through this agony?" She sounds despairing but also dismissive at the same time.

I am sitting at the table, fiddling with the pistachio nuts in a big bowl.

"How is Dave about your decision not to have the baby?" I know the answer, of course, but I want to hear what she has to say. I also wonder whether she has changed her mind. I am hoping and praying that she and Dave will work it out and be happy together, so that she no longer feels like a threat to me.

"He's coming round to it, but no, he's not happy. I think he understands, though, that it's not the best time for us to be having a child. We'd have to move out of the flat. We couldn't have a baby in a one-bedroom flat."

"You could, until the baby is about one. It could sleep in a cot in your room."

"Yes, but you know what I mean. It would be so cramped."

"Not really," I argue. I can't stop eating nuts, and I'm piling up the pale shells on the surface of the table. "I don't understand. Lots of people have babies in one-bedroom flats."

"You just want to give me a hard time," she says

boldly, sitting up now, shifting to the edge of her chair. She is almost toppling off it with indignation. "Just because you don't have to worry about one-bedroom flats, just because you think... In fact, what do you think? Tell me."

My heartbeat is quickening and there is a throbbing in my chest as I realise that I am going to speak my mind, but strangely I am not at all scared of confronting Tara; someone has to. She's right, though, I don't have to worry about living in a one-bedroom flat, and for a moment I wonder if I should offer her money.

"I just think it's odd to be thinking about aborting your baby when you have a loving husband who desperately wants a child."

"He may *think* he wants a child, but he would leave it all to me. I'd have to take maternity leave and be cooped up with him and the baby on the days he doesn't work."

She hasn't raised her voice, but she looks really angry.

"I don't think he would leave everything to you. Once he was introduced to his own child, of course he would get involved. Only a truly lazy, ineffectual man would do nothing for his baby."

"Don't be so judgemental," she snaps, and I'm reminded of my mother during one of her insane rages, but I am not afraid of Tara, not worried about what she may think of me, as I was earlier in the year. In fact, I am no longer worried whether she is a good friend or a bad friend, or even a friend at all. She strikes me as manipulative, self-pitying, indulgent and selfish. I have other friends, better friends, friends who care about me and who care about their children. And yes, I am judgemental and pretty hung-over, but someone has to defend this unborn child. There is a risk of a child losing its life because Tara can't make the effort to look after it. Perhaps I wouldn't be so harsh if she had been a better, less complicated friend. I know she's depressed, but then who isn't now and then? Aren't we all depressed at times? Tara glares at me; she looks as though she may cry.

Sam is back with a cup of steaming tea. He senses the difficult angry silence that hovers in the air.

"What's up?"

"Nothing," says Tara, standing up and pulling her shawl around her like a little old lady. I am suddenly so repelled by her that I can't even look at her. "I have to go in," she says.

"Was it something I said?" Sam calls after her.

"Ask Jen."

She goes off and he looks at me quizzically, and I shrug. "It's about the baby," I say. "We have different views as to whether she should go ahead and have the baby."

"Ah. But she's the mother, shouldn't she decide?" He sits down opposite me at the table. "I want her to have it," he adds.

"Yes, of course she has the ultimate decision. I know I should apologise. But I lost three babies, so it's hard for me to understand why anyone would knowingly abort their own child, unless they were raped or very young and on their own… "

"You are quite harsh on her, though," he decides.

"Yes, perhaps I am harsh. It's not really any of my business, I guess." I regret my outburst.

"Well, I think you should apologise."

"I'll go and speak to her. Don't worry about it. We're just having a go at each other, I suppose it was brewing…"

"I thought we were all old mates," he sighs and kind of laughs too. "I got it completely wrong."

"Yes, we are mates and that is why we are having a row and speaking our minds. We wouldn't bother if we had just met and didn't care about each other. I just want to shake her and pull her out of this mood she's in, where she thinks nothing is possible and everything is difficult."

"I'm sorry if it's anything to do with me; perhaps I shouldn't have invited you all here together."

Sam stretches and then bends over and pulls off his tee shirt. He is standing before me, flicking it back and forth against the palm of his hand.

"Look, don't worry, Sam. Please don't let this stop you enjoying yourself."

"Look at it from my point of view. I've got Dave locked up working, Tara having a crisis, Jack in bereavement for his ex-wife, and a mate who's engaged to a mad woman. And let's not forget your boyfriend who's abandoned ship… I mean, what am I meant to think? Then there's me, of course, recently divorced. Talk about a group of dysfunctional friends. I mean, it's crazy." He finally puts his shirt down and I laugh and immediately feel lighter.

"Sorry, Sam. Sorry you've had to put up with all of this."

"About last night –" Sam starts.

"What about it?"

"I'm sorry if…"

I take another handful of pistachio nuts.

"There's nothing to apologise for. It's probably me who should apologise," I say, opening the nuts and putting the shells in my empty hand.

"Well, nothing much happened, did it?" he asks. "You didn't do anything that warrants an apology." His tone is light and carefree, whereas my mood has become heavy and urgent.

"No, not really." My hand is now overbrimming with pistachio shells.

"Good. I can't shake the feeling that I did something wrong."

I can hear the children heading towards the terrace.

"You see," I say, putting the shells into a terracotta ashtray that he hands me, my heart banging in my chest, "I've always loved you Sam." Once I've said it, I instantly wish I hadn't.

"And I've always loved you," he says, opening a lager bottle, missing the point, missing the meaning, or if he's not missing the meaning, he's pretending to, which is worse, somehow, and more humiliating.

"We're really good mates, aren't we?" His voice sounds growly, and he's looking at his watch.

"Yes." I look up at him and I know that he'll never understand. My feelings for him were never reciprocated. Yes, I know this for sure now. I've always known it really. He really loved Tara, in the true sense. He loved me as a friend, but he's never been in love with me. All the old hurt, the wound, is gaping again now, and I am close to tears and so angry with myself for letting it happen. I am frustrated that I still have feelings on this subject, even now when I am in a relationship with Marcus and we have a son together. I wasn't even thinking about Sam until he called to invite us to Italy.

He ruffles my hair. "You're a real babe," he says. "And I want you to make up with Tara. And let's have some fun around here, OK?"

Then he leaves me with my cup of coffee and I hear him shouting after Tara. I decide then, finally, at that moment, never to embarrass myself again around Sam. In fact, after this holiday I don't think I will see him again. Once I've decided this, my mood momentarily lifts, but crashes back down again when I realise how unrequited my love for him has been.

I am still sitting at the table when Tara comes and sits down next to me. I wonder if Sam has sent her to find me. She has piled her thick, dark blonde hair up on her head and changed into a white kaftan top. We both apologise at the same time, and she says, "Please don't judge me any more. You don't know what it is to be me. "

"I'm sorry, Tara. I'm projecting my feelings onto you. It's all about me and my miscarriages and not really about you at all."

"Can we make up?" she asks, smiling at me.

"Yes, we can," I say, hugging her. There is no harm in being friendly but when this holiday ends, I probably won't see her again either.

Miranda comes onto the terrace pulling a pink suitcase. "We've decided to leave," she says.

"Really?" Tara asks. "Why?"

At that moment, Toby comes through. He's wearing

a white shirt and trousers and he joins Sam in the garden. Miranda leans against the table. Her hair is pulled back tightly, and she has grey circles under her eyes. She wears a navy jacket with gold buttons and pressed three-quarter-length white trousers. She taps her foot up and down. "We've decided that we need some time on our own, the holiday hasn't being going well for me. We're going to spend a night or two at a hotel and sort a few things out."

"Well, good luck," I say.

"I have to calm down and slow down," she says, biting her nails, "but for some reason, I can't seem to do that here. I talked to Jill. She found me by the fig tree and she said that if I wasn't happy here, perhaps I should leave, and it suddenly seemed like the obvious thing to do. Toby agreed with me."

"Did you find your bangle?" I ask, glancing at her wrist and thinking how inappropriate it was of Jill to advise Miranda to leave.

"No, I must have left it at home," she says.

It seems ungracious to leave so suddenly. Sam has only been here 24 hours. Toby kisses us all goodbye and mumbles apologies, and squeezes my hand, saying he enjoyed talking to me. We walk towards their car and wave them off. Toby rolls down the window, and then hoots the horn and waves his arm out of the window.

We gather around the terrace table, while the children are playing hide-and-seek indoors.

"That was odd," I say.

"Yes." Sam is drinking a cup of coffee. "Toby has decided that he's going to call off the wedding."

"Good luck to them," Jack says. "Definitely wiser not to get married at all."

"Don't say that!" Tara exclaims! "We're newly married!"

"Maybe I meant 'better not to get married if in doubt'," Jack says, "but honestly, I don't quite see the point of getting married. We were married but my wife still had an affair. I've lost the best woman I have ever known. I should have forgiven her, of course. But being married didn't help us. And God, Miranda was a handful! I can quite see why he backed off."

"She wasn't great last night," Sam concedes, "storming in like a diva, swearing and then storming out again. What was that about?"

No one replies. "So where are they going?" I ask, watching a wasp hovering around my tea.

"He's taking her to a restaurant to tell her that he wants to put the wedding on hold, then he's going to drive her to the airport, put her on a plane, and then probably come back here. I think he just wants to soften the blow. He definitely doesn't want to get married."

The wasp is crawling around the rim of my tea-cup, and I'm wondering when it is going to fall in. I think of her sitting on the aeroplane with all her plans shattered. I imagine her ringing her parents to tell them the news.

"Poor girl," Tara says.

"Yes, but probably better to split now rather than wait till after they're married," I say.

"Yes, better than waiting for a mortgage, three children and an indifferent sex life," Sam laughs.

I am not surprised that things between them haven't worked out. She just seemed so unrelaxed and intent on changing poor Toby, and making him something she wanted him to be, rather than appreciating the man he actually is. It makes me think about my relationship with Marcus. I behave as though I want him to be someone who never leaves my side. But actually, the opposite is true. It wouldn't suit him to be a "house-dad", baking bread and making fairy cakes with Alfie.

"Yes, she'll be all right," Dave says, stretching his arms in front of him, "Wow, I'll tell you something, though. I've worked really hard here. Haven't worked this hard since I was sent on the campaign trail with Tony Blair. I think we should all go somewhere for the afternoon. Maybe visit the chapel that Jill was telling me about."

We agree that we all need an outing. We haven't been very adventurous. We make our way towards the pool and pass the morning reading and swimming. The pool area seems quiet and less crowded without Toby and Miranda, but Sam sits right next to Tara and I try not to notice. I sit by myself and read and then I stand up and ask Jack if I can take some photographs of his children for my photographic agency. He wants me to come for a little walk around the garden, so we go off towards the stream and sit down on a beautifully carved bench. It is a perfect day, the sky is almost cloudless and there is a slight breeze. Jack lights a cigarette and asks me if I like him, and I reply, "Of course."

"Jen, I really like you," he says. I understand that this is some kind of declaration, that he likes me more than just as a friend. I don't know what he expects me to say, or how he wants to proceed, but I'd like to get up and move away from the bench. This can't be happening, I think, but then again, I am not that surprised that it is, because of our kiss in the pool and Jack feeling sorry for himself because his wife has a new lover.

"Listen, Jack, I live with Marcus, we have a child together," I say gently. I look down at my shorts. My legs appear to be browner and slimmer than they did a few days ago. I glance up at the cloudless sky and pull my dark glasses down and wish for a second that it was Sam saying this. I wish it was Sam. I know instantly that it's wrong to think like that. What's wrong with me? Sam doesn't love me; he never has – why am I still behaving like this? I'm hoping Jack and I can get through this exchange quickly and move on to something else.

"Yes," he sighs, "I know. Didn't stop my wife," he laughs.

"And look what happened," I remind him. He takes my hand.

"Please ignore me. I'm a silly old fool. Forget this happened and don't let my blunderings ruin our time here."

"No, of course not."

We hug because I'm fond of Jack, and while we are hugging, Alfie appears. He's been crying and he says he fell over and didn't know where I was.

We all walk back together and I spend an hour taking photographs of the children by the pool and become immersed in my task and forget everything else. I remember with a guilty pang sitting on Jack's lap, and wonder if my motive was partly to stir up Sam. I shouldn't have done it and I was sending out the wrong signals to Jack. I take photographs of the children jumping and swimming, and pushing each other in to the pool. Potentially, I can make some money from these photographs. Picture editors will ring my agency and ask for photographs of happy holiday children by a swimming pool and hopefully they'll want mine, of a moment captured, a happy, sunny day.

We gather for lunch. I have cooked some eggs and cut them in thin slices. I have washed the lettuce and opened jars of anchovies and capers and placed them in a lovely glossy pattern around a red plate. My salade niçoise looks as though it's going to be photographed for a magazine.

At lunch the mood is definitely lighter. However Tara doesn't appear and Dave says she is feeling sick. Sam sits next to me and we have fun chatting and playing guessing games with the children. Alfie has insisted that we play something called the animal game, in which someone, usually him, chooses an animal and we have to ask him questions to find out what kind of animal he is thinking of.

After lunch, we put on *Tom and Jerry* for the children and then, one by one, we slink away for a rest. I love this part of the day. Lying on the crisp sheets, with the shutters half-closed, and then reading, before curling up on my side and maybe falling asleep. On this occasion I fall asleep for about ten minutes and then wake at up with a start at 3.30. I go downstairs to find the children still watching television.

"Where's Maud?" I ask Jed.

"She was hear a minute ago," he replies. He is transfixed by the television.

"Maud!" I shout through the house. When she doesn't reply, I walk out onto the terrace.

"Maud!" I shout louder.

I have obviously woken Tara, because she comes down the stairs and senses my anxiety, and now we are running towards the swimming pool.

There is a large plastic boat floating in the pool and it's bobbing near the side. There is a dark shadow underneath it, and I sway a little with shock. From the edge, I push the boat away and find Maud floating face down. I've often heard the expression "my heart missed a beat", and now I realise that's exactly what happens. My heart falters in its rhythm and I sway again from the shock. Tara jumps into the water fully dressed and drags the limp, lifeless body to the side of the pool, and then I pull Maud onto the concrete. Her face is grey and her lips are blue. Tara is now out of the water, kneeling over her, breathing into her mouth and pumping her chest, but I am rooted to the spot. I should get Jack; I should find Jack. I am sure that Maud is dead. "Do you think she's dead?" I whisper to Tara, and her look tells me yes. I am dizzy at the thought of having to tell Jack. Tara's face is the colour of paper.

"Get Jack. Get Jack now," she says to me, keeping

her tone low and steady.

I want to say, "I can't tell him; I can't tell him his daughter is dead." I think of Maud's sweet little voice and begin to cry.

Tara shouts at me, "Get Jack!"

I turn around with dread and begin to run to the house, but it's as if I'm watching myself and this is happening to someone else. My legs are weighed down as though I'm running in a nightmare. I run to Jack's room, and he's asleep face down on the bed. I shake his shoulder, and he grunts and sits up and senses that something is wrong. "What?" He looks at me anxiously. "What?"

"Maud, it's Maud. She's had an accident down by the pool. We don't know how long she's been under the water."

"My God," he says quietly. He grabs his dressing gown and he's running and asking me to call an ambulance. I go down to the telephone in the kitchen but don't know the number for an ambulance in Italy, so I call Jill's number, which is still displayed prominently on the board, and kind of sob with panic down the phone and ask her to call one. She says she will, and that she is on her way. She says everything will be all right, but I am not so sure. I look in on the children and they are still watching the DVD. They haven't even noticed that Maud is missing.

I run back to the pool to say that the ambulance is on the way, and find that Tara is still breathing into Maud's mouth, while Jack stands over her. He's moving his lips, perhaps he is praying. After one long, minute, Maud is coughing. "We have to take off her clothes," Tara says, "and cover her in a blanket."

Even though she has coughed, she is unconscious. Jack is sobbing and swearing. He rushes off to find a blanket and meanwhile we cover her in swimming towels. Tara manipulates her onto her side into what I vaguely remember is called the recovery position. She tells me that because she works with children, she has to renew her first-aid course every year. I don't know what we would have done if Tara hadn't been here.

Dave and Sam arrive to say the ambulance is on its way. Dave has a fixed, worried expression on his face and Sam is on his mobile, trying to get the number of the hospital. Dave says that Jill rushed from her house and was able to talk to the ambulance drivers in Italian and guide them to the house because they got lost. "They should be here soon," he says.

Two men eventually arrive by the pool with a stretcher, and Jill follows behind. Both men are dark and purposeful. They have brought what looks like oxygen and a respirator. Jack is talking to them in English, and one of them speaks a tiny bit of English – enough to reassure Jack.

They lift Maud onto the stretcher and Jack takes her small, lifeless hand. The taller, more hirsute of the two men turns to Jill and says something in rapid Italian. From Jill's translation, we learn that they are worried that she could die of the shock, but people, children, can survive if their lungs are not filled with water. So I am hopping from foot to foot, hoping and praying that Maud's lungs are not filled with water. They can't be filled with water. "It will be all right," Tara says, in a very responsible and strong voice, and this is the first time I have seen her as teachers and children must see her in her professional life.

Jack is firing questions at Jill about how far the hospital is, and whether Maud will be seen straight away. He climbs into the ambulance and Jill somehow ends up going too, as she has offered to carry on helping Jack with the translation. He is sitting in the back with his head in his arms. The door is still open and he asks for a glass of whisky. But before I've had a chance to look for the bottle which is apparently in a duty-free bag in his room, they are off down the drive. The lights are flashing and the siren wailing. It's oddly unsettling to hear that sound in this silent rural landscape. And while I watch the ambulance careering down the dusty path, I'm sure I see a bird of prey circling overhead and I hope that it is not an ominous sign.

After the ambulance has gone, it is unnaturally calm

and quiet. Dave, Tara, Sam and I stand in the drive for a few minutes without saying anything. My breathing is still irregular and my heart is beating hard and fast. Sam says he is so upset that he can't sit still, so he is going to go for a run to try and clear his head. He thinks if we are to be of any use to Jack, we need to be strong and together. Tara offers to keep the children occupied and also tell them what happened. "Thank you," I say. Something has shifted in Tara. I don't really want to go inside yet, and be with the children; I need to gather myself. I admire her strength. She has been strong and focused through this whole drama, while I have been jittery. When Dave says he is going to meditate, I ask if I can go with him. "Of course," he says, wrapping his arm around my shoulders, "of course you must."

He leads me along a stony path towards a eucalyptus tree in a faraway part of the garden. We sit down under the shade of the branches. 'Wow," he says, "that was heavy. Very heavy."

"And it isn't over yet," I say, and then I begin to cry. He comes and sits next to me and draws me to him and I lay my head on his shoulder. "It was a miracle that she didn't die," Dave says. "She must have fallen in only seconds before you arrived."

"Let's hope so. Let's hope she doesn't remember anything."

He kisses the top of my head as though I were a little girl. "Let's stay positive," he says. "If we think about a positive outcome, there is sure to be one. I have to keep thinking that," he says. " I have to keep repeating that she is going to be all right, otherwise I fear the very worst. I also have to keep myself sane while Tara is messing with my head. I have to believe she is going to have the baby." He sounds confident for the first time on this holiday.

"I'm sure she will," I say, wanting to reassure him.

We sit for a while with our eyes shut, just breathing. He gives me specific meaningless sounds to repeat, *shi va ba, shi va ba, shi va ba*. I close my eyes and repeat the sounds over and over again until they reverberate in my head. After a while I feel sleepy, but at times my mind becomes distracted, and pulled back to other things: the colour of the water in the swimming pool when I first caught sight of Maud, her body floating there, my heavy legs as I ran to find Jack. I open my eyes to see that Dave's are still shut and he's really concentrating, and for a moment I want to giggle. He has instructed me to go back to repeating the sounds if my thoughts drift off, so I keep doing that, focusing on *shi va ba*, until I am heavy and empty and very still. Soon I am seeing geometric patterns in all colours and every chirp of birdsong or rumble of a distant car seems loud and significant but not intrusive. When we finish, it's been half an hour, although it feels like five minutes, and I am invigorated and refreshed and my heartbeat has slowed down.

The children are in the kitchen with Tara and they are making a fruit salad. Tara is in her teaching mode, firm but kind, and very much in control. In fact, oddly, she seems to have come alive. Jed asks me about Maud. He wants to know if I've heard anything.

"No, darling, we haven't heard anything more."

"Will she die?" he asks me.

"No," I say firmly. "She won't die." And I pray that it's true, but now I am more sure, more hopeful. I have to explain that he won't be able to talk to his father while he is at the hospital with his sister because hospitals are very strict about letting people use telephones.

"Can I speak to Mummy?" he asks. He can only recite the first part of her mobile number, though. "I hope she's going to be OK," he says. "I do love my sister you know, even though we fight sometimes."

I have a flash of Maud lying limp in the pool. I remember my first glimpse of her, with hair falling across her eyes, and biro scribbled all over her arm. She's here, aged four, without her Mummy and she's being so brave because there is no doubt that Jack is a little gruff with her. She seems shy, but also at times she can be quite outgoing. She will be so cool when she's a teenager. Boys will fall in love with her... The sound of the telephone interrupts my thoughts.

I run to answer, in case it's Jack. It's a woman, who says hello in a breathless voice and introduces herself as Ellie, Jack's wife. She says she can't get through to Jack now, as he's in the hospital, and she is presuming he is not allowed to use the phone. She wants to know what happened as she's only had a brief conversation with Jack from his mobile while they were on the way to the hospital. I can hear that she's on the edge of tears and that she is only holding back because I am a stranger at the end of the phone. I fill her in with as many details as I can manage, about what happened to Maud; perhaps I edit a bit, because I don't want to alarm her. I can imagine how she feels. In my fantasy celebrity questionnaire my answer to the question, "What is your greatest fear?" is always "Something happening to Alfie".

She asks to speak to Jed. I call him over and hand him the receiver, and he says nothing but "yes" and "no" for a while. I'm half-listening and half-making a cup of tea when I hear him say, "See you soon, Mummy. Bye."

"Is she coming here?"

"Tomorrow morning," he says with a small smile. "You will like her, you know. She's really nice."

We play Monopoly with the boys and I'm finding it

hard to concentrate. Jed has to keep reminding me that it's my turn. Tara is strangely energised by the situation. She is like a toy that has been wound up and springs into action. She is making Jed laugh by doing impersonations of him and Maud. She has found a small silver yoyo in the bottom of her bag and she is letting the children play with it.

Alfie says he would like to swim, but we are not quite ready to take the children to the swimming pool. Jed says he doesn't want to swim anyway. The afternoon drags, and only Sam finds that he is relaxed enough to be able to go down to the pool and read. At about 6.30, the telephone rings and Tara and I both run towards it. I let Tara pick it up and stand inches away from her. She mouths at me that it's Jack and I know after two or three sentences of her saying, "Oh good, oh, thank God", that Maud is not dead. She carries on talking to Jack, but gives us the thumbs up. I gasp "Thank God", and let out a scream of joy, and for the first time since we found Maud, I breathe properly. Tears come to my eyes and I wipe them away. Tara says goodbye to Jack and hugs me and then cries out "Yeah!" Jed wants to know what's happened and we tell him.

"Awesome," he says rather coolly, but he's pale and there are dark bruise-like shadows under his eyes.

Tara tells us that Maud is sitting up in her hospital bed

and she's drinking a hot chocolate. The specialist was worried that she would develop hypothermia, the danger being that her body would go into shock and she would die of a heart attack. They kept her in a heated blanket, but now she is ready to come home. We are all so happy that we actually go around hugging each other and laughing. Sam comes back from the swimming pool with soaking hair and a towel wrapped loosely around his shoulders, and when he hugs me, so close, I can smell the zesty tones of his aftershave. He pours himself a drink and says that he's very relieved, very relieved indeed.

Tara speaks with her mouth full of banana, "Jack says that Ellie is coming out tomorrow morning to be with Maud, if that's ok with you, Sam?"

"Yes, of course. That should be interesting," he winks at us all, and I wink back.

The day has shaken me. Sam and Tara and their absurd flirtation no longer seem important – nothing much seems important, except poor little Maud. We are all having tea on the terrace when Marcus appears with a small suitcase. He's wearing a suit and a silk scarf and a white shirt. I am genuinely surprised to see him. I had forgotten in all the drama that he was returning today. I stand up to kiss him. Sensing the strange atmosphere he asks "Has someone died?"

"Well, actually," Dave quips, "someone nearly did."

Marcus flings down his battered brown briefcase. He falls back into the white chair. He looks tired and crumpled and tanned. I would like to hug him and kiss his dear face because I am tired of being suspicious and cross with him. I am so happy to see him after the terrible uncertainty of today and my doubts and regrets over Sam.

"Who nearly died?" he asks. We fill him in with the details, each adding our own interpretation of what happened. Marcus stifles a nervous yawn and fiddles with the strap on his suitcase. Alfie comes in and sits on his lap and Marcus pulls him close to his chest. "Every parent's worst nightmare," he declares. He stands up and fetches himself a glass of water. He asks where Miranda and Toby are and Tara explains that they have left. He jokes that he is surprised that so much has happened since he's been away and then he laughs, but no one laughs with him.

He goes into the kitchen, and Alfie and I follow him. He sits down at the table and I hand him a beer. "Bit of a sense of humour failure around here."

"You do realise what nearly happened here today?"

"Yes," he replies. "Sorry to laugh, it was just nerves."

"Alfie, we need to talk," Marcus says.

"What?" Alfie asks.

"You mustn't – and I repeat – you must not ever swim or play around the pool without an adult. You know what happened to Maud."

"Yes, I know. Tara told us."

"Haven't you said anything?" Marcus turns to me.

"No, I haven't had a chance, but we're talking about it now."

"We're all safe then," Marcus says. "Let's have a hug."

We stand, hugging in a circle, warm and close and snug. I am ashamed to think how treacherous I have been to have kissed Jack and to have desired Sam and to have imagined that Marcus was unfaithful.

We hug a bit more before releasing ourselves. Alfie is drinking a glass of water when he says, "Mummy and Jack are really good friends. They are always chatting and whispering and Mummy sits on his lap." My face warms up with the beginnings of a blush because what he says sounds so awful.

"Oh really," Marcus says. He studies me, searching for the truth.

"Alfie saw me sit on his lap for a moment at lunch when Jack was feeling sorry for himself."

"It was more than a minute," he adds cheerfully.

"Alfie," I say, trying to control my urge to shut him up, "why don't we play a game?"

"You two play a game," Marcus says, "I'll take a

234

shower and get out of these clothes. Perhaps we can have a chat later?" He looks at me and I nod in response.

Nothing significant has happened between Jack and me, although I am aware that I have been flirtatious with him. Much more has happened in my imagination with Sam, but Marcus will never know this. I want Jack to like me. I like his presence and I think he's funny and sad, but there is nothing more than that going on. We go to the table in the sitting room and Alfie puts the Monopoly set down. He grabs the silver shoe, while I choose the hat.

"Listen, Alfie. I sat on Jack's lap because he was sad. It doesn't mean anything."

"Why do you keep talking about it?" He looks up at me. He's right, of course. I'm now making an issue of it, instead of saying nothing. I am making it into an event.

"Why don't you get Jed and see if he wants to play too?"

He groans and sighs and I can hear Marcus on the stairs chatting to Tara. It's hard to hear what they're saying. I have the impression they are talking quietly on purpose, which makes me uncomfortable and anxious.

Tara offers to supervise the children's baths, as Jack has not yet returned from the hospital. I wander on to the terrace, where I chat to Dave, and I know that Marcus will be brooding about Alfie's remark. While we talk, Marcus comes back onto the terrace and asks if he can speak to me.

Marcus and I go off together to the garden. He walks quite fast ahead of me and stops abruptly by the gazebo. He invites me to sit down, while he stays standing. He says that he has the impression that there is something going on between Jack and me. For some reason I blush.

"What is this about you sitting on his lap?" he asks in quite an unpleasant tone.

I laugh. "It was nothing, Marcus. Really, it was just that he was looking forlorn at lunchtime and I went and sat on his lap for a moment." I sound dismissive, as though he is mad to question me.

But he doesn't appear to listen to me or to take any notice of what I am saying. He says that he sensed immediately that Jack was interested in me. And he adds that Jack pisses him off. I protest at this point and tell him that it is true that I do like Jack, because he's funny and charming, but there is nothing between us.

"Well, even our son has noticed," he points out.

"He's just a little boy," I laugh. "Jack is depressed about his wife. She has a new boyfriend."

He suggests that we go for a walk. I think about how wrong it feels to leave the boys, but Marcus seems so angry and insistent that I tell him that I will go and ask Tara. I rush up to the bathroom to see how Tara is getting on with the children. I wish I could stay here with the boys. I don't want to walk with Marcus. Jed and Alfie are playing with some Lego, while Tara is reading a magazine. She tells me to go; she is happy for me to go. She says it will be good for me to spend some time alone with Marcus. She says she finds it relaxing after the stress of the day to watch the children. "Give me a hug," she says, and I breathe in her rose-scented hair, and wonder if I trust her.

I go to join Marcus and we walk up the track, but we don't walk hand in hand but side by side, and he is a little ahead of me, and I watch his city shoes kick up the dust. We have reached the end of the track and the heat has cooled. We begin to walk down the hill towards the village. He tells me he has no time for Jack. He looks angry. His brow is furrowed and I want to laugh because I am a little scared. When Marcus is angry, he can remain uncommunicative and cold for much longer than I can. I can't stay angry for too long, because I find it exhausting and unpleasant.

When we arrive at the village, we stop at the bar. It's crowded with mostly local men, although a group of tourists sit outside at a table. Marcus admits that Jack's obsession with cooking is infuriating. He says he has never met such a competitive man. I don't remind him about how competitive he can be – how he broods for hours if he loses a tennis match. I don't say that he is just as eager to impress with his cooking as Jack is.

A moody teenager with a rock-and-roll tee shirt and an earring takes our order. We ask for beers and olives, and Marcus wants a cup of coffee too.

The beer and olives arrive on a small tray and I dip my hand in and out of the olive bowl, and take a sip of the delicious cold beer. Marcus says he doesn't like the way Jack talks about himself all the time.

"Marcus," I soothe, taking his hand, "darling, you mustn't get so worked up."

We are sitting side by side on two small chairs and behind us is a whitewashed wall. A little boy with a deep tan is playing with a Game Boy, while a crowd of children huddle around him.

"I love you and you alone," I say. "I want us to be close again."

Marcus takes my hand and draws me to him. I lean against him and he strokes my hair and I begin to cry, very silently, because I know there is hope and because it's true – I want to be close to Marcus again; I have been wanting to be close to Marcus again for a very long time.

"What is it?" he asks. The children are staring at me. I wipe my eyes with a scratchy napkin and I sniff.

"I've been so lonely," I say.

"Yes. Me too." Marcus sits up straight in his chair and then finishes his beer and summons the boy with the earring.

I am surprised that Marcus admits this; I don't think of him as someone who is lonely – he seems too busy.

"I miss you," he says, "very much, but I'm on a mission. It's only a matter of time before I'm 50."

He asks the boy for another beer, using a splattering of Italian and a little bit of mime.

"You're only 38."

"38... 50 – soon I'll be dead."

He stands up. He looks so serious and good-looking in his navy tailored suit.

"You've hardly been at home. On my birthday, you got your secretary to ring me and buy me a present. You left the holiday, our rare chance to be together. I'm sure the Japanese would have understood the concept of a week's holiday."

"No," he says, "I don't think so, not when I am doing such a big commission for them. I don't think they do understand. They only take one holiday a year."

I have finished the olives and I'm still hungry. I mustn't be so greedy.

"There is so little time," he goes on, "I have so little time, and when I think about it, I realise how much time I've wasted. I have a good opportunity now, and something has to give. It's true that I don't

239

see you and Alfie as much any more, but this is my last chance to make some real money. It's not so long now before I'll be old. We'll need money when we're old." He leans back as he says this, and stretches out his legs. He looks tired.

We begin to giggle at the idea of him being old.

"Please understand," he begs. "I have to use this time to expand the business. Why don't you enjoy this moment of financial security? Would you really prefer to have me at home every evening at six but worrying constantly about how we are going to pay for all our outgoings?"

I think about this for a moment; part of me would like to go back to how we were, but I can't admit this. It would make him feel as though all his hard work was for nothing. "You're right," I say, "it's good that you are doing so well and I really appreciate it." I feel like someone taking advice from a self-help book, but it's true, I do appreciate everything he is doing.

He orders a sandwich and another two beers without asking me if I want one. I explain to him that I'd like to put on a show of my photographs, and he seems enthusiastic about this idea, but then he asks about Alfie, and wonders how Alfie will cope if I commit to a show.

"Of course he'll cope," I say.

"But who will help him with his homework?"

"I will. I don't need to work ten hours a day."

"But I know you," he says. "Once you're committed to a show, you'll be too busy to stop work at 3.30."

He's right, of course. We will need to find someone to help with Alfie. But, I reason, Alfie is sure to benefit from all my hard work and sense of purpose. "Alfie will benefit from me being busy and fulfilled," I say.

"Really?"

"Do you wish you were married to someone who stayed at home and prepared delicious food and made the house smell of scented candles?"

"Yeah, right." he says, "like I would tell you."

"What are you saying then?"

"No, well, yes... No. Oh, for fuck's sake, Jen, no you're not that kind of wife. You're a woman with a career, a son, a house, and I do accept that. I know I moan about the filthy hall carpet, but actually, in a way I think it's great that you're happy to stay in our beaten-up old house and that you don't care whether I make a lot of money. But I just want a good life for us and for Alfie and I suppose because I'm away so much, I feel more secure knowing you're at home making sure everything is OK."

"I know."

We laugh again.

"Do you trust me?" he asks.

"Yes," I say, finishing the olives. "Well..." There is

a question I still have to ask him, just to make sure, and when I think about asking, my heart begins to thud and I feel a little sick. I want to ask him if there is anything between him and Tara, although I know he will be angry.

"What?"

"Is there anything going on between you and Tara? Could the baby be yours?" I say the last part in a rush, the words just tumbling out of my mouth.

"Me and *Tara*?" He bangs his glass down on the table. He sounds outraged.

"Yes, you and Tara, you're so..."

"What?" He looks indignant, even hurt.

"I don't know, just so secretive... I just thought, well she's been so strange about the pregnancy..."

"Me get Tara pregnant? No, of course not! She's just got married, for God's sake. I don't even fancy the woman! She's your friend... Christ! What do you take me for?"

"I know, I just..."

"What?"

"Well, you told me that you met her for coffee and now I'm saying it out loud, it does sound totally ridiculous that I should jump to conclusions, but the other night, when I found you both talking at two in the morning, it did seem strange, particularly when you both stopped mid-sentence as I appeared and you were talking just now on the stairs, I just…"

Marcus takes my hand. "My love," he says, kissing it, and reassuring me. Then he laughs. "Yes I can kind of see where you're coming from but please…You have an overactive imagination. Nothing is going on."

"Why were you talking to her just now on the stairs?"

"She was telling me how awful it had been when you found Maud. She said she had never been so scared. But she said the incident had sharpened her sense of her priorities in life or something like that. Look, to be honest, I don't find her attractive; she's a bit of a whinger and she always seems a bit frail, and more importantly, Dave's a mate and you're my wife. I find her quite boring. Honestly, love, believe me. The most we've done is have a coffee that day we bumped into each other, and we talked the other night. It was late, but I was up and she came downstairs."

I am yawning but I do believe what he is saying.

"You need a rest. Why don't I look after Alfie tomorrow? And you can take it easy?"

"You need a rest more than I do," I say. "You've been working."

"No, I don't want to rest – I want to enjoy myself."

I lean on him and shut my eyes. I almost believe that he doesn't even find Tara attractive.

I would like to tell him what Jack said to me, just to

be totally clear and honest with him, but I can't risk it, not after we seem to have come to an understanding – and sometimes being totally honest is not a good thing. We sit for a while and watch the locals in the bar. A couple of elderly men wearing caps are playing chess on the table next to ours, and we watch them for a while in a soothing, companionable silence.

Alfie and Jed have asked if they can stay in the tent in the garden tonight. We have said they can, because we want to keep them happy, particularly Jed, of course but we've told them they are not allowed to go anywhere near the pool. I think Jed is still in shock. He's quiet, and well behaved, but seems mournful behind his big brown eyes. We are getting the tent ready when there is a commotion on the terrace; Jack is back.

I run towards him, and gather up Maud and give her a kiss and a hug. She seems shy and subdued. Jed runs over to her and puts his arm around her.

"We're home," Jack says. His tee shirt is crumpled and so is his face. He opens a bottle of wine and pours himself a glass. "Maud is shocked," he says, "but she's out of danger. Jill is making her some soup and she'll have an early night."

I kiss and hug Maud and when she says she hates soup, I offer to get her something else. "Just wait here," I tell her.

The kitchen is quiet; Jill is cutting up onions and I call out to greet her. She turns around to say hello. I explain that Maud doesn't like soup, and she says, "I've started it now."

I am surprised by her response, and say that the adults would love to have the soup but I am going to make Maud something Alfie loves when he's feeling low, which is soft-boiled egg, taken out of its shell and mixed in a bowl with small bits of bread and butter.

Jill takes off her apron, "Well, it's been a long day, I've spent all afternoon at the hospital with Jack. I'll be getting home now." She gathers her things together, wipes her eyes, which are streaming from the onion, walks to the door and says goodbye, but she is curt.

"I didn't mean to upset you," I say, rushing after her. "I just wanted to spoil Maud, make sure she eats something, after the ordeal."

Jill turns around, "You know best, I'm sure," she replies and she carries on walking without turning back. After she's gone, I glance at the abandoned onions and I am shaking. Nothing much was said, but she was so cold.

She is already starting up her car. She is probably exhausted after the trip to the hospital. I finish chopping her discarded onions and start boiling eggs and peeling carrots for Maud. She trails into the kitchen and sits down.

"Mummy is coming to see me," she says, "and she's coming the day after this day."

Good, I tell her, putting the egg mix in front of her. She doesn't use her spoon, but picks up the bread with her fingers.

We talk about the hospital, and she says she fell in the pool and that Jack held her hand. We sit and talk about her mummy, until Jack comes in to find her and takes her off to bed. I hear him telling her a story about a brave princess as he carries her up the stairs.

I read Alfie and Jed an adventure story about a boy overcoming some kind of beast, then they climb into their tent with torches and zigzag beams across the roof. I go upstairs, change into a loose pink kaftan, brush my hair, which is dry from the sun, and slather cream on my limbs. After the children are asleep, we have dinner. Jack is quiet and hasn't offered to cook, so Marcus is in the kitchen tonight. He's making something with aubergines and Parmesan and sweet-smelling herbs.

Sam has changed into a white shirt and beige trousers. He is talking to Tara in a hushed voice out on the terrace. For a moment I strain to hear what they are saying, but decide I may hear something that I shouldn't and I am tired of being suspicious. I find Jack in the sitting room, smoking and reading a magazine. Dave hasn't come down from his bedroom yet.

When everyone has gathered on the terrace, Marcus calls us to sit down, and presents his vegetarian dish. Dave appears and says he finished editing his book and can't improve it any more. He's had enough. He wants to join the holiday. We toast Dave and we toast Jack and then, as a last silly gesture of goodwill, we toast each other in turn. Jack looks anxious and tells us that he is going to pick up his wife from the airport and will take the children. I almost offer to look after them, but after the incident today, decide not to.

We have just about finished the aubergine and the table is quiet, when Sam says he's heard from Toby. Toby has decided to go home with Miranda, rather than return here.

"Wow!" Jack exclaims. "He's going to have a tough time with that woman."

"Yes," Sam agrees, "but she's recently been diagnosed with breast cancer. She kept it from everyone, including him, until they were on their way home."

"You mean he will marry her, because she's ill?" Jack grimaces. He sounds astonished and unsympathetic.

"I don't know if he'll go that far… I have no idea, but he says he must escort her home. He would have liked to come back, but he can't now."

"It seems so ironic," I say, "that she should get cancer. She eats so healthily. She pays such attention to her diet."

"You don't want to marry someone just because they are going to die." Jack says.

"That's horrible Jack," Tara says, clearing the plates into a pile.

"Yes, I know," he admits, "I don't know why I said that." He leans back in his chair and then forward again, and pours himself a glass of water. He looks a little embarrassed.

He coughs. "Look I realise what I said was a little harsh, but it's clearly going to be a mistake to marry someone because they are ill. Marriage is a long, hard road. Being a father is the most life-changing event of my life. I've made terrible mistakes being a husband and a father. Terrible." He pauses, but before we've had a chance to respond, he rubs his face with his hands and goes on. "My little girl nearly drowned today. I'm going to be a more committed father in the future. I think I've had a pretty laissez-faire attitude in the past," he admits. "Jed disappeared last year because I wasn't around. I think my wife is going to kill me when she gets here. I presume she'll want to take the children home. She may never allow me to see them again without a chaperone. God, how ghastly."

"It was an accident," I say as we carry dirty plates and dishes to the kitchen.

We are sweeping food into the dustbin when he

says, "She's had swimming lessons and she seemed so confident. But, of course, she's still used to wearing armbands. I shouldn't have left her for a minute."

"But don't forget she was meant to be watching a DVD."

"Yes. But she's so small." He stands there looking so lost and upset.

"Don't dwell on it, Jack," I say, "Come on," I take his hand and lead him through the door.

We come back to the terrace and sit down at the table. Jack breathes out heavily.

"I am a *hopeless* father, I will never forgive myself." He stops abruptly and wipes his eyes. "I just didn't imagine she would ever wander down to the pool on her own."

"Steady on, old man," Marcus says, handing him a bottle of wine. "It could have happened to any of us."

I nod my head and take a mouthful of salad, but it's true: Jack has struck me as a father who is not that aware of what his children are doing.

"Jed disappeared last summer, and that was really my fault."

"What happened?" Dave asks.

"It was a year ago exactly. Ellie was busy opening a café, and I was meant to be looking after the children down in the country. Jed was playing with a friend and disappeared. They had taken a tent and a duvet and gone off exploring and we couldn't find them for 36 hours. We searched up and down the nearby beach, along the roads, knocking on people's doors, driving around all the local villages. Eventually, the police came and we were all questioned. Ellie and I felt awful as we had been arguing a lot that summer and we knew that Jed hated it when we argued. Of course, she was right in the middle of her affair with the neighbour at that point. Our au pair, Petra, eventually found him, camping in some woods at the bottom of someone's land. The people who owned the house were away at the time."

"Wow!" Tara exclaims. "How frightening."

"Yes, it was. Awful. Poor Ellie. At the time, her mind was on this damn neighbour, but at that point I had no idea. And naturally I blame myself for not being more vigilant. Well, I'm going to be from now on. And I wanted to ask you, Sam, whether Ellie could have Miranda and Toby's room?"

"Yes, of course," Sam replies. "I'll get Jill to sort that out."

We are eating cheese and figs when I tell them how Jill had abandoned the soup she was making, and how curt she had been, to the point of rudeness. Sam says he finds her strange and a little sad and suggests that perhaps she is tired. Dave says that she's a sweet old thing, who's been bringing him cups of tea and snacks while he's been working in his room. Jill unnerves me. It was strange of her to advise Miranda to leave the holiday and when I say this out loud, Dave responds that she probably saw how unhappy Miranda was.

Marcus prods a lump of cheese on the end of his fork. "You're overreacting," he says.

"She's pretty harmless," Jack agrees. "It was good of her to come with me to the hospital. It can't have been fun. She really was great."

It's true she has been so helpful and I am the only one who thinks she is odd; no one else has seen that cold, rude side of her. Sam thinks she's probably having a hard day. Tara suggests that perhaps she's lonely and depressed.

"You're right," I concede. "She's probably just having a hard day."

We linger at dinner a little while longer, but we don't stay up as late as we usually do. I think we are all exhausted after what happened today. My eyes are heavy and my limbs too.

After supper, Marcus and I walk to the swimming pool and lie down on the grass and stare up at the sky, which is lit up with hundreds and hundreds of stars. Marcus sees a shooting star, and then another, but I can't see any. The crickets are very loud in the stillness. I snuggle into his shoulder and he pulls me closer and hugs me tighter and suddenly we are kissing. We haven't kissed like this for a couple of years, and although at first it seems strange to kiss my husband, after a few minutes, I lose myself in the kiss and I'm enjoying it. We are lying side by side, after the kiss, when we hear voices approaching.

It's Sam and Tara.

"You have to leave me alone, Sam. It's not going to happen between us. You have to believe me."

I almost don't dare breathe.

"So why did you come and visit me?"

"It wasn't just you I was visiting. Remember that? It was my aunt too. I was visiting my aunt, and we met and..."

"Yes, but... what about when I first arrived here and you were all over me...?"

Their voices trail off, and we can't hear any more.

We stand up, walk back to the house and talk in whispers about what we have just heard, which is shocking and strange, but not that surprising given the amount of flirting and whispering and huddling in corners that has been going on between them.

"There must have been something between them really recently," I say.

"Sounds like it," Marcus replies.

"Do you think they were having an affair?"

Marcus shrugs. He's not that interested, but I am

satisfied because it sounds as though Tara wants nothing more to do with Sam.

Alfie hasn't slept in our bed for two nights now. If this continues, it will be a major breakthrough in all our lives, worth coming to Italy for. I am heartened and have hope for my relationship. I yawn and stretch in the luxury of the space between us, and lay my head on Marcus's chest and he wraps his arm around my back. I haven't done this for a long time and it is lovely. Tonight before sleeping, I thank God that Maud is not dead.

THURSDAY

Marcus and I wake after eight, without a small body between us. For once, one of us is not up early – sitting with Alfie, watching him while he eats his breakfast and wishing we were still asleep. We lie in bed, talking. He pulls me towards him and soon we are kissing like we were last night. I breathe him in, touch his skin, stroke and clutch at his neck, and he grabs me and kisses me all over and soon we are making love, slowly and then quicker without any sense of strangeness but just love and longing and need. I have yearned to be close to him for so long, without knowing how to be. Afterwards, we lie side by side, silently holding hands.

By the time we are up and dressed, Tara has given the children breakfast and Alfie is reciting his five times table to her. Alfie greets us with a huge beaming smile, but he doesn't make demands, he doesn't climb on us, or tug at our chair or ask to be taken swimming as he usually would. He is excited about his night away from us in the pop-up tent.

We are the last ones down for breakfast. Dave sits next to Tara with his arm protectively around the back of her chair. We are helping ourselves to cereal, when Tara, who is eating mouthfuls of bread says, "I'm pregnant, I'm having a baby. Just to explain, why I've been so tired, and..." she continues with her mouth full, "that is why I'm eating so much."

She takes Dave's hand. "That is why you may have thought I was tired and listless, well, more than usual anyway," she laughs. "I know I'm not an exactly energetic person."

"That's brilliant, Tara," I say, playing along, but pleased that she's made the decision.

"Congratulations," Jack says, patting her on the back. Marcus gives her a thumbs-up sign but Sam, who is at the top of the table, looks angry and sad. He finishes his cup of coffee, then stands up and walks off into the garden. He seems dispirited and dejected. I turn to Tara and congratulate her and smile, but shrug at the retreating figure of Sam.

"I'll tell you about it," she says. "Later."

"What's up with him?" Dave asks.

"Maybe he's got a hangover," Tara suggests.

Jill comes onto the terrace with some secateurs and says she is going to do a bit of pruning. It's strange that she's here, as the gardener came yesterday. I haven't seen her since the incident in the kitchen yesterday, but I smile at her, and she smiles back.

"The garden could do with a good going-over," she says firmly.

Her speech has quickened and her eyes are very bright. She is wearing white trousers and a beige tee-shirt. She heads off and stops when she reaches Sam. I watch them chatting and wonder what they are talking about. Tara looks out over the garden towards Sam and then she says she'd like to talk to me. Jed is teaching Alfie how to play chess, so it seems like a good time to get away for a few minutes. I am eager to hear what Tara has to say, and I know she will say something about Sam.

We go up to her bedroom and look out of the window at the hills, which change colour according to the time of day. It's hot in her room, and I switch on the overhead fan and lie back on her bed and wish now that I could be in the pool or paddling in the cool stream. The bed is covered in a plain white bedspread. The room has grey walls, calm white curtains and a wooden floor covered with a rug in geometric patterns the colour of plaster.

'We are friends, aren't we?" she asks anxiously.

"Yes," I reply, matter-of-factly. "Of course." I sound a little hard and cold, but that is how I feel. "What made you decide to have the baby?"

"A combination of things. I realised how fragile and precious life was after seeing Maud nearly drown. But there are also things I need to explain to you."

She kicks off her flip flops and sighs, "Sam telephoned out of the blue one evening, a few months after the wedding and we just started confiding in each other. He was having problems with his new wife. She was upset that he wasn't nearly as available as she wanted him to be, and I was disillusioned about being married and worried that I wasn't feeling deliriously happy, which I now realise is so naïve. So we had something in common."

"No marriage is going to be happy all the time."

"I know," she wails, with a funny smile. "I can see that now, but I did expect to be happy so soon after getting married."

"Well, I haven't been married, so I can't say."

"Are you sad about that?"

I think for a while before replying, "Sometimes I am, yes."

"Have you asked him why he doesn't want to get married?"

"He says it is nothing personal towards me. He married a French girl when he was 25 and felt as though he had been taken hostage. He was suffocated and imprisoned and desperate. Marriage didn't work out, and he doesn't want to risk our relationship, which he says is fine as it is."

"Maybe you have to believe him," she says.

"Yes," I reply, thinking that her response is lazy. "Anyway, what happened with you and Sam?"

She looks down at her hands. "He started ringing more regularly. At first it was about every two weeks and then it was once a week, and finally we were talking nearly every day. He drew me in, as though I was the only person in the world that he could talk to. He started talking about all sorts of things. He had become kind of obsessed about his mother abandoning him when he was a child. He thought that was why he couldn't get close to a woman, which is what I had thought when we first broke up. Our conversations became quite addictive and I began to check my messages and wait for his texts. It was as though we were having an affair but without the sex. I knew it wasn't right, but tried to justify it by telling myself he was just a friend."

The fan is whirring around and its hard to hear what Tara is saying as her voice is very quiet. I turn off the fan but it becomes hot and stuffy in the room and we decide to go to the stream. We smother ourselves in sun cream, and find our sun-hats. I am half-impatient and half-dreading what Tara has got to tell me. We reach the stream and sit down. It is lovely here and the church bells ring out, as they always seem to do while I am sitting in this spot. This time they are striking the hour.

"This week has gone so fast," I say to Tara. "We've only got two days left." I can hear a tractor in a neighbouring field and the chorus of crickets.

"I know," she says. "Actually, it's quite a relief," she giggles and is suddenly so endearing. We laugh and I am relaxed and quite happy. Tara tells me that when she was depressed, she began to look forward to Sam's calls because he was good at listening and making her feel like the most important person in the world. He sympathised, and soon she was wondering why she had ever left him.

"You left him," I remind her sternly, "because he went to his ex-girlfriend's 30th birthday party."

"Yes," she says, "but actually, I began to wonder why that had mattered so much."

"It mattered," I retort, "because he lied to you, or omitted to tell you the truth, and he went to see his ex when he was meant to be in a loving relationship with you."

"You're right, I know, but you know how it is. Sometimes I just think the timing was wrong."

Tara is wearing a frilly, 50s bathing suit, and she looks eccentric and very English with her pale translucent skin. She says that about two months ago, Sam told her that he was coming to London on a business trip and persuaded her to meet him at his hotel for a drink.

"He probably made up the thing about a business trip," I suggest, picking at a piece of grass and smoothing it over my lips.

"Maybe," Tara blushes, lying elegantly on her side. "We met at a hotel in Holland Park. He was sitting in the bar and when he stood to greet me, we hugged and it was so good to be with him again. Dave was going through a particularly bad patch, moaning, and working till very late and drinking too much and we were bickering all the time. Sam just seemed so dignified. We sat down at a table in a corner. He ordered us whisky sours and told me about his divorce. He was quite upset, and well, I drank too much. I rather naively presumed that being married was enough to put him off wanting me. I went to his room because he said he had something for me."

I laugh at this and so does she. "*Hello!!* You must have known that going to his bedroom would have been dangerous."

"I know," she says, "I know. He had this huge room

with a balcony and a vast double bed. It was all so luxurious compared to our tiny flat. I was weak, Jen, really weak."

"You kissed him?"

She nods. "And more."

"God!" I exclaim. I am used to seeing this kind of thing happen in television dramas, or reading about it in book. Despite thinking I no longer cared about Sam's affection for Tara, I still have a little residue of jealousy welling inside me.

"Everything I've said stays between us. Right?"

"I promise," I say.

Tara looks so serious beneath her hat. "This is one of the reasons why I was apprehensive about having a baby, just in case the baby wasn't Dave's."

"It did cross my mind," I admit.

"What, that the baby wasn't Dave's? What made you think that?" She pauses. "Look, we've talked about this before. I've told you there is nothing going on between me and Marcus. You've got to believe me. Did you really think me capable of that?"

"Well, perhaps for a moment, yes. I just wondered, because you were so adamant that you didn't want a baby, that's all. It just made me wonder why, and when I found you talking very late the other night, it made me think something odd was going on. Plus that coffee you had with him. It all seemed so secretive."

"I promise you - there was – there is – nothing be-tween us. I mean, if the baby belonged to anyone other than Dave it would be Sam, but I know now that Dave is the father – I've rechecked the dates."

I nod because I no longer suspect her baby belongs to Marcus; in fact, I'm embarrassed that I confronted her. "So anyway, about Sam." I prompt.

"He called me the day after the hotel incident. He bombarded me with calls. I finally called him back and said it could never happen again. We both agreed and he said he hoped it wouldn't affect my decision to come here. We had already bought the tickets. How would I have explained to Dave that I had completely changed my mind about coming to Italy? I couldn't tell him the truth. I wouldn't have been able to. He would have been too hurt. Sam and I didn't talk much in the month before we came, but I couldn't stop thinking about him and our night together. If I'm truthful, I wanted to see him again, just to really make sure that I wasn't in love with him and that I hadn't made a dreadful mistake marrying Dave. Dave has been so depressed about all the rejections from his publishers that when Sam arrived with his smooth, easy air of success, he just seemed so much more appealing."

She stands up, and I follow. We walk nearer to the stream to dangle our bare feet in the water.

"He wants me because I am married. That's all."

I am biting my nail. "Maybe he's always loved you."

"He's really putting the pressure on me. You won't believe the things he has been saying."

"Like what?" My heart is thundering inside me, because I want to confess to her about how I loved Sam. I am eager to know more though, like someone who is getting to the end of a book and is reading faster and faster, but the news that he loved her so much, or still does love her so passionately, is still bitter to hear.

"He said that after I left him, he rented a flat near to mine, in the hope that he would see me."

"No!"

"Yes and he said that even though our affair wasn't long, I am the only woman he's ever been in love with."

"Really?" I fiddle with the silver bangle on my wrist. I can't think how I ever thought he'd love me or want to kiss me, or why I ever imagined that I loved him.

"Yes, that's what he said," she continues. "He says he googles my name, although nothing comes up. I never realised that he still thought about me all these years later."

"He's probably just revisiting the feelings he had for you because of his marriage not working out."

"You're right, of course. I know."

She lies back down on the grass. We hear laughter

coming from the terrace.

"It's just so difficult knowing that he's here and that he's poured his heart out to me, and that I can't reciprocate or tell him what he wants to hear. I think he rented this villa as an excuse to see me."

"So we've all been invited to disguise the fact that he really wants to see you?"

Tara laughs, "No, not that bad. He loves you, Jen; you know that. But he does want me to leave Dave."

"Oh," I say in a small voice because I don't really want to hear any more.

"Don't be upset, Jen. I'm sure he wants to see all of you too. But he's quite obsessive."

"Yes," I say, "you're probably right. How is Dave now?"

"He's good and you know what? I needed to go through all of this to see that I'm married to a lovely man. I've rechecked my diary and realised the baby must be Dave's. I was using the fact that the baby could be Sam's as an excuse, because I wasn't sure I wanted a baby, or that I could cope with one, or that I even wanted to stay married to Dave. But since Maud nearly drowned, I've changed my mind. It's been a kind of epiphany for me, which sounds odd, but it's true. I am now totally sure I do want a baby. I am ready, stronger and more optimistic Jen; I don't know why. I think because I'm now brave enough to have a baby. I'm just so relieved and happy. But I've explained to Sam that the baby definitely can't be his and he doesn't seem able to accept it."

"Why? You only had a one-night stand."

"Yes, I know, but he really wants a baby and he really wants one with me." She looks genuinely concerned and still so pale beneath her straw hat.

"I'm glad it's worked out for you," I say, taking her arm, because whatever has gone on between us, I still can't help but like Tara and I appreciate her honesty.

We both stand up and walk to the pool, to find Marcus and Sam and the children. Dave apparently has gone for a walk. Sam is reading and he waves languidly. I slip into the water and flip onto my back. I manage to do a length of backstroke, while looking at the sky. I race with the children and get splashed, then climb out and lie on my lounger. I fall asleep and when I wake there is only Sam and me left at the pool.

"Where are the children?" I ask.

"Marcus has taken them to the village. He didn't want to wake you."

I stand up and pull a towel around me, and he puts his book down, sits up in his chair and asks how I am. I say I'm fine, sad that the holiday is nearly over. He reminds me that we have the rest of today and tomorrow too and even half of Saturday, as none of us have to leave until lunch-time.

He comes over to my lounger. When I roll my neck, he asks if it's tense and I reply that it aches a bit. He sits behind me and begins to massage my shoulders. At first his hand feels clammy and I don't want him to touch me, not after all the recent news, but soon I am relaxing into it. He asks me to lie down, which I do, and then he's massaging me, properly, his hands kneading deeply into my back, smoothing out the bumps and knots, and I'm lulled into a kind of stupor. I'm worried that Marcus will come back and find me being massaged by Sam, but Sam is so good at the massage that I soon forget to worry.

He is fluttering his hands over my back and I sense that the massage is coming to a close and I don't want it to, and I have the bizarre thought that I would do almost anything to stop it from ending. I roll over and thank him, and he's staring at me, without saying anything, which is strange and unsettling.

"Jen, I'm so glad you're here," he says.

"Thank you so much for inviting us."

Then I sit up and he hands me a glass of water. I drink it down, and still we don't say anything.

"Tea?" he asks.

"Yes, that sounds great."

We are in the kitchen making tea, when Sam tells me that he has had a long conversation with Jill. I watch him make the tea and stir a lump of sugar into his cup.

His hands are strong and narrow, his fingers long. His shirt is open and his chest is smooth as it always was, and he wears the same old battered St Christopher on a gold chain that he always wore. He seems so lost and sad.

We take our tea to the benches at the side of the house. "She came to visit me in the garden," he says, "and asked me if I was OK. Then she went on to tell me that I was a very generous host. I said I was very happy to have my friends here and that I had really wanted to see them all."

"Or was it that you wanted to see Tara?"

He looks at me quickly and then looks away.

"I wanted to see Tara, yes, but I also wanted to see you, Jen, and Jack and all the others."

"But is it true?" I begin and then stop because Tara has asked me not to say anything to anyone.

"What has she told you?"

"No, not very much, very little…"

"She shouldn't have," he says.

"Please don't tell her we've had this conversation," I beg.

"No, I won't. We haven't really said anything any-way."

"Have you always loved Tara?" I've asked it now. I've always wanted to.

"Yes, since I met her, yes."

"Or do you think you love her because she dumped you?"

"Perhaps," he smiles. "Perhaps. But anyway, I can't have her. She's a pregnant married lady. I haven't been able to commit to anyone. I have never had a happy lasting relationship, but I want a child. When she first told me she was pregnant, I was convinced the baby was mine and it seemed so right." He smiles at me, but it is a sad smile. "I want to be a dad and have a family. I've been running away from the idea of it, because of what happened when I was a baby, my mother leaving and all that, but when Tara became pregnant, it all fell into place."

"You will be a father if you want to be," I say, taking his beautiful hand and placing it in mine. "You will be. You just need to find someone who is unmarried and not pregnant."

"Like you?" he smiles.

I don't reply, because I know what can happen with Sam. I can get swept along with him right to the edge of the precipice and then he'll push me off and watch me fall.

"Do you mind not being married, Jen?"

"No." I am not going to tell him the truth. He has no right to know. "Marcus and I have a child together."

"But would you rather be married?"

He is wearing dark glasses. I can't see his eyes. For

a small second, I wonder if he has the audacity to flirt with me, now that he can't have Tara. I want to get up and leave.

"I am happy as I am." There is something else I want to say to him. I want to say, you could have had me, when I was available, but I will not say this; it is all too late now. There is no point.

I shift further away from him on the bench and stretch my legs in front of me. "So what about Jill?" I ask. "What did she say?"

"She just wanted to make sure I was OK. She said I didn't look very happy, and that I should be enjoying my holiday."

"Didn't she say the same kind of thing to Miranda? I think it's quite invasive."

"No!" he laughs. "I think she is genuinely concerned about us."

"But…" I am going to say something negative about Jill, but decide not to. Instead I say, "We'd love to thank you for this holiday and take you out to dinner tomorrow night."

"Thanks, Jen. That sounds lovely. Will we get Jill to babysit?"

I shake my head. "No, I don't think so. I don't want to be obligated to her any more than we already are. I'll see if I can find someone else."

"I'm really glad you're here," he says, pulling me

towards him and giving me a hug.

"Me too," I smile at him.

"Jen," he says hesitantly, "about our time in Rome, it was…" and at that very moment, the moment we are going to talk about Rome, when he still has his arm around me, Marcus appears with the children trailing behind him. Alfie has chocolate ice cream all over his face and the other two are holding plastic toys.

"Have I interrupted something?" Marcus sounds cross.

"No. We're just discussing Jill."

Marcus is mouthing something at me, which I can't understand, and pointing in a dramatic way at the door. "She's just in there," he says under his breath.

"Oh really?" I whisper back and make a *shhhh* mime at Sam, placing a finger over my mouth.

"She's here," I whisper.

"Who?" he asks loudly

"Jill."

"Why are you whispering?" Jed asks.

"Hello," Jill comes out to join us, holding a dust-pan and brush. She seems enlivened, happy even. She's changed out of her gardening clothes. Her hair is pinned on either side with kirby grips, like a small child. She is wearing pink lip gloss and a kaftan top in candy pink and bright yellow.

"I just thought," she says, "that I would prepare a

269

picnic for today." She is smiling widely, so widely and with such a fixed expression that she looks like a sad clown, with that droopy face and huge sad eyes.

"A picnic?" Jed and Alfie scream. "Yes!"

"We'll be all right, Jill," Sam says. "We have Ellie arriving. We may just have a quiet snack when she gets here. Don't go to all that trouble for today."

"I've already started on the picnic preparations. I've made a Spanish omelette and some chocolate brownies. It's ever so lovely having a picnic up at the ruins." She fixes Sam with a sad but determined face. "I'd really like to do this for you," she says, looking directly at him.

Sam looks puzzled, "Ah… right, but we won't be wanting to go anywhere today, as Ellie is arriving. It's so kind of you, though. We could have a picnic supper?"

Jill looks crushed, as though she is about to cry. I notice that Marcus is very sullen. He stands with his arms crossed before leaving the terrace.

"Let me talk to the others," Sam says, "and see what they would like to do. Perhaps we could have the picnic by the pool."

"I see," she says, looking up at Sam with a mixture of awe and desperation.

She puts the dustpan and brush away with a great clanking noise. "I'll just bring over what I have already prepared," she says, opening the door, ready to leave, "then you can do what you like with it."

She sounds flat. Sam goes after her. I hear him thanking her for the food, on the hot driveway. I hear them talking but can't hear exactly what they are saying.

Her car door bangs and Sam comes back into the kitchen. He shrugs.

"Well, we didn't *ask* her to make us a picnic. It seems odd that she took it upon herself to do that for us. She says she made a picnic for the last family that rented the house, and they invited her along to share it."

"I find her behaviour really strange," I say.

"Yes, it is a bit," Sam admits.

Jack appears in a flurry, with a leather bag across his shoulder and the two children trailing behind him. He has shaved and changed into a pink shirt, cream trousers and pale canvas shoes. He's drinking coffee and asking me if he looks OK, and now the children are dragging him towards the door, because they are going to pick up Ellie.

"I'm sure she despises me," he whispers with a sigh. "She'll never forgive me for what happened in the pool."

"Where is she going to sleep?"

"Jill didn't prepare the room that Miranda and Toby stayed in after all, so she's going to sleep in my room and I'll camp with the children. Jed wants to sleep on one of the blow-up beds."

"I'm sure she will forgive you," I say, kissing the children goodbye. They are barefooted and have un-brushed hair, and I shout at Jack to wait while I find their shoes. I run into their bedroom and find Jed's red trainers under the bed and Maud's little pink sandals in the shower room. And then I see a notebook lying open on Jack's bed in which he's scribbled, *Ellie arrives today, not in the best circumstances, but still we'll be staying a couple of nights under the same roof and I have to tell her what a terrible mistake I've made...* I avert my eyes as it is obviously wrong to be reading something quite so private. I deliver the shoes to Jack and he says he'll be back by lunchtime.

We all come out to wave them off, and then they are gone, and for a moment I am sad. I think it's unlikely that Ellie is going to be very civil to Jack, particularly if she has a new boyfriend. I try and imagine what it would be like if I was separated from Marcus and heard that Alfie had nearly drowned in a swimming pool. I'd probably blame him. It would be hard not to, especially if we had broken up. I often wonder how couples survive the death of a child.

Marcus has relaxed. I can tell, because he is wearing army-style shorts and a green tee shirt. He says that he has discovered from talking to someone in the village where to buy fish and good cheese. He would like to prepare lunch for everyone. I remind him that Jill has already made some things for us, and he says we can have her food later.

I go and change in my cool, still room. Alfie complains because he doesn't want to come on a shopping trip. He is moaning when Tara comes into our room. She offers to take him to a little fun fair she's spotted in a town nearby and he says he'd like to go. Apparently, Dave wants to go to the post office now, as he's finished his changes and is going to send a disk to his agent. I give her a hug, because I know she hasn't been unfaithful with Marcus, and I'm pleased that she seems to have come through something. She's more the Tara I remember. She even hugs differently now. It's so strange. I put on my treasured yellow kaftan that Marcus brought back from a trip to Morocco when he was working on a hotel garden outside Essaouira.

Marcus watches me as I come down the stairs, but he doesn't say anything. He tells me to wait while he gets his camera. I wander onto the terrace, where Sam is sitting. I sit down and he turns to me and says, "God, you look absolutely gorgeous. Wish you were mine." I am about to say something back – like, you could have had me all those years ago – when he comes over to me, and as he stands over me, he gently rests his hand on my head. Marcus arrives at that moment, with cameras hanging around his neck.

"Well, goodbye," Sam says as he moves away

from me. "See you later."

"Is there anything you want?" I ask.

"Beers."

I almost offer to invite him along with us, but just want this time alone with Marcus.

"Want to come along, mate?" Marcus asks. "Have a little threesome?" He's laughing, but his voice has an edge to it. "Nah," Sam replies. " I've got to make a few business calls."

As we drive away in the car, I don't say anything at all. I buzz down the window and look out and let the hot air brush over my face. We drive for several miles along winding roads, until I begin to feel a little sick, and for a moment, I regret that Marcus and I are not young and free and able to drive on for ever. We arrive at a town that has a market set up for the day, with stalls selling tomatoes and aubergines, whole salami and straw hats and balls of mozzarella cheese. It's very hot and I have the start of a headache. We find a stall with fish laid out on slabs of ice. Marcus spots some monkfish and says he knows a good recipe for monk-fish paella. We buy chillies, garlic and tomatoes, and then a selection of delicious cheeses, but we do this mostly without talking and Marcus does not hold my hand and he buys everything very quickly, as though he can't wait to get back. Finally, after buying some olives, he suggests that we have a coffee.

The main piazza where the market is set up has three cafés but they are all full. So I follow Marcus down a side street. He strides ahead of me, without waiting for me to catch up. We find a restaurant that agrees to give us coffee, and we sit inside. While we are waiting for the coffee, Marcus drums his fingers on the table.

"It's been a strange holiday," I say.

"Has it?"

"Well, haven't you noticed?"

"Yes," he admits. "This morning I was thinking that it was all worthwhile because we seemed to be communicating again."

"We were," I laugh, but he's not laughing back. "We are."

Our coffees arrive with a little biscuit on the saucer. Marcus stares through me.

"What is it?" I ask, concerned now that he isn't saying anything at all.

"This morning I thought we were getting on really well; we had a real connection. We talked, we made love; it was good. Then just an hour or so later, you are holding Sam's hand and looking into his eyes. Then just before we left, he was stroking you hair. What's going on?"

I'm laughing now, a little nervous. Before this holiday Marcus was never the jealous type. Or maybe he never had cause to be jealous.

"I was just comforting him. He's upset about Tara. He thought the baby was his. You know he's got this real thing about Tara. He bought a flat just to be near her. He wanted to be a dad. I think it's all really heavy for him."

I eat my biscuit, even though I don't particularly want it. I sip my coffee, which tastes so good that I drink the rest of it in one gulp. I have a small camera with me, and I pick it up and take a picture of Marcus, hoping to deflate his mood, make him laugh in some way.

"I've seen him operate. And you've fallen for it. He's a slimy bugger. Don't you remember telling me once how in love you were with him? What do you think I am? Why are you flirting with everyone on this holiday? It's really cheap."

"Marcus, please. It's not what you think it is. Honestly."

"Well, what is it? What is it with you and Sam?"

"Nothing, nothing."

He's looking through me in such a penetrating way that I imagine he can see right into my mind. He knows that in my dreams I kissed Sam and wanted him. I take his hand but he pulls it back as though he's been burnt.

We drive home in silence. Marcus has turned on the radio and the tinny pop song blasts out, though the reception is bad and it crackles. He doesn't say anything as I fiddle with the knobs and he doesn't reply when I say how sorry I am. I look at him every now and then, at his crinkly uncombed hair and the jut of his jawline. I notice his bitten nails on the steering wheel.

When we arrive back it's about one, and we hear voices on the terrace. The group has gathered for drinks before lunch, and Ellie has arrived. The first thing I notice is that she is very pretty, but not in a threatening way. She is slim, a little taller than Jack, and she is blonde. Her hair is slightly wavy with ringlets, and she has oval-shaped eyes. The children are draped around her and Jack is by her side, looking quite uncomfortable. Jack introduces Marcus and me, and she thanks me for talking to her on the telephone.

"It was such a shock," she says to me. "Something I've always dreaded happening. I am furious with Jack. I had intended to take the children straight back to England, but they really wanted me to stay here with them until Saturday. This isn't the first time I've left Jack in charge, and something like this has happened. Jed went missing a year ago, while Jack was looking after the children in the country. I'll never forget the drive down there as I prayed to God that we would find him."

"I can't imagine anything worse."

"This was far worse. It was awful hearing the news

about Maud, not knowing whether she was going to make it, and not being able to get to her straight away. I don't want to be in that position again. Ever. I can hardly look at Jack right now."

Jack joins us. His brow is covered in beads of sweat. "Sit down darling," he says. "Let me get you a drink."

"A cup of tea would do," she replies.

"Cup of tea it is then." He shuffles off and Ellie turns to me and says that Jack is being really humble and apologetic about his carelessness with Maud. He would never usually fuss over her like this. When they first met he would cook for her, but by the end of their marriage he was cooking only as a kind of performance in front of guests. "He would never make me tea," she adds. "It just didn't occur to him." She is laughing as she says this, but I imagine it can't have been easy.

I want to tell her that Jack would do anything to have her back and that he's really sad, but we've only just met and it seems a bit inappropriate and it is none of my business either. Marcus is drinking beer and playing backgammon with Alfie. I'm not sure whether he is still angry with me, but I suspect he is. I can feel him near me, unforgiving and tense.

When Jack returns, Ellie is checking her mobile. I notice that Jack is peering over her shoulder. Tara joins us and says that Alfie loved the fair.

"He probably ate too many sweets and I bought him

an ice cream. He joined a gang of boys who were playing football, and had a few goes on a helter-skelter."

"What is bright, Mummy?" Maud asks, tugging at
Ellie's dress. "Daddy says I am bright."

"Bright, bright is…"

"Clever," says Tara.

"Yes, clever."

"Do you know what?" She looks up at me.

"What?"

"I have nits."

"Really?" I burst out laughing and Ellie laughs too.

"Can they jump through knots? I have lots of knots.
They may be stuck. Mummy thinks I have nits though.
Can they fly?"

Marcus has started the paella when Jill arrives with
her picnic food, which turns out to be a box of brownies.
She offers me one and it is rock-hard and I can hardly
bite through it. Marcus is cooking the rice, and I am un-
wrapping the fish. We are not talking but we are cooking
side by side. Jill is wearing a bathing suit and a kaftan.

"We're cooking paella for lunch," Marcus says.

"I'll cook the paella," she says, washing her hands,
and then putting on an apron. "I'm very good at
paella."

"Well," Marcus replies, "it's just that we bought all
this beautiful fish and cheese, we'd –"

"Don't worry," she interrupts, "I'll do it and I'll

make meatballs for the children." She's already taken the fish from me. I am about to pull it back, but stop myself as it seems too aggressive and I'm a little wary after the incident with the soup. Marcus shrugs at me. At least he is communicating. It is hot in the kitchen and palpably tense. I take off the apron I had put on and leave.

I walk out of the door and return to the garden, where I find Tara and Dave wrapped around each other. Jack is pacing up and down. He's sending someone a text. I fetch my camera and take some photographs of Tara and Dave together, but I am unsettled and angry that Marcus and I can't cook together.

"Ah, there you are." Jack beckons to me and whispers that Ellie is having a shower. He's found a text on Ellie's phone from someone, he shows me what is says:

Hope you arrived safely, everything fine this end. The cat is missing you. Can't wait to get my hands on your gorgeous hair again.xxx

"See," he says triumphantly. "The lover has moved in."

"I'm sorry, Jack."

"Yes, well, so am I. I suppose that's how it is now. And it's all my fault. I have been so stupid. I only have myself to blame for this mess."

"You have to put her phone back," I hiss at him.

Jack walks over to the long table and leaves Ellie's mobile at a casual angle.

We hear Maud crying and Ellie trying to soothe her, and then we see Jed running in with a pair of swimming trunks on his head and he's shouting, "Captain Underpants... Captain Underpants!" He's laughing hysterically and Alfie is running behind with not two but three pairs of pants on his head. They collapse onto the sofa screaming. Maud runs in, naked apart from a pair of socks, and laughs a surprisingly deep infectious laugh for one so tiny. Then Ellie appears in a black bikini and a black hat. She's wearing clogs with heels. She picks up her mobile, reads the text and smiles.

Jack is slumped in an armchair looking morbidly depressed. He sighs loudly.

"Did you open my text?" Ellie asks Jack.

"Yes, I thought it might be from my mother".

"Why would your mother text you on my mobile?"

"I've no idea. She's always trying to get hold of me any way she can."

"Jack, that is absurd. Please don't read my texts again."

"So who is this man who misses your hair?"

"None of your business." She won't look at him.

Jack sighs and pleads with Ellie to tell him, but she's not giving in.

Sam walks up the stairs from the garden. He's been swimming. He comes up to me and gives me a big wet hug and at that very moment, of course, Marcus arrives and says in a jocular way, "Can't you keep your hands off my girl?"

"You should make a decent woman of her," he says laughing. "I would."

"Oh, I see. You mean marry her and then leave her a few months later."

I imagine that 200 years ago, this encounter may have turned into a duel.

"I'm joking, mate." Sam is taking this in his stride. "Actually, I came to find Jack. Jack, we must have a word about the film. We haven't spoken about it."

"Odd joke," Marcus mutters. I'm not sure what to do or where to look, so I sit down and pick up a magazine.

"Good man, I thought you'd never ask." Jack stands up and they walk off together to the kitchen and return with a couple of beers.

"Wow," says Jack. "It's like world war three in there. I've never seen so much smoke."

"She seems to be using a lot of wine," Sam says. "Anyone know what she's doing?"

Marcus laughs and I am relieved. I tell them about

shopping with Marcus for the best fish and cheese, how we had wanted to make paella and how Jill had somehow managed to take over.

Jack and Sam wander off into the garden together. Marcus is now reading. Tara and Dave have gone off to town, so Ellie and I take the children down to the pool. We lie side by side, but she is keeping her eye on Maud. After a while, she sits up and takes a long drink of water.

"It's strange being here with Jack. I was so angry, but I've calmed down a bit now," she says.

"Yes, it must be strange. But I really understand why you were so angry."

"We haven't been in the same house for nearly a year."

"Look at me, Mummy!" Maud shouts to her mother as she flings herself into the pool.

Ellie claps and shouts at her to be careful.

"Did you miss him? I mean, before all this happened."

"From time to time. I miss his cooking. I'm a useless cook. I can't even boil pasta. I overcook it or undercook it. And, of course, there are other times when I miss him too. Do you cook?" she asks, changing the subject.

"I never get a chance to," I reply. "Except when Marcus is away, which is actually most of the time these days, so yes, I do cook, but not imaginatively."

"Lucky you," she laughs. Her skin is pale and flawless and her crinkly blond hair is untidy but sexy.

"What else do you miss apart from his cooking?"

"Jack is very funny and sweet" she says, relaxing a bit, "but he thinks about himself all the time. Before we split up, I felt smothered by his company as though I was drowning and couldn't breathe freely. He's a huge character to contend with, and can be very selfish. A friend and I were starting a business, which he didn't support. I'd given up a career in film because it was so hard to juggle with the children. He didn't believe that we would make any money; he thought it was just a hobby. And of course we have made money. Well, we've just begun to and we're opening another café."

I congratulate her and watch Maud swimming in her armbands right up to the deep end. "Will you stay?" I ask.

Ellie stands up and walks over to where she is swimming. "Yes, I think so," she says.

"Have you been lonely?" I ask when she sits down, warming to her more and more. She is so open and charming, and has just enough sense of humour and self-deprecation to make her interesting too.

"Yes, very, though I have a lodger now, so it's not so bad. But let me tell you, it was Jack who wanted to split up, not me. I behaved rashly. I fancied a man who moved in across the road. In retrospect, it was like a teenage crush. A ridiculous dare. I knew what I was doing was wrong, but couldn't stop. Jack was ignoring me. I just wish Jack had forgiven me, but he wouldn't or couldn't. I was turning 40 at the time – it was probably a mid-life crisis."

"I think..." I pause.

"What?"

"I think he still cares for you very much."

"Yes," she twiddles her finger around her hair, "but he loves himself more. He thinks about himself more than anybody else. How could he have let Maud out of his sight?" She frowns.

I pull my hat further down over my head as the sun is burning.

"They were meant to be watching a DVD."

"Yes," she says a little sadly. "I suppose the same thing could have happened to me."

"Or me," I say.

"It feels sort of wrong to be here, though. We shouldn't really be together in the same house, and yet it also feels wrong when the children only have half their set of parents at a time."

At that moment, Jed climbs out of the pool. Despite having been in the sun for nearly a week, he's still white and pale like his mother. He's wearing goggles and flippers and he walks in them towards us. He sits on his mother's lap and she strokes his hair. "It's great having you and Dad here together," he says. "I wish you could be together all the time."

Ellie continues to stroke his hair as she gazes into the distance. I wonder whether she is thinking about her lover.

Jack walks towards us, rubbing his hands together. He has cheered up; he is standing taller. He pulls up a wooden chair. "Great news," he says. "Really good news. Sam is setting up an audition for me in Hollywood, on my long weekend off. Private jet."

"Really?" we both exclaim at the same time.

"No – joking, but upper class and champagne all the way."

"Better than the dog food advert," Ellie jokes.

"Oh, definitely. Have you forgiven me? Even the tiniest bit?"

"A tiny bit."

"Well, good luck," I say, standing up. I should probably leave them to have a chat together. "Just going to the house for a drink, anyone want anything?"

"We'll be up in a minute," Ellie says.

I walk up the hill. I can hear the familiar rumble of the tractor from the neighbouring hill and the incessant sound of a dog barking, probably one that has been tied up. Sam is walking towards me with his arms outstretched. He stops when he nears me and gives me a huge hug, which takes my breath away. I breathe into the warm sweat of his chest.

"Sam," I say, gently pushing him away. "*Don't.*"

"What?"

"Marcus keeps finding me holding your hand or you stroking my hair, and it's making him uncomfortable. Didn't you pick that up just now on the terrace?"

"Don't see why," he says. "And you?" he winks. "Does it make you uncomfortable?"

Suddenly, for the first time ever, I want to get away from Sam.

"Yes, it does a little, because of Marcus. He's my boyfriend." I sound childish and silly.

"Everyone but me has a boyfriend or girlfriend or a child. I'm an affectionate person. I've always been one. If you can't hug a friend, you may as well get a dog."

He carries on walking towards the pool before I've had a chance to respond.

I continue up to the house. My instinct is to turn around and call out to him to make him feel better, but I stop myself.

The table is set. There are meatballs steaming on a big red plate and Jill is carrying in a huge casserole dish. Dave puts a large salad bowl on the table and Tara is already sitting down with Alfie. Ellie arrives holding both her children's hands.

"Can I sit next to you, Mummy?" they both ask.

Jack has put himself in the middle of the table. I am sorry that neither of his children appear to want to sit next to him, so I do. Sam comes back from the pool with the mobile he had left behind. He sits opposite me, but I avoid his glances. Jill sits down on the other side of Jack.

"Did we invite Jill?" he whispers.

"No, she just sat down."

Sam pours himself a glass of wine and raises it. "To Jill," he says loudly.

"To Jill!" those of us with glasses repeat.

She then proceeds to hand out dollops of paella. She gives Jack and me a huge plateful, and when I ask if I can have a smaller portion, she replies, "Just leave what you can't eat," and I feel like a small child being reprimanded by a teacher or someone else's mother. She doles out meat balls for the children and then before I know it, she's grating our carefully chosen, expensive cheese onto the meatballs.

"STOP right there," Marcus commands as he comes in with another salad. He very gently prizes the aged Asiago from her hands and then goes back to the kitchen and replaces it with a lump of very ordinary cheddar.

"I'm sorry,' she says in a voice that sounds as though it's on the edge of hysteria. "What have I done?"

"This is for grown-ups," he replies quite sternly.

"It's matured for up to year and is very expensive and should not be used for grating on a kid's meal."

She looks as though she could murder him, but says, "Oops, I didn't know. Ever so sorry."

"Well, now you do," he smiles at her. For the moment he is calm, and unnervingly cool.

My plate of paella is swimming in oil and wine. She has butchered our beautiful fish. It's overcooked and the rice is sticking together in hard lumps. It is inedible, too salty. After all our shopping, I could cry. I could cry, anyway, when I think about how Marcus is being so cold towards me and I imagine – in fact I know – that Marcus will be livid. He takes his cooking very seriously, as Jack does. This revolting lunch will ruin his day. Marcus takes a mouthful and then a deep gulp of wine. I try to catch his eyes, but he won't look at me. Jack takes a mouthful and makes an expression of disgust. He wants to talk to Ellie but she is engaged in conversation with Dave. If a magazine questionnaire asked me what would be the worst meal of my life, this would be it.

Tara and I pick at bread and talk about baby things. We chat about giving birth. Like most women talking to birth virgins, I smooth over the birth experience. I know that Tara is terrified, so I omit to tell her about the insufferable pain, which for me, as I imagine for everyone else, was like pushing a watermelon out of a hole the size of a pinprick, accompanied by a terror that my body would split in half. After the tears and the rips and the exhaustion, there was the fear that I wouldn't know how to look after my baby. I don't describe the overwhelming first weeks of having a new baby, when your breasts are hard like unfriendly bricks and so painful that you cry and wince, and I won't tell her that sometimes when the baby sucks your nipples, the pain shoots through your body like a knife.

Instead, I describe the bond you have with the father of the baby, and how filled up you are with love for the newborn. She tells me about Dave's need to have a family. It turns out that he has no relationship with his parents and nor do his siblings. "It's just so sad," Tara confides quietly, "that his parents were unable to approve of anything he did. Whatever he achieved, they couldn't congratulate him, or encourage him – particularly his father – and from the age of twelve he grew to hate them. I think having a baby will be so healing for him." I digest this news. It always strikes me as so strange that everyone has so much going on just below the surface of their lives. All that history, tangled like wool.

"What did you think about when you first looked at Alfie?" Tara asks.

I tell her that I remember looking at him, just wanting to protect him, and not wanting him to experience any pain. I quickly realised that it was too much to think like that; being consumed with those kinds of thoughts could drive you insane. I tell her that she will love her newborn child. Then I change that, because actually some women aren't filled with love instantly; some take months to bond with their baby, so I describe that too. It's comforting to know that you can't necessarily be expected to love your baby the moment it appears and that you may not be able to. Lastly, I tell her that there is nothing like having a child – it changes you as a person, you feel complete and more ready to give and receive love. You become less selfish, more giving and more fulfilled.

"What is that love like?" Tara asks, shifting the gluey rice around in the oil on her plate.

I tell her that the love is exhilarating and painful at the same time. This is the downside of having a child: the eternal fear that they may die before you and that you will never be the same again. Tara listens to me quietly, her eyes wide, and when I've finished she cries a little. She wipes her eyes and holds onto my hand, and I am touched by her warmth.

"I once heard someone say that parents are destined to love their children more than they love you. Do you think that's true?"

I think about what she has said and sip a glass of wine.

"At the moment, I am the centre of Alfie's universe, but that will change, of course. When he is a teenager, his friends will be more important than me, and then later he will love his wife."

Everyone helps themselves to salad and bread and no one is able to finish their paella, except Jill, who has second helpings and tries to offer us all more. The fish is tasteless and has the texture of chewing gum. She's holding a glass of wine and swigging it back. She quickly helps herself to another glass, and then another. She is verging on the grotesque. Her mascara has smudged a little and so has her lipstick. She is starting to look like a carnival clown, caught in the rain.

We watch her, and I can sense that everyone is slightly repelled by her behaviour. The children have all asked if they can get down, and they've gone off and found themselves ice creams and are now sitting in a huddle at the other end of the terrace. Jill confronts a couple of us to ask why we haven't eaten her food. She is becoming more and more overbearing; the scene is ugly and distasteful. I begin clearing the plates, hoping to get to the end of lunch, and Sam picks up the empty wine and water bottles. We have a rushed conversation in the kitchen. It no longer seems right to be cross with him. There is too much going on. He says he's not going to ask Jill to leave quite yet, as there is bound to be a scene. We will rush the rest of lunch and then offer to drive her home as she is clearly drunk. I like talking to Sam about something practical. I like to see him taking charge when there is no chance of him making innuendoes, or teasing me, or giving me false hope. "I'm going to call Dad after lunch and have a chat about Jill," he says.

Luckily, she hasn't been able to destroy all the food. Sam and I bring out the cheese and more salad, although it is tempting just to leave lunch and go and lie down somewhere. Jill wants to know if we like the garden and which bit we like best. But she sounds aggressive rather than interested, demanding rather than charming. Her voice is slightly slurred and it's louder than usual. She is flushed in the cheeks and shiny. She's asking for wine and thrusting her glass at Sam. He says we have run out. The kirby grips have fallen out of her hair, and the kaftan is slipping a little off one shoulder. At one point she knocks a glass over and then suddenly she is talking to Tara and she is crying and the table goes silent and we are all listening. "Oh, it's my husband," she sobs. "I do miss him so very much." She's really crying now and Maud is asking, "Why is that lady sad, Mummy?"

"What is wrong with her?" Alfie asks me.

I take the children to the sitting room and find them some sketch pads and colours.

I'm in the kitchen fetching juice for the children,

and Jack is in there with Sam, talking to Jill. "I'm in such pain," she moans, clutching her stomach.

"Sam, why don't you talk to your Dad," Jack suggests. "Maybe he will suggest that Jill takes a break."

Jill doesn't answer for a while because she has her head in her hands. "No, don't disturb him," she says finally. "Not now, not when I'm in this state. I'll be fine tomorrow."

Jack offers to drive her home, but she says she'd prefer to drive herself. I linger in the kitchen, opening cupboards, pretending to look for something.

"I think you need to sober up," Jack says. He hands her a cup of coffee and sits down next to her. Sam and I leave the kitchen and join everybody at the table.

"Well, well," Sam says. "What a cabaret."

"What are we going to do with her?" I ask.

"Poor old thing," Dave says.

"Jack is dealing with her."

"Good!" Ellie smiles. "He's good with older women. He has so many fans of that type. He's had one particular fan called Jean for years and years, and one of the reasons we broke up was because Jean remembered his birthday and I didn't."

We laugh. We clear the table and find Jack ushering Jill out of the house, and into her car, but she refuses to let Jack drive, insisting on driving herself.

We decide to visit the lake for a picnic tea. We are

still hungry after the disgusting lunch. Marcus wants to stay at the house and when I try to persuade him to come, he is dismissive. On the way, we stop for bread and salami at the village shop and the children make us buy some overpriced chocolate eggs with plastic presents inside. As we drive towards the lake, I'm thinking about Jill, and how unnerving she is and what a relief it is to get away from her.

We set out our picnic things on a large white cloth by the lake. There are a couple of bare-chested teenagers selling boat trips, and Sam and Dave offer to take the children out on pedaloes, while Jack stays to chat to someone about his travel arrangements to Los Angeles. We girls sit in a huddle stretching our legs in front of us. We gossip about Sam, and I confide about how he always wants to hug me. Ellie says how sad he seems and Tara agrees in a quiet, knowing way.

Sam, Dave and the children return from the boat trip and we start tearing off bits of bread, and eating it with salami, and we drink beer, and eat some more. Jack talks loudly, and throws bread for the birds. The sun glistens on the water, and the children's shrieks seem to echo in my head. The children swim in the lake and then spend quite a long time, throwing stones into the water. As Sam is rubbing suncream on to his arms, I ask him whether he's spoken to his father about Jill.

"I can't get hold of him at the moment. I spoke to

my mother, and she said that he's playing golf and will probably call her tonight. He's somewhere without a signal."

I'm lying reading my book, when Jack comes and lies next to me and begins to moan about how cold and detatched Ellie is being. She won't talk to him, or tell him anything, or explain who the text is from. I think Jack is quite an obsessive person; the way he smokes, and uses his telephone, and talks too loudly and too much. I tell him that he shouldn't really ask her who the text is from because it's private.

"But it's haunting me," he says. "I have to know about the boyfriend."

"Well, I suppose you could ask her straight out."

"I asked who the text was from and she refused to tell me."

His mobile rings. "Ma, how lovely to hear you," his voice booms out over the reservoir. It's early evening now, and swallows are diving into the water to drink. "Yes, Ellie is here, she's fine."

"Yes." He pauses. "Mother, that's not really anything to do with you."

"Ellie?" he calls out. She's now paddling with Maud in the water. "Mother wants a word."

Ellie raises her eyes and shouts out, "Can I call her back?"

"Can she call you back? Yes, she will."

We sit and watch the sunset, and I begin to miss Marcus and feel quite angry that he is being so difficult and not trusting me. Sam, however, has apologised for being arrogant and unsubtle. He seems to have made up with Tara too – at least he is not ignoring her any more. We pile back into the cars as the sun is dipping and drive home to find that Marcus has made us all supper. He is wearing espadrilles and he's put one of Maud's red hairbands in his hair.

"Please forgive me," I whisper to him in the kitchen. "Please. I didn't mean to flirt with Sam, and it doesn't mean anything. It really doesn't."

Marcus doesn't reply. We walk back to the dinner table and we sit down opposite each other. Marcus has made us a simple vegetable soup, and it's delicious.

Sam eats his soup in silence and Dave asks him what he's thinking about.

"I had a nightmare last night," he says. "I dreamt you were all laughing at me, and you left me somewhere, and I overheard Jen saying that I was an asshole and you all agreed. I am an asshole, I know it."

He leans his head against the palm of his hand. At first, we don't make a move. I am worried that Marcus will accuse me later, behind closed doors, of being too keen to comfort him.

"I don't think you're an asshole, " I laugh. "That's just not true!"

He lifts his head, laughs and apologises. I know he's not just upset about the dream. It must be hard to be so completely rejected by Tara. I think he really wanted to believe that the baby was his. In some mad, obsessive way, he wanted to make a completely new start after his divorce. Dave goes over and pats him on the back, and then we each take a turn to thank him for the holiday. Marcus takes my hand, which is a sign to say that everything is all right between us.

Sam cheers up and our conversation turns to Jill.

"She's behaving very strangely," Marcus says. "Almost as if she's having a sort of nervous breakdown."

"I know," Tara agrees, "or maybe she is someone who can't take her drink."

"For sure," Sam says. "She is a *bad* drunk."

"What happened when you drove her home?" I ask Jack.

"Well, she didn't let me drive her home, remember? She got in the car, and drove herself home."

"God, I wonder if she ever got there?" Dave laughs.

"I've left a message for Dad," Sam says. "He'll be back on Saturday. I'm going to talk to him. There's definitely something wrong. I don't think she's well."

I am yawning now and although it's not late, it's been a long day.

"Goodnight, all of you," Sam says, getting up from

the table. He looks exhausted.

"Night, Sam," I blow him a kiss.

"Night, Sam," the others call out.

We sit around the table for a while longer, discussing our plan to visit the garden that Marcus wants to see tomorrow. Jack and Tara go off to make tea and coffee. I stand up and say goodnight, and Marcus stands up too. We check on Alfie and Jed, who have set up their tent near the stream this evening. They are still awake, playing Lego with light from a couple of torches they have balanced on boxes. We say goodnight, but Alfie doesn't want to be kissed.

In the bedroom, Marcus and I open the shutters and look out at the stars and hear the crickets strumming.

"I'm glad we came on this holiday," Marcus says, "despite the bad start."

"Yeah, me too."

"We were really stagnating but now things seem to be moving again."

"Yes – and Alfie is out of our bed!"

"Got our sex life back – and long may it last."

I nod, and lean forward out of the window. I crane my neck to look at the stars some more, but Marcus pulls me back, and I giggle and I think he's going to kiss me, but instead he takes my hand and leads me towards our empty bed.

★

FRIDAY

It's our last full day here, and it's a spectacular morning. The sky is clear and blue, but there is a slight breeze. The children went to bed very late and the house is quiet. Marcus and I are in the kitchen. He's wearing boxer shorts and a tee shirt and his hair is a mess. I love the tattoo on the inside of his arm, a little star and a crescent moon. I like to see him like this, slow and peaceful, reading the paper and drinking coffee. I drink tea and sit next to Marcus on the large comfortable sofa. I stretch out my foot and think it's lovely here, but I'm ready to go home. Marcus is reading an old newspaper when I hear the children beginning to wake up and I decide to walk down the hill to the shop for croissants and perhaps a toy for Maud as she's not allowed wheat. I borrow a hat and put on my trainers and some suncream, and set off down the drive and down the hill to the village. I swing my arms and hum a song from an American musical.

There are morning sounds coming from houses on the outskirts of the village, unfamiliar Italian pop songs from the radio, water running, people talking. I pass a clutch of hens, clucking around a hen house, and two young boys whizz past me on bicycles. I am caught up in my own thoughts when I see a red car approaching.

It slows right down and draws to a halt.

It's Jill, a different Jill. Her hair is brushed, she's wearing large sunglasses, and a bright green top.

"Good morning, Jill," I greet her.

"Hello," she says, all bright and cheery. She's leaning towards me and I can see down her cleavage to the top of her breasts and the red ridges on her chest.

"I'm just coming up to the house, and bringing a bag of lovely fresh croissants."

"Oh! Thank you. I was just walking down to the village to buy some."

"Well, no need now," she says cheerily. "Why don't I drive you up the hill? It's already hot."

She seems to have forgotten what happened yesterday. I don't want to get into her car, but now there is no reason to go down to the village. I have an irrational fear that she may run me down if I don't do as she says. She's ruined my morning expedition, my mellow stroll, and I wish she'd stop coming to the house. I climb in reluctantly. She moves some papers from the front seat. The car smells of synthetic roses.

She drives up the hill. I look at her sagging underarms and I ask her where her house is. She turns the radio on and hums to the tune; she opens the window and looks out. She has no intention of answering my question; perhaps she didn't hear. I try another one. "How are you feeling? Any better?"

"Can't complain. Are you all set for leaving Sunday?"

"Actually, we're going tomorrow."

"Of course you are. So how shall we celebrate your last day?"

"Well, we've got a plan to go to a garden about an hour's drive away."

She asks me which one and I tell her vaguely where it is, but I don't tell her the name of it because I don't want her to turn up. Maybe I am being paranoid, but I don't think so. She says she's always wanted to go. She tells me how much she loves gardens, and gardening, but I resist inviting her. The pressure to ask her is bearing down on me, so much so that I have to open the window.

We drive the last few minutes in silence. She parks the car and pulls the handbreak up rather violently. She breezes into the house ahead of me and dumps the croissants on the terrace table and I am childishly resentful that she has ruined my plan to give everyone croissants. The children clamour around her. Jack looks up from a paper and asks how she's doing, Ellie thanks her and Sam takes a croissant and gives her a thumbs-up.

She asks us what we are doing today, even though I have told her in the car. Marcus says we are going out, but doesn't elaborate. She sits down at the table and pours herself a coffee.

"We're going to a garden, Jill. What are you up to today?" Ellie asks as she joins us.

"Oh, I've always wanted to go to that garden."

None of us say anything, and the silence is embarrassing. Luckily, Jack's mother calls on his mobile.

While we are distracted, half-listening to the phone call, Jill says cheerio and leaves the house, almost slamming the door. She has bought the kind of croissants I don't like, dusted with sugar and filled with cream. I pick at the corner of one.

"I think she's really sinister," I blurt out. "I really do. She's giving me the creeps I think she is capable of something weird, even violent.'"

"Well, she can't be that weird," Sam says, "or Dad wouldn't have let her be the housekeeper. She's worked hard. She definitely wanted to help us, and make sure we had a good stay. She's babysat, cooked, tidied, cleaned and helped Jack. Perhaps we should have asked her out for the day; I mean, she did step in at the last moment and all that."

I am fingering the croissant, tearing off tiny bits of dough. Why doesn't Sam see my point of view?

"She doesn't seem to have done any cleaning," I say. "I mean, she's cleaned up the kitchen after babysitting, but she hasn't cleaned our rooms or anything. She didn't make up a bed for Ellie, or clear up the bedroom after Miranda and Toby left."

"We'll see what Dad has to say when he's back tomorrow."

"She just needs to stop drinking quite so much wine. Speaking of which, I must buy some wine to take home," Dave says.

"She's just very needy," Marcus says, "and probably drinks too much. She means well."

I'm sure they are wrong. I think she is distasteful and strange, but I don't dare say this.

Marcus and I talk about Jill in the car on the way to the garden. We discuss what it is about her that is so unhinged. Alfie asks what unhinged is, and we say that somebody who is unhinged is a little sad and crazy, and thinking about that, I begin to feel a bit more sympathetic towards her. "Maybe she is claustrophobic," I suggest. "She's living in a small Italian village, where she doesn't appear to have any friends."

Marcus managed to upgrade the car when he came back from London. The air-conditioning is so cold that coming from the heat into the car is like diving from a sauna into the Baltic Sea. We have a sat nav, and all sorts of gadgets that we don't need. We drive for about an hour before we find the entrance to the garden and we don't speak much. We climb out and wait for a couple of minutes for the others. We traipse to the entrance and pay our money and because we are quite a large group we are given our own guide.

Lorenzo looks about 90. He has a lovely, almost toothless smile, and speaks a little English. He's very stylish and well dressed in grey trousers, a short sleeve shirt and a panama hat. The garden is lavishly decorated with statues and flower beds in geometric patterns. There are fountains and topiary labyrinths. It is beautiful and so peaceful. We follow Lorenzo through the gardens while he talks to us in Italian and I am pleased that I can understand almost half of what he says. Sadly, the house is not open to the public, the wooden shutters closed in a tantalizing way across all the windows.

On the way home, we stop for a long lunch at a pizza restaurant near the road. This is what the Italians do so well – a simple, inexpensive lunch: thin-crusted pizza, green salad, coffee, fresh orange juice and ice cream. We drive home with all three children in the back and play "spot the red car/yellow car" until the children get bored of the game. Maud falls asleep against the window and we arrive at the villa at about four. The little tabby cat welcomes us by meowing and wrapping itself around our legs. There is a slight breeze and the tops of the trees dance.

The first thing that we notice is that the key is in the door of the kitchen.

"The kitchen is really messy!" Maud shouts out.

My heartbeat quickens as Sam rushes past me and through to the hall. The kitchen is exactly how we left it, with a few breakfast things in the sink and cereal packets left on the surface next to the oven, but I hear Sam swearing from his bedroom. "Fuck!" he spits as he comes into the kitchen. "My bedroom's been ransacked and my passport is missing."

We clamour around him in a small huddle and Jack asks him if he's sure. He says it was on the small table by his bed and now it's gone.

"Is anything else missing?" I ask.

"No, I don't think so."

We follow him up the stairs to his bedroom. The bedcovers are on the floor, and all his books and magazines are strewn on the bed. There are papers everywhere and the contents of his briefcase are dumped in a pile on a chair. The scene makes me shiver.

"There's no sign of a break-in," Jack says, "so who's got a key?"

"Jill is the only one that I know of." Sam says.

"Jill? Why would she want to take a passport?"

"No, it can't be her," Sam says, "She wouldn't want my passport."

"Hang on… What about the missing money?" Dave says. "Remember the euros that went missing."

I have a picture in my mind of the gold bangle on Jill's wrist. Miranda lost a gold bangle.

We are milling around in the kitchen, trying to find a number for the police station. I telephone the number that Jill has left on the fridge, but it rings and rings until it rings off. Sam calls his mother, but she knows nothing about anyone called Jill. His father is still without a signal on his golf trip and his mobile is going straight to answering machine. I hear him tell his mother it's urgent and she says there's nothing she can do until he's back tomorrow. We realise that none of us actually know where Jill lives. Jack calls the police station and speaks to them in English, then passes the phone to Sam, who has limited but slightly better vocabulary than I do. They want him to come to the police station and fill in some forms.

We all search our rooms, but can't find anything missing. Marcus and Sam drive to the village to make enquiries. I search with an increasing sense of suspicion and neurosis. It is a horrible feeling, to be searching a house after a burglary, and I feel as though I am being watched. I am thinking about the ring I lost that Jill miraculously found. I wonder whether the burglar has taken books, paintings or money. I go through my wallet, and then remember that of course, I had my wallet with me.

The children, particularly Maud, are fascinated by what has happened.

"Can a woman be a burglar?" Maud asks Ellie, and

Ellie replies that yes, but not often. Jed wants to know if the burglar got in through the roof, and we tell him that the burglar probably walked in through the door. I wonder if anyone else but Jill has a key, and if so, who?

"I'm scared, Mummy," Maud says to Ellie, curling into her lap like a kitten.

"Don't be scared, angel," Ellie says, kissing her hair. "We're leaving tomorrow, and whoever came won't come back now."

I think back to when I first met Jill. Was there anything strange about her? I remember all the food she bought us, and how kind it was of her to babysit and how she really helped Jack when he needed her. But there are other traits to her character: her sudden surliness, her insistence on cooking the paella, the amount of alcohol she drank during that lunch, her desperate need to be included. I wonder if she has been a housekeeper before. How well does she know Sam's Dad? He can't have hired someone he'd never met. He must have seen references. We should make a report to the police.

We sit on the terrace playing Monopoly with the children, waiting for the others to come back from the village, but I am unrelaxed and I'm not really thinking about the game as I push my little silver boot around the board. Jed has to keep reminding me to take a chance card or pay a fine, or collect my rent. The game is still going strong when, about an hour later, Marcus and Sam return and tell us that they have found out that Jill is definitely not from this village, and although the shopkeeper and a couple of others have seen her around, no one seems to know where exactly she lives. They say they had a pretty futile visit to the police station and tried to fill out some forms as best as they could. Marcus says that the man at the desk has promised that he will send some officers to the house, but we don't know when.

Ellie and I are making the children's supper, when Jack slips down the stairs. He shouts out in pain as we hear him tumbling and we find him in a crumpled heap on the floor. Ellie helps him up and he leans on her heavily. "Ow!" he keeps saying loudly. "Ow! Be careful." Ellie sets him up in the sitting room with a newspaper and a cup of coffee, with his leg resting on a small stool. He wants Ellie to call a doctor, and I show her the list of numbers pinned up on the kitchen board.

Ellie would like me to speak to the doctor, as she doesn't even know how to say hello in Italian. The mobile number goes straight to answering machine and I leave a message in my shameful Italian. Then we go back to peeling carrots. Ellie tells me about a disastrous holiday they had together when their marriage was falling apart. Jack arranged for them to go on a romantic break to Scotland. It was pouring with rain and they drove through a storm, around and around twisting roads, until Ellie threw up and they had to stop by a church. Jack slipped on the threshold and twisted his ankle and insisted on being driven three hours back to casualty in Glasgow. When they arrived, he took one look at the people waiting with their ripped mouths, swollen ankles, black eyes and threatening tattoos, and decided that actually, he didn't want to go to casualty. And so she had to drive all the way back to the hotel room he had booked above a noisy pub. "It's just a cry for help, all this slipping over," she says. "He just wants my attention. And now he's got it, of course."

A doctor telephones the house, and he speaks perfect English. He says he can come to see Jack. Jack is very pleased to hear this and settles back while we wait on him. I bring him some sliced salami and Ellie brings him a cold bottle of beer. About half an hour later, the doctor turns up on a Vespa, just after the children have put on their pyjamas and are settled in front of a Disney film. He's travelled from the nearest town, and he's wearing a pink shirt, navy-blue linen trousers and navy-blue loafers. He speaks to Jack and after examining him, says that his knee is not broken, just bruised, and suggests putting arnica on it, which he happens to have in his bag.

"I see," Jack says, wincing. "Are you sure I don't need an x-ray?" He sounds disappointed.

"No," the doctor laughs, "there is nothing broken, I can assure you."

The doctor has very dark black hair, smoothed back, and tanned skin. He has a large hooked nose and he wears cufflinks. He is calm and softly spoken, neat and reliable, like an aeroplane pilot or the concierge at a smart hotel.

Ellie winks at me. "So darling," she says to Jack, "not so bad as you thought?"

"No, but still painful," he moans. "Still very painful. Doctor, can you give me a prescription for painkillers?"

"You can take aspirin," the doctor says. Ellie and I snort with laughter.

"Why is it funny?" he asks, smiling and revealing teeth so white they seem unnatural.

"I think Jack was hoping for something stronger. Perhaps something more like morphine."

"Morphine! *Non e possibile.*"

We give the nice doctor some cherries and a cup of coffee, and he thanks us profusely. I ask him about Jill but he has not heard of her. He says there are a lot of English people living around here; he sees a few now and then, but he can't remember Jill. He says good-bye, and Jack stands up with a great deal of groaning to wave him off. Ellie finds a walking stick in the hall, which Jack uses to hobble around on.

We were planning to take Sam out to a farewell thank-you dinner but haven't got round to finding a babysitter, so we have dinner at home instead tonight. We've eaten our way through some leftovers and had a kind of huge picnic – mozzarella and tomato, *spaghetti vongole*, cold ham, some peaches and figs with mascarpone, and now we are drinking fresh mint tea.

"This is stranger than fiction. It's truly bloody weird," Dave says, referring to Jill.

"I found Jill frightening," I say. "She seemed great at the beginning, but she became more and more scary."

"She's very screwed up, that's for sure," Tara agrees. "I mean, if it was her who ransacked the house, it's so creepy that she ingratiated herself with us. She did all that babysitting and all those chores, and brought us food, only to steal from all of us. How wretched. How sad."

"We can't be absolutely sure it is her," Sam says reaching out for the large disk of bread and the plate of cheeses and grapes. "We are presuming that she is the only one with a key."

"That's true," I say. "There could be other people who have a key."

We hear someone calling out "*Coooee!*" from the front door. It's Jill.

"Oh my God," I mouth. "What are we going to do?"

Sam stands up very coolly and goes to greet her. None of us say anything, but my stomach swirls downwards in a tunnel of nerves. Sam comes back onto the terrace with Jill.

"We've had a burglary," Jack says immediately. "Not a very nice way to end our holiday. We've been trying to reach you, in fact."

"Oh, that's terrible," she cries, looking suitably shocked. "Just terrible. I'm so sorry. I've never heard of such a thing around here."

"You should have seen my bedroom," Sam says. "I don't know why they targeted my room and took my passport. Now I'm trapped here. Well, I won't be. I'll get my PA to find out if I can use my driving licence to get back to the UK."

"Yes," she says. "Oh, I'm so sorry Sam. That really is a nuisance."

"More than that," Sam says.

"Oh, Sam," she says. "Awful for you. I'd like to take a photograph of you all before I go." She plunges her hand into her big basket bag and retrieves a throwaway camera. We are all standing around but none of us make a move. We are not in the mood for a group photograph taken by Jill. She stands back, sighs and takes a photograph of Sam, who is standing in front of

313

her, but he is scowling and doesn't bother to smile.

Her eyes are large and round, great, dull, murky pools in her face. "It's awful," she repeats. "Well, I'll call the police. I just stopped by to say goodbye, as I know you're off in the morning. So it was nice to meet you all, ever so nice. And I brought some tomatoes from the garden."

I feel as though I am dreaming.

"Where have you been?" I ask as she's walking towards the door. "We've been looking for you in the village."

"Oh, but I'm not from the village," she says, turning around to face me. "I live about five kilometres away. I told you that."

"Oh, right," Marcus says. "Which village?"

"Why are you asking, do you suspect me?" She twists her head from side to side, looking at each one of us, but not really directly, which is made worse by her squint.

"Well, how shall we put this?" Jack ponders, surveying her. "As you know, Jill, we've had a burglary but there are no smashed windows or broken locks and you appear to be the only other person who has a key."

He's brave to say this and I watch Jill's face closely. Her eyes narrow slightly and for a moment, she looks as though she may spit.

"How do you know?" she asks, looking a bit put out. "I don't know what you're saying. I'll have to have a word with Philip. I hope you're not accusing me of something."

"He's unavailable until tomorrow," Jack says.

"Well, we shall have to wait. Now, if you don't mind, I'll be off. Honestly, I just came to say goodbye – the cheek of it. There are plenty of others who have a key."

She's in the kitchen now, gathering her things together, and she's angry and brittle.

"Do you think we should make a citizen's arrest?" Tara asks me, giggling nervously.

"No, we can't. We don't have any evidence. What would we do? Where would we keep her?"

Jill calls out, "I'll be going then."

We gather at the front door, watching her getting into the car. We hear her switch the engine on and drive off, a cloud of smoke whisking up behind her.

"Has anyone called the police?" Dave asks.

"They said that they'll send someone to the house. Do you think we should have detained Jill? It has to be her," Tara says, putting on her dark glasses which make her lips look so red against her pale skin.

"Maybe not," Jack replies. "I mean would someone who has just robbed a house really come back the same evening?"

315

"Doubtful," Dave says. "Unless, It's a double bluff. Is it a double bluff? Or a double-double bluff?"

"Ellie, can you help me to bed?" Jack asks his ex-wife. Ellie helps him up and they walk slowly towards the door, and I hear him telling her to be careful. Marcus calls the police, and they say they promise to send two officers over in the morning. He says he did try to persuade them to come immediately, but his Italian wasn't quite good enough.

Sam double-locks the front door and we all go around closing and bolting the windows. It's been a strange, disturbing and eventful day. In our bedroom, I search again to see if there is any cash missing from my wallet and check that the jet black necklace and set of silver bangles are still in the hidden pocket inside my suitcase. I put my hand into my jacket pocket where I know I left a ten-pound note. It's still there. I glance at my finger, pleased that I didn't leave my eternity ring on the little shelf above the bath.

Marcus joins me. "I don't think it was Jill. She's too daft. I mean she drinks too much and she's definitely barking mad, but she wouldn't be stupid enough to come back here after opening the door and taking our things."

I think it's Jill, but what he says makes me doubt that I'm right. "It must be someone who has a key. We know that."

"Yes," he says yawning. "We know that. Do you think we'd make a good detective team?"

I laugh at Marcus. He is a handsome, funny man and I'm pleased to have him all to myself after years of Alfie squirming between us.

"Do you think whoever it was will come back and kill us all?" I ask in mock terror, although I am a little afraid.

"Yes," Marcus says, pulling me over to his side of the bed. "Let's have one last fuck before we're all dead."

SATURDAY

I am up early and go downstairs to find Jack alone on the terrace. He's wearing beige chinos, a pale blue polo shirt and a large expensive-looking watch on his wrist. It's our first cloudy, dull day, and it seems right that we should be leaving, particularly now that the end of the holiday has coincided with a burglary.

"Good morning, Jack." My voice sounds hoarse.

"Good morning, darling," he says a little flatly.

"What's up?"

"Well, poor Sam was up late worrying about his passport, and hoping he hasn't ruined our summer by asking us all here."

"Poor Sam, I must talk to him."

"Yes, do, and Ellie still won't tell me about the boyfriend. I keep imagining how excited she must be to be returning home to him."

"You never know. It could all be over by this time next year. Have you managed to ask her about him yet?"

"Well, no," he says, standing up, with a grimace of pain. "I can't really bear to hear the answer, but she wouldn't tell me about the text. I think she's embarrassed to admit that she has a lover. Shall I make coffee?"

"Yes, please. She's very fond of you, I think," I say as I follow him into the kitchen.

"Not that fond. She treats me like the family pet." He sits down at the kitchen table, stretches out his bad leg and groans.

"You have to open yourself up," I suggest, sitting down next to him. "Tell her how hurt you were when she had the affair. Just say that now you've had time to think, you see that it was a terrible mistake to end the marriage. Tell her how sad you are and how much you miss her."

"Yes, maybe I should have tried that; but is there any point now? It seems a bit late, She is flying back with us, though, so maybe I'll invite her to lunch when we're back. The only problem being that she might not agree to have lunch with me. Well, my dear, it's been a pleasure to have spent so much time with you. Will you make an old wounded soldier a cup of coffee?"

"Yes, of course, you charmer. I can't wait to get a signed photograph of you so that I can auction it off at the school fair."

Jack laughs. "Ellie used to tease me because I send out photographs that were taken twenty years ago! Well, at least six years ago, anyway."

"Do you really? Why?"

"Because I don't have any good ones of me now – well, flattering ones anyway. And I looked better six years ago. Actually, Jen, I'm looking to redo my publicity shots. Would you be interested?"

"I'd love that. I really would. That would be such fun."

"We'll make a date to chat about it."

After making the coffee, we take it out onto the terrace, and Tara joins us.

The children are demanding breakfast. Ellie comes to the table. "I'm all packed," she says. "Three pairs of knickers, two vests and a bathing suit. And I've done the children. So, Jack, we'll fly back together," she says, "like the old days."

"Yes, that'll be nice. I'll look forward to that."

The children are having breakfast when Sam's father, Philip, telephones. I speak to him briefly and then call for Sam. He comes on to the terrace and takes the telephone.

"Hi, Dad. We've been trying to reach you. There's

been a bit of a crisis. Someone stole my passport. We think it could be Jill... Jill, the housekeeper. Beth? I don't know about her, but there's one called Jill. Yes, she's been around the entire week." He pauses as he hears what his father has to say. "Oh, really? No, she's been in every day. Yeah, late fifties, droopy eyes, kind of greying blonde... What? OK, Dad." He walks into the garden and out of earshot.

"Right," I hear him say as he comes back to the terrace, "OK, well, I wish you'd said something. She's been up to some strange shit."

The children finish their food and Ellie offers to take them off for a final swim. Tara decides to go with them. I'm sitting with a cup of coffee, when Sam sits down and takes a cigarette out of Jack's packet.

"You don't smoke," I say.

"No, but I've just had some very strange news." He lights the cigarette and takes a deep drag.

"What?"

"That woman, Jill. Dad apologises. It turns out she's not some random housekeeper, she's an ex-girlfriend of his. They went out together briefly years ago, and he's been trying to help her get her life back on track, or something like that. She's been in a bit of trouble with the police in the past, but was meant to have reformed. He's going to try and track her down and then get back to me."

"Oh right," I say. "How weird of him not to say before. I mean, why didn't he?"

"I've got no idea; he was probably embarrassed. Maybe it was a one-night stand or something. He probably didn't think of it. She was only meant to let us in."

"Yes, maybe he didn't want to upset your step-mother."

Sam frowns, "Maybe..." He is about to say something when his mobile rings again, and again he walks off smoking his cigarette, while I sit and wait. Then seeing that his conversation with his father is taking a while, I decide to make a snack for Alfie.

He comes to find me in the kitchen. "Come outside Jen," he says in a strange, strained voice. I follow him onto the terrace.

"Well, that's really it. That tops all news. I've heard something that's going to blow your mind." He sits down, legs splayed, and sighs.

"What?"

"Jill..." He pauses, and puts his head in his hands.

"What?" I imagine that she has been found dead or that she's turned herself in.

"Well, first of all she's not called Jill, she's called Beth, and secondly – I don't quite know how to say this."

"Go on," I prompt him.

"Well, that woman, Jill, is my mother. You know, just before Dad rang back, I thought for one mad second that was the case, but just dismissed it as too crazy."

"What?" I can't process the information – it is just so unlikely that I think he must be joking, but I can see from his strained expression that what he has told me is not at all funny.

"You mean Jill is your mother, the one you've never seen until now?"

"She's my mother!" He's laughing and kind of sneering.

"I can't believe it. Your mother!" It's shocking that such a strange wayward woman should be the mother of the man sitting here before me, the man I loved. It doesn't feel right.

"Are you sure?" I ask.

"Yes. Yes, I'm sure." He sounds impatient.

"How are you sure?"

"Believe me," he says, "this is no joke. My father told me everything. Jill is really Beth, my mother, the woman he had a relationship with. I was the result."

I am not certain how to react to the news. It doesn't seem real. It's like a scene from a movie, a strange denouement to a French film. It seems incredible that Sam and Jill are related, because Jill is flabby and sad-looking and Sam is handsome and strong. I am waiting to see what Sam will do next. I imagine that he may smash the big yellow ashtray on the floor, or grab a bottle of whisky. The silence between us is stifling and awkward.

"Are you all right?" I know immediately that this is a stupid question.

He shakes his head in response. I am wary about hugging him. Every time I am close to him, Marcus seems to appear, as if in some scene from a farce.

"I'm not," he says, blowing his nose on a paper napkin that's been left on the table. "I've always wanted to put my birth mother out of my mind and have nothing to do with her. I didn't want to hurt my stepmother. But now that I've met my real mother, what the hell am I to make of her? She's mad. It makes me doubt myself – I mean, potentially I'm capable of being mad too. The idea that she is my mother repulses me. Do you understand?"

I nod that I understand but I can't imagine what it must be like to suddenly meet your mother as a grown man, and not to be prepared for the meeting in any way – and to discover that she is pretty odd too. I really want to touch him, not in a sexual way, although I am drawn to his vulnerability and it appeals to me. I walk over to him, but just as I am nearing him, he stands up and backs away, and even in this strange situation, it feels as though he is rejecting me. His mobile is ringing and he picks it up, "Hey, Dad. No. I'm taking it on board… A load of shit to deal with. Yeah, I'm with my friend Jen… It's just so fucking strange Dad. You shouldn't have let her into the house even to see me. She's unbalanced. What were you doing with her?" He walks to the other side of the terrace and sits down. "She can't have changed that much." He is now listening to something his father is saying and nodding, though his face is still contorted. "Yes, I know. I'm sorry, just shocked. Sorry, Dad." They talk for a couple more moments, while I worry about how to deal with all of this on the day that we're all leaving.

He gets off the telephone and comes back to sit at the table with a sigh. "He can't get hold of her," he says. "Her phone is ringing and ringing, no reply."

"When did she leave you?"

"Dunno exactly, I think when I was about three months old." He takes a drag on the cigarette and then stubs it out. "We spoke about it once, don't you remember?"

"Yes, yes, I do remember."

"Dad has always said that she couldn't cope – with a baby, with him, with anything, so she just took off. She apparently got into trouble in some village in England for stealing things, silly little things. She inveigled her way into people's lives, offering to babysit and help out, like she did with us, and then they discovered that she'd taken things – hairbrushes and that kind of tat."

"She also makes things up," he continues lighting another cigarette. "That's what Dad said. 'He also said he's always felt guilty that he let her go like that – that he didn't try harder to make her stay or find out what was wrong with her.' Sam is blowing the cigarette smoke out in quick and ferocious circles. "It would have been better if she'd come out with it. It would have been more honest. The fact that she's taken off like some fugitive with my passport is too weird. I mean, what the fuck does she think she's doing with my passport? She's trapped me, made my life hell now."

I have never seen Sam like this. I've never really seen him being real and truthful. I've definitely never seen him so distraught and angry at the same time. Dave comes onto the terrace and sees Sam looking anxious and says, "What's up, mate?" Sam tells him what's happened and it's almost like he's recounting the plot of a film; in retelling the series of events for the second time, he now seems detached, even bored, and there is a strange indifference to his tone. Dave, like me, is incredulous and offers to take him for a walk. Sam stands up and kind of lets out one strangled sigh and then he and Dave go down the steps into the garden.

I go to the bedroom and pack the last few things into my bag. I sit on the bed and wait for Marcus to get off the telephone so I can tell him, warn him what's happened. But he talks on and on, and at last, in exasperation, I point at my watch, but he ignores me and, with rising irritation at his refusal to stop working, I leave the room and make my way back to the terrace, where Sam is talking to Jack and Dave.

"I think she had a job in a hotel or something, and then she was made redundant or maybe she was sacked. I'm not clear. Anyway, Dad is renting her an apartment in a town nearby. She found out that I was going to be here and begged Dad to let her see me. At first he said no. He knew I wouldn't want to see her and he knew that she was a bit loopy. Then, when the housekeeper left, she asked if she could let us in, but she wasn't supposed to do any more than that. Dad says she pleaded with him – she was desperate to see me, just for a minute. He said he was weak and just wanted an easy life. He believed that she would just let us in and leave it at that."

"Quite naïve of him," Jack says, "to think that once she was let in, she would just disappear."

"Yeah, I know. He called her, just before he went away, and she said she had seen me once, and what a great man I was. Dad knows that I've always refused to have anything to do with her, so he was really apologetic, in fact, more than apologetic; absolutely, resolutely embarrassed and guilty, but he doesn't think she'd take my passport."

"Absolutely extraordinary," Jack says. 'Hard to believe it's true. It seems so odd that your father agreed that she could let us all in. With her history."

"I suppose it's hard to say no to a mother wanting to see her son," I say, imagining that if I was in the same situation I would probably be desperate to see my child. "It must have been wretched for her to have lived all these years without seeing Sam. Maybe she couldn't cope when you were a small baby because she had undiagnosed post-natal depression. Maybe everything that's happened to her since then is because she's never been able to accept the idea of leaving you and not knowing you." I stop now, realising that I may have said too much and that Sam doesn't want to hear this. "I know I'm jumping to conclusions; I'm sorry. It's just a guess," I finish quietly.

"But she didn't get in touch," Sam says, sounding angry, pacing up and down the terrace. "She never bothered to tell us where she'd gone. I didn't hear from her until I was fifteen years old. Then she disappeared again. She got back in touch with Dad about a year ago."

"Honestly, maybe she was too depressed." Jack gulps down a coffee in one and glances at his watch.

Sam is at the steps of the terrace staring out into the garden. I don't think he's listening to us.

"And ashamed," I add. "Perhaps she was depressed

and ashamed and just miserable somewhere."

Sam turns around; he looks exhausted.

"This is such a lot to take in," I say and immediately regret making such a fatuous comment, but it's hard to think of the right thing to say in the circumstances.

"I'm in shock," he says. "I'm not that happy with the way Dad has dealt with all of this. Why did he arrange to let her see me? As though I was some kind of monkey in a zoo? Why did he give in to her? I've already got a perfectly good mother. He should have consulted me."

Sam is lighting another cigarette, and Dave is standing behind him massaging his shoulders.

"She was desperate to see you," I say. "She's probably been desperate all these years. It must have driven her slightly crazy. Now I think about it, she seemed upset when you weren't here right at the beginning. She kept asking when you'd arrive."

"And now she's gone again. That's it. It was never meant to happen."

"Your dad gave in to her because she pleaded with him; don't forget she was only meant to be here for a few minutes," Dave says.

"She had to return," Jack adds, "because she found out you wouldn't be arriving for three days into the holiday. I imagine things may have turned out differently if you'd been here the first day. "

Marcus arrives at the breakfast table with wet hair and a smooth shaven face.

"So I know what I'm going to do," he says. "I've got it all worked out. I'm going to put up posters all over the village. Look, I have a mobile photograph of Jill. Underneath it will say: Large, middle-aged, depressed thief with a shelf of a bosom, a droopy chin and even droopier eyes. Looking somewhat like a cow —"

"Stop," I beg, grimacing.

"What?" Marcus looks at me.

"Turns out she's my mum."

"What the fuck? Jill?"

"Beth," Sam says. "Jill is in fact Beth, who is my real mother. She was desperate to see me. It's a long, long story."

"Jill the housekeeper is really Beth your mother. Is this some kind of sick joke?"

"No, Marcus," I say. "No, it's not." I feel a stab of irritation. I am perhaps unreasonably annoyed that Marcus hasn't sensed the mood, the gravitas of the situation.

He looks around at our serious faces. "I can't get used to it," he says. "Hey old Man, I'm sorry, I obviously had no idea. Are you sure? I thought you had a mother?"

"I have a stepmother. Jill or Beth is my real mother.

I spoke to Dad. She's been living nearby for about a year. Dad is helping her. When she found out I was coming here, she begged to see me. She contacted me once when I was fifteen and I refused to see her because I didn't want to upset Mum. I've always known my stepmother as Mum."

"Wow," Marcus says, sitting down. "So your father told you all this."

"Yes, just now on the telephone."

"Sam, mate," Marcus says, "if there is anything we can do…"

"Nah," he replies. "This is something I have to deal with. I should have dealt with it when she contacted me when I was fifteen. It's just come back to haunt me. She sent me a letter and I didn't even open it. I was still angry with her and threw it away. Then I became curious about what she had written, but by then it was too late, so I tried to forget about it. It wasn't meant to be, you know?"

Sam is slouching on the chair but suddenly pulls himself up. "Look, we have to call the police and tell them we made a mistake. She's my mother after all."

"But wouldn't it be a good thing to track her down? She sounds unstable," Marcus says.

"Yes, but I'll find her. I don't want the police after her. Poor old sod."

He goes to the kitchen to make the call and Dave

says, "Is this for real?" His eyes open really wide and his voice is high and hysterical.

"Well I've just blown it. I was so rude about her," Marcus mutters.

"Well she's a freak," Dave whispers. "I mean really, really odd."

"She's ill," I say, "that's for sure. I think she had post-natal depression and never got any help for it, and things escalated, well, who knows? But I know if I'd been separated from my child, it would haunt me."

Sam is back on the telephone, asking his father to call the police, as his father speaks better Italian than he does. Jack, Sam and Dave are sitting around the table and I decide to join Tara and Ellie and the children by the stream, partly to get away from the intensity of the strange situation.

They are sitting in a circle, playing a card game, and I tell them what's happened in a hushed, urgent voice. Tara and Ellie are both as surprised as the rest of us and Tara plies me with questions. I tell her as much as I know and we talk about the theory of the post-natal depression. She somehow manages to turn the conversation round to herself, worrying that *she* will get post-natal depression after the birth of her child. I am irritated by how self-absorbed she still is and I stand up conscious that we have to leave soon. She gets up too and they all follow me back to the house.

A few minutes later, Sam says he managed to convince the police that we don't need an investigation and he thinks they have understood. "I'm so sorry," Sam says. "I'm sorry that I've dragged you all here and you've ended up having things stolen and children who've nearly drowned and you've had to put up with my mother masquerading as a housekeeper. I don't know what to say, really."

"I don't think it's been a complete disaster," I reassure him.

"Are you sure?" He's kind of laughing and crying at the same time and I go over and sit next to him. Tara sits on his other side and takes one of his hands and I take the other. I'm sure Marcus won't mind, as Sam really needs to be taken care of right now. We sit for a few minutes and Tara says "Poor baby" to Sam, and he smiles sadly. Then he says, "I did once catch her in my bedroom just doing nothing much. She said something about how she was looking for her mobile but now that I think about it – it probably wasn't true. "

"Also," I say, "she did seem quite flustered when she looked at the photographs of your father and stepmother when we first arrived. And remember how weird and inappropriate it was when she took your photograph?"

Marcus arrives with two of our suitcases. He's

followed by Alfie, looking spruce in a polo-neck tee shirt.

I don't want Sam to go home thinking that this has been a holiday from hell because although things have gone missing, and Maud nearly drowned, and Toby and Miranda broke off their engagement and Marcus had to go home and finally strangely, terribly, Sam found out who his real mother was, we've all become much closer during these last seven days, and things in our lives that were stuck or not working are shifting and moving again.

"Sam," I say, "in some ways this holiday has been great. Well, maybe not for you, not this business with Beth, but –"

"No, it's OK," he interrupts me. "I don't think of her as my mother, not at all, not even now that I've met her. I'm going to deal with it, all of it, in my own time."

"This week has been great for me," Tara tells him, "I've finally managed to accept the fact that I do want a baby and that is a huge issue resolved for me and for the future of our marriage."

"Oh, and I've thought of another one," I add. "Alfie… Alfie no longer sleeps between us. You have no idea what a good feeling that is."

"I've been able to work on my book in these beautiful surroundings," Dave says, "and I received good news here. Two pieces of exceptionally good news."

"OK," Jack booms in a loud, exaggerated American accent, "if we're all going to share, I've got something to say. Ellie, I love you." She looks up at him, from across the table. "I want to say how really sorry I am that I behaved like a prat after *le scandal avec le neighbour,* and how ridiculous it was that I was so unforgiving. I want to tell you how much I've missed you. I was really hurt, you see. I was just too damn proud to have you back."

Ellie is blushing and she looks shy, perhaps embarrassed, that he has declared himself in front of all of us.

"Jack, it was my fault too," she says a little coyly. "I've missed you as well."

He stretches out his hand to her, "Have you really missed me, darling? But what about the boyfriend?"

"Boyfriend?" She sounds astonished.

"The man who sent the text about the cat; that man who can't wait to see you."

"Oh, him!" Ellie laughs. "You were being so nosey, I didn't want to tell you. That's my lodger. My gay hairdresser, Ali. He's broken up with his boyfriend and is staying at mine till he finds somewhere else."

"Oh, relief," Jack says laughing. "I can't tell you what relief. The gay hairdresser. Of course."

We are all clapping and cheering and thanking Sam

again. He manages to smile, and he looks pleased for a moment, then his smile fades.

While I am collecting Alfie's baseball cap and my wet bikini, I consider the fact that I am closer to Marcus now and that we've opened up to each other for the first time in years. Dave and Tara are having a baby, and Ellie and Jack will probably get back together. Perhaps Sam will find that being single for a while will make him stronger. Maybe discovering that his mother was unstable and didn't have the resources needed to look after a child will give him some peace and enable him to find someone he can commit to. When Marcus has finished packing up the car, he gives me a hug, and Alfie actually thanks Sam for the holiday without being asked. We are almost ready to leave when we hear a car drawing up in the drive.

It's Beth, and my heart begins to flutter and thump but before there is time to think about it too hard, she is on the terrace looking forlorn and wretched. Sam stands up, and at first I think he may walk off in disgust; but he falters for a second and as she comes towards him, he opens his arms and he hugs her – politely, without immersing himself in it, patting her on the back as though she were a small child. I wonder if he's embarrassed or disgusted or just numb with shock. Or is he feeling some familial love for this woman, his mother whom he has never known?

"I'm just so sorry," she says, standing back and looking up at him and then around at all of us. She's crying and the tears are smudging her powdered face. "I came back to apologise. I took the passport and the bangle and the money. I could see that you weren't drawn to me as I was to all of you. And I especially wanted to be close to Sam. I don't know why I took the bangle and the money; I can't explain it. I wanted to be part of the group and I couldn't find a way in, a way to make you notice me." She is talking very quickly. We are expecting Sam to say something or do something, but he remains silent until at last he says, very quietly, "Thank you for telling us."

"It's all right," Jack says, stepping forward and taking her hand. "You're very brave to come here and tell us. We appreciate that. You're a good woman, you know. You helped me that day Maud nearly drowned. I couldn't have done it all without you."

"Thank you, Jack," she replies, sitting down on one of the bamboo chairs. I pour her a glass of water and hand it to her. "I'm Sam's mum," she announces, looking around at us.

"Yes, we know," Jack says. "Your son told us; his father told him." He gestures towards Sam, who nods his head slowly, but doesn't look up..

She takes a big gulp of water and she looks pleadingly at Sam. "I wanted to see you but Philip asked me not to say anything; he said it would be too much of a shock. He made me promise, you see.

"I just had to see Sam, though," she continues, looking around at all of us, "I had to see him; not being able to tell him that I am his mother made me stressed and too tense. It's like something is simmering in me, just about to boil over, and for a few minutes after I've stolen something, the tension goes away, but then it comes back again, and the sadness too. Don't ask me why – it's a kind of illness. I took all sorts of little things that I've already put back. I've taken things from people before. I never know why I do it. Something comes over me, like a kind of rush that blots out the wrong and right of it. I've done it to people I like, people who trust me, and I'm cursed afterwards with this terrible guilt, a terrible guilt that stops me sleeping... I'm returning the things I took from you now. "

She pulls the things out of her pocket and puts them on the table in a pathetic little pile.

"Thank you, Beth," I say.

"Why did you take the passport?" Sam asks.

"I just..." her lip trembles and she starts to cry again. "I just didn't want you to leave. I've been so lonely and sad. Like something was missing, a part of me, like a limb. The thought of never seeing you again was too much. I've missed you so much. I could never risk having another child, not after what happened with you. I'll never forgive myself. I'll take this trouble to the grave, you know."

Sam's hard, distant expression melts away. He looks up at her. "I understand that," he says quietly. "I'll stay in touch," he promises. "I really will."

He gives her another hug now, this time with more feeling and warmth. She hugs him back as if she never wants to let him go.

It's time to leave and even though it seems like a really inappropriate moment to go, Sam assures us that he will be fine. In fact, he would like some time on his own. I am in a reflective mood as we say goodbye to everyone. Sam hugs me, but not in a weird flirtatious way; a real, friendly hug, warm and embracing. I walk towards our car, and hurl our suitcases into the boot. We get in and I pull on my seat belt and wave at him. He is standing on the stairs, with Beth just behind him. Marcus hoots the horn and waves his arm out of the open window. It's been a holiday that we will all remember, I think, as we bump down the track for the last time, while the wasps buzz at the windows and the cicadas strum, strum, strum.

We return to our house by the park, which now seems dusty and small and dark. The cat has disappeared even though our neighbour came in to feed her, but everything else is still and settled, as we left it. We have been home for about twenty-four hours when Sam telephones late at night. He has had a long conversation with his father again, who has organised for Beth to see a doctor in London. Sam says he's going to keep in touch with her. He may see her when he's next in Europe, but he says he's wary of getting too close.

After the telephone call, life goes back to normal. It was fun sharing a house with all the others but it's a relief to be a family again. The wine drinking, the late nights and living through so many dramas have tired me out, even though on reflection, it was an important week, a definite turning point for all of us.

The cat sloped back meowing and looking huge; she must be getting fed at several different houses. Marcus now refers to her as the "old slapper", or "slap" for short. Alfie has started Year 3 at school, Marcus is submerged in meetings and Jack has already commissioned me to do a series of portraits. The house no longer appears to be small and dusty and dark – quite the opposite – sunny and spacious. The weather is warm and blustery and it's good to be home.

Eleven Months later:

We are back in Italy, but in a different villa from the one we were in last summer. Yesterday Marcus and I got married. It was a beautiful London day; warm but not too hot. I wore a lavender-coloured dress, and carried lavender husks inside my evening bag. The music in the church was soulful and uplifting and saying the vows in front of our friends and family has added a profound aspect to our commitment. I'm tired but happy, not glum like Tara was with her post-marriage gloom. I feel cherished.

It's been a year of change, and being here in Italy again, is making me think about those seven summer days, when all our lives were touched in some way. Jack and I have become friends since that holiday last summer and my career has taken a new twist. I did a series of publicity shots for him, and Sam liked them so much that he said he would use them as the official photographs for his big blockbuster film about a detective who helps children solve crimes. Sam says it will be as popular as Harry Potter and Jack will become huge. Sam hired me to take official portraits of all the stars, and now other actors I've met through Jack have also commissioned me to take their photographs, which means I am busy and making more serious money.

Sam is calmer now, somehow more authentic. I no longer find him alluring or yearn for what could have been. My misguided feelings for him have diminished almost entirely. I think this is partly because on holiday in Italy, I understood that he had never been in love with me, whereas before I had always been quite sure that it was just that our timing had been wrong.

I think Jack nudged Marcus to propose to me and he did so last New Year's Eve in a cottage in Pembrokeshire. It was minutes into the New Year and we were watching fireworks across the valley when he asked me to marry him. It was ironic really, because by then, I had stopped worrying about whether he wanted to marry me or not; it didn't seem to matter any more. But I said yes, of course. On New Year's Day, we went to a small chapel and just sat there in silence, for half an hour, wrapped up in our own thoughts while Alfie played with a remote-control aeroplane outside.

Tara had her baby, a little boy called Joe, and asked me to be godmother. She's on maternity leave and she's turned out to be a good mother, perhaps a little over-protective, but very warm and tactile. She says she's tired but has learnt to meditate. She now meditates to fall asleep during the day when the baby is sleeping. I'm not sure that meditation is meant to send you to sleep, but Tara says it really works for her. Dave's having a book launch next Thursday for his new book, *The End Game,* that he was working on in Italy. Jack and Ellie had a rapprochement after the holiday. It wasn't an instant reconciliation – it took a while, but they decided to give it a go and went to couple counselling for a few months. The other day, Jack told me that he is consciously more tolerant and less selfish. "I talk about myself a little less," he said. "I now write about myself instead," he laughed. "Did I tell you I'm writing an autobiography?"

Alfie is staying with Jack and Ellie while we're away, and it's strange because now that Marcus and I are here alone, I rather wish they were all here with us. But that's the nature of the human condition, isn't it? We always want what we don't have, even though what we *do* have is usually just right.

ACKNOWLEDGEMENTS

I would like to thank the following people – my agent, Peter Staus, editor Vanessa Webb and others who read drafts and made comments: Dominique Lacloche, Josa Young, Kathleen Baird-Murray, Maggie Phillips and as always Deborah Susman, Gillian Greenwood and my husband, Luke White.

Kate Morris is the author of three novels. She lives in London with her husband and two children and writes a weekly marriage column in *The Times*.